Sidereal Time

D0111030

Also by Christopher Meredith

Fiction

Shifts
Griffri

Poetry

This
Snaring Heaven

Sidereal Time

Christopher Meredith

seren

seren
is the book imprint of
Poetry Wales Press Ltd
Wyndham Street, Bridgend, Wales

© Christopher Meredith, 1998
The right of Christopher Meredith to be identified as the Author
of this Work has been asserted in accordance with the
Copyright, Designs and Patents Act 1988

ISBN 1-85411-239-2

A CIP record for this title is available from
the British Library

All rights reserved. No part of this publication may be reproduced,
stored in a retrieval system, or transmitted at any time or by any means
electronic, mechanical, photocopying, recording or otherwise
without the prior permission of the copyright holder.

*The publisher works with the financial assistance of the
Arts Council of Wales*

The characters and situations in this book are entirely
imaginary and bear no relation to any real person or actual
happening.

cover: detail from 'Eternity the other night' by Arthur Giardelli

Printed in Plantin by Creative Print & Design Wales, Ebbw Vale

LLUN

Eight see nine tee eleven ee then, yes, then four ell, sorry, ten ell, and after grub seven see for a double and oh shit lower six double hist oh, oh Christ and enterprise denterprise in my dinner. That's the trouble. Once it's full on a Monday you're stuck the whole bloody year. Entist. Dentisprise Thursday. Dentist Thursday. Denterprise in my dinner, that's, yes, today, and openeve Tuesday then inset was it? something about? And dentistset Thurs. But a full Monday and enterfuckinprise through dinner. (Sorry, Mel. Lunch.) Ben's minder, owe two weeks. Phone home about Kenny. Happy birthd. Not till Friday. Oh no not yet not half way yet. But double hist lower six. Have word with Brace. Must. Bastards.

Then the furrow and fret of herself smoothed and became the eggshell matt of the bedroom ceiling. Sarah stared at the lath of light which fell upward across it through the chink at the top of the curtains. The rosiness of the lath faded in some precise Newtonian relation to its distance from the source. The rosyfingered dawn. Rosy fingered Dawn. Like something from a sexy novel.

But god is a boring author. Every chapter starts like this with the cliche of waking. Reacquiring the self, reinhabiting the husk, coming to. Coming too. (No that's something else.) No technique there. No feel for the ruthlessness of taut narrative.

It, the lath of light, must be shifting slowly like a clockhand. Unticking finger of smooth clockwork. The sun, the sun. Somehow it made her think of music. Something starting soft and getting louder. Vaughan Williamsy, or that one Mel liked, Daphnis and Chloe, that reeked of voyeurs' semen. Trust him to like that. God's triumphal crescendo. The sun's finger pushing in my room.

Her hand, in her crutch as usual when she woke, rubbed against the tampon string.

A garden shut up. A fountain sealed. Won't need one in today. That's done and one good thing. Upset Mel's rhythm yesterday.

My rhythm upsetting his. Moon at odds with the sun. Back to normal next time. Sunday's fuckday as Monday's washday, or used to be.

Her mouse, Ben called it. His tail hangs out, Mummy, so you don' lose him.

The finger of sunlight didn't look as if it moved. Perhaps there were moments when everything stopped. But Mel's breathing continued, hoisting the duvet then letting it down slowly. He was lying on his side with his back to her making a ridge between her and the window. The air flowing in and out of us time after time. How count what flows? You count days. Could count breaths. But the sun's always rising somewhere. Remember when we had clocks that ticked? Jerky little jumps like a child on stepping stones. First you're in one place then – tick – suddenly you're in another and a bit of the stream's behind you. Tick. No. Time comes down a wire now at two hundred and forty volts. A smooth passage of electrons. The river itself, not jumps across it. Process, not occasion. The clock radio, soon, with a blocked road and a war, will remind me I connect with all the fury and mire.

Then, Mel's sighing indrawn breath checked itself and the hoisted duvet stopped. Stopped at its parochial zenith. Funny how sleepers do that. The rhythm suddenly gone, disobedient to the moon, tides, everything. How long could he hold his breath? Till he died? She looked at the carefully razored line of fair hair on the nape of his thick neck. Real and dead as a waxwork.

She rolled back and looked up.

Through the chink there was an extraordinary patch of vivid green sky, ruddled at its eastern edge. Okay, god. Bad at narrative but a dab hand with the descriptive bits. The roseate finger held its place. It lay frozen as if it had been airbrushed on the ceiling. She held her breath and watched and nothing happened.

I've escaped.

She breathed again to make sure she could. Her hand, still at the palpy flesh around the string, clutched.

There are moments when it stops. Only me left. No lower six double hist. No enterprise. The Starship Enterprise stopped still in midnothing. The ship of fools icebound.

The vivid green with the ruddled edge didn't change. The finger of light didn't shift.

I have escaped. Congratulations, god. You've finally done something interesting. I.e., nothing. Dreaming when dawn's left hand

was in the sky. Dreaming of dentists and knotted timetables. No.
No eight see. No today and no tomorrow. No flow except my own.
Moon alone sailing. Dreaming when dawn's left hand. Miraculous
escape. Parting the Red Sea.

She felt the moisture on her kneading fingertips.

The rosyfingered dawn. No need to phone home. No steel probe
pinging at the old amalgam. No lower six double hist. No hist,
even. The death of history. No birthday. No marking of arrival at
the half way mark. There's a thought. The death of death. Oh yes.
Rosy fingered Dawn and Sarah fingers Sarah. My dab hand
dabbing.

She looked back to Mel. Man of stone. The pale orange hairs
short and unreally uniform were individually visible on the fat
razored nape. And all those little pits of reddish flesh where other
hairs might come. He was in his beige pyjamas with the dark
chocolate collar. Very Mel, them. It might have put her off, but it
didn't. She watched herself watching him as her hand worked,
worked, and all the world stood still as the airbrushed lath. Under
the hoisted duvet, inside the beige cocoon all his ridge of flesh was
hanging, that way fat men are so you're not sure where muscle
ends and fat begins. The scoop was hanging between shoulder and
hip, an illusion of there being a waist on the upper side. At the
front his belly would be depending roundly from him on the bed.
Men his size always look as if they've got small dicks even if they
haven't. Must be dispiriting to look around the hill of gut and see
that silly little flap of stuff.

She slid her free hand over his hip, broad as her own. She could
see the back of his ear, part of his cheek with the irritating neat-
clipped beard. Felt forward, kneading her hands in unison, one on
him and one on herself, felt down over all the unresponsive beige-
clad skin. The skyfinger stood still and still he didn't breathe. Felt
down through the little peeing vent in his pyjamas for the silly flap.
Her other hand parting the Red Sea, reversing waterfalls and
behold, Moses with his rod. Yes. Yes. Charlton Heston with a
weird perm and highlights. Oh yes. Dreaming when dawn's left
hand was on my thigh, the white hand of Moses on the bough. The
promised land. But Omar didn't hold with gods or miracles.

Her hand found his penis but it was disappointingly thickened
and half erect. She'd wanted to stroke the flaccid dink she saw
bobbling under his belly when he walked.

As she stroked, it stirred and he groaned out all the indrawn breath and the rosy skyfinger moved smoothly across the ceiling. The film unlocked and ran.

Spellbreaker. Things do revolve. You can't escape.

The rose yellowed in some precise Newtonian way as her bit of earth revolved towards the sun. The world had resumed its constant melting rearrangements. Awake, my little ones, and fill the cup.

'Mummy.'

She moved her hands quickly and wiped her fingers on Mel's beige back. When she turned she saw Ben in his teddypatterned pyjamas standing in the open door.

'Hello, little un. Awake already. Goodness me.' She unruckled her nightie and pushed back the duvet for him.

He climbed in and clung close like a baby chimp, made her aware of her heat and bulk. She realised she was sweating a little. He must be able to smell her.

He pressed his tiny nose against her throat.

'Are we on a day off day today.' His voice faded back into sleep as he said it.

Mel had rotated onto his back and was making a noise like a tractor idling, scratching in half sleep at the places where she'd tickled him. He stopped and switched the idling engine off and she sensed his body stiffening. His usual prelude to the matutinal fart, which mostly began quietly and built to the nonexistent god's triumphal crescendo. This one, though, leaked out inaudibly to humans. She imagined nextdoor's dog waking and fetching its lead. The methane would pervade the room subtly with its beige smell.

The skyfinger had wagged to a new angle on the ceiling and shifted to a buff glow, the colour of an unwelcome envelope.

'No, lovely. Not a day off day today. Bloody Monday.'

★

With Ben spectating detachedly around her thigh as they stood in the toilet, Sarah demoused herself.

She tugged the tail and it came away easily. Together they inspected the sleeked snout. Winedark and glutinous. She saw Ben imitate her face, raising the nose affecting slight disdain. Wrap. Bin.

'You want to watch that' Mel said passing the open door, his beigeness ruffled but his hair maddeningly neat. 'Children copy. He'll be trying to stick one of them up his bum.'

Ben laughed and told him it wasn't a bum it was a babyhole and men didn' have a one of them.

'I think your daddy's joking' she said. 'Now you have a go at your morning poo while mummy dresses.'

She left him in position and placated with a toy, squeezed alongside Mel at the sink to wash, and went nightieless before the wardrobe mirror. Mel had opened the bedroom curtains, ensuring the folds hung evenly. Now he would be attending to his beard. He treated his face like some formal Jacobean garden. Face hair was cleared into geometrically exact walkways and piazzas. There were rectangular pieces shaved down on each cheek and two symmetrical arbours of intricate shape on either side of the triangular wedge of hair he permitted underneath the centre of his lower lip. He shaved his neck to leave a parabolic clearing as though this might make it look as if there was still some sure point where chin ended and neck started. He probably spent more time shaving than most men who had no beard at all.

She checked her eye across the workclothes laid on the chair then looked at herself in the glass, haloed in the pale gold of early October sun.

This is the scene where I look in the mirror. Oh come on, god.

The halo made her strawy hair look a bit golder. Nicely out of place. She put her glasses on and the fuzz diminished. All those folds, hanging not evenly at all, sharpened into focus.

My fate is to look more and more like some carved fertility figure the less and less I feel like one. Not tick but flow and look at the flow, like something melted and reset. Or not reset. Melting slower that your eye can follow. Process. But then, the veeshaped thicket looks okay. No absurd bobbly dink. Nicely unkempt. Proper beard. Thou art a fountain of gardens, a well of living waters, and flowing streams from Lebanon. Spikenard and saffron, calamus and cinnamon. Deep romantic chasm athwart a cedarn grove. Yes. Old Sol could still do something with that. But the rest. Hanging gardens more like. Everything yielding to gravity. When you get to thirty four your tits give up and head for the floor.

'Mummy. I done two plops.'

And that breaks the logjam. All to do with gravity and forces acting. What was magically stopped moves. All that shit released. There's the mire, where's the fury?

She started to dress, could hear the radio talking lowly.

'Mummy.'

'Yes, lovely. That's very good. Wipe you bum now. Daddy'll help.'

Eight see books back. Do the last few now. Take the lesson to talk it over. Nine tee worksheet on *Joby*. Eleven ee orals prac. Christ. Noise. Four ell carry on from books then ten minutes for food and enterbleedingprise. Read up for lower six double break-time and now. Modern or medieval? Who cares.

She looked at the red numbers on the clock radio, the flow counter, dimmed by the pale gold air. If the kettle wasn' on in the next ten minutes the whole day would slither out of control. Fill the cup. All of a slither anyway, only happening too slow for the eye to follow.

She fingered the thickness of the gusset in her knickers.

Put a liner in for today. Worksheets. Where? Shelf in staffroom? Top of cabinet in the stockroom? Table in staffroom with all the dirty cups? Christ. On the draining board? Oh Christ. Slithering onto the smirchy floor. The photocopied bulletpoints fanned out under indifferent feet. Chucked out by the caretaker. No. On the shelf surely. That's what we are. Slitheriness. The inconsequential heaving processes at the bottom of muddy water. Gloop. Hard, fixed things like stars, when you look up through the water, are bobbly bits of jelly. What could be magisterial reduced to slither and chimera. And is there any sight less magisterial than fat woman in underwear with tights hitched up over the wombbobble? Blancmange shovelled into a string bag.

'Daddy.'

'I'm shaving' Mel called. She could hear how he held his mouth sideways presenting relevant facial area to mirror.

Giving form and occasion to the spilly slitheriness of process. Occasions just arbitrary markers in all the spill of things. Fictions to make it bearable.

'I'm dressing' she called back.

Counting birthdays. Might as well count the telegraph poles. But there must be occasions. Real ones, critical ones, not just markers. Sperm meets egg, beak breaks shell, that sort of thing. Flashpoints and nodes. The plop point at which what was you stops being you and falls away to muddy the waters. But that's back to process. Nothing seismic. No big deal. Mel. Ben. Me. Hair. Shit. Blood. Having teeth out. From the slither years on there's the slow striptease of the skeleton, the falling hair and floorward flesh. So the halfway mark perhaps is something real. Thirty five Friday. Christ.

'I'm shitting' Ben called.

She buttoned the cuffs on her pale blue blouse and brushed the place where her hips ought to be on her sensible black skirt.

'Good boy' she said. 'I'm coming.'

★

When Shattock sat next to her in the staffroom, Sarah opened the week to view diary in her lap so as to conceal the twin planets of her knees. The black ink wafflegrid of her timetable blared from the opened page.

'Why are the women's bogs so smelly in this place?' he said.

'Morning, Ryan' she said.

The moonfaced electric clock above the door was dragging its minute finger close to twenty five to. She picked up the last five 8C books she still hadn't marked from the floor by her foot. It was like that thing about ironing trousers. However long you spend on them there's always one leg left over you haven't done yet. Always a book left to mark. And Brace would be in soon talking about Finding a Way Forward.

Her red pen dipped on the fractured blue biro text. Mark. Tick. Trying to corset chaos.

'He spelt *business* right' Shattock said.

'What?'

'*Business.* He spelt it right. You put a ring round it.'

'She.'

'She then. Poor handwriting for a girl. She got it right though.'

'Oh. They always spell *business* wrong. They put bu-isness, like nuisance, or they forget about the sin in the middle. Shit.'

'No. Smelt like piss to me.'

Sarah tried to correct the wrong correction then gave up and looked around.

The slanting morning light was doing cruel things to the faces of the forty-odd teachers in the room, even the two new from college who looked like they were in year ten. All faces simultaneously adroop and tense. Some marked, some talked, some stood staring at the noticeboard above the urn by the sink. All with the weight of a new week on them. Peter, her head of department, half sat propped on the edge of a table with his arms folded, listening to the other English specialist, Eunice. Peter spent a lot of time listening to Eunice. He was a decade or two younger than she was, and came from nowhere to take the crown she'd thought would fall on her head when Craddock retired. Peter soothed her hurt by listening and nodding a lot every morning, giving her exactly half the sixth form English teaching. Sarah never got a sniff of that since she came back after Ben.

Through the metalframed windows the soft light made the shoulder of hill hazy and flat. The room was on the first floor so you didn't get kids walking past. The racket of morning voices meant you couldn't hear the main road nearly a mile away where two valleys joined, but she could just see the traffic flowing Cardiffward along it. Arterial. Mel had gone up the other way by now, to the quarry. He'd be there looking silly in his collar and cuffs with a pot belly and a hard hat.

In front of her sitting at the tables citied with bookstacks and scummed mugs were May and Gron. Gron's grey Zero Mostel hairdo was not yet awry. By the afternoon at least one dragged forward strand would unpeel itself and streamer back on his jacket collar. He was talking in his usual undemonstrative way to May whose clutched mug eclipsed the lower part of her wrinkled face, making her eyes look even more concerned.

'– so it was a heart attack, officially' Gron was saying.

May, who lived fifteen miles away, hadn't caught up yet evidently.

'The pong was so bad this morning I actually went in and had a look' Shattock said.

'Had a look for a smell' Sarah said. 'In the women's toilets.'

Gron broke out of his serious sentence. 'You pervy bugger, Ryan Shattock.'

'Well, I was worried somebody'd died in there' Shattock said before he could stop himself. His thick cropped brown moustache buckled as his lips tightened.

'It is bad though' May said, letting him off. 'I've stopped hanging my coat in there.'

'The men's nextdoor don' wiff at all' Shattock said, recovering. 'Just Dettol and soap.'

'It's the natural superiority of the male species' Gron said. There was a time when he would have paused to suck his pipe but you couldn't smoke in the staffroom any more. 'Cleaner. Leaner.' Gron was fatter than Mel. Another suckless suckpause. 'But not meaner.'

'Either you mean male *of* the species' Sarah said, 'or some feminism's rubbing off on you.'

'Typical nitpicking English teacher' Gron said. 'Anyway, nothing feminine's rubbed on me for a very long time.'

'And there's damp in there' May said. 'I'm going to mention it to Mr Brace.'

Sarah had hung her coat on the stand by the damp patch that morning. The grey paint was cracked and curled away from the walls in elegant scrolled cartouches like an old manuscript. The layers of paint underneath were wet and bubbled. In places you could see the oozy pink flesh of the plaster.

'Gron' she said, 'I need a word with Brace too. This lower six history stuff is crazy. I can't do it.'

'You'll be okay, gell. Don' worry. Just follow Perrot. He'll see you through.'

Perrot, three inches thick between hard covers, was by her foot next to 8C. *The Dawn of our Times: Spirit and Structure of Tudor England.* D.M. Perrot, Senior Master somewhere expensive with letters after him like the chemical formula for something damaging to the environment.

'It's not my subject. I only just scraped a pass myself. The kids know more than I do.'

'Highly bloody unlikely. Although I have heard some of them in that group can read this year.'

'They take the piss.'

'That's an occupational hazard. Look, lovely girl, work from Perrot for now and when it comes to essays let me see em before you hand em back. Keep one step ahead and play it like a pro. Act like you know what you're talking about and they'll believe you.'

'It's because she does some Special Needs for me' May said. 'If you teach dull kids the kids think you're dull.'

'The little bloody snobs' Gron said. 'Look, come and have a chat with me dinner time and we'll work out the next one or two sessions.' He pulled his chair closer and dropped his voice. 'The thing is, don' tackle Brace. You know what he's like. What he'll say is: all right, if you can't cope combine your group with Gron's. Good old Gron'll do it. Brace don't care if there's thirty odd in a sixth form group if we're daft enough to do it. He knows we'll just work our nuts off – sorry – and get em through it. That'll be six history lessons a week down the Swanee that we'll never see again. If we can just hang on this year he's bound to appoint next summer.' Something in her face made him add, 'If not before.' He moved back and spoke louder to include the other two. 'Good god. It's October already. Before you look round it'll be half term. What did old Schwarzkopf say. We've just got to hunker down for a bit. With Eileen gone it's looking dodgy for the history department. You know him. Any old reason to whittle staff.'

'Poor old Eileen' May said.

Shattock laid his chiselled hand on the exercise book on Sarah's lap. 'We've got a meeting lunchtime remember' he said. 'In B13. Quarter past. Enterprise. Okay?'

That was why he'd sat by her, to remind her. The twin planets tightened against one another. She felt the mesh of her tights biting. 'Yes' she said. 'Sorry, Gron. I've got a meeting.' She picked up three inch thick Perrot and used it to ease Shattock's hand off her lap. 'I'll have a sneaky look now.'

'No problem, lovely girl' Gron said. 'Mustn' upset the captain of Enterprise.' He looked at Shattock. 'Aye aye, Cap'n Kirk.'

Shattock did not return the salute.

'Watch out.' Sarah looked at moonface. 'The big hand is on the eight. Any second.'

Mr Brace the head, all of thirty eight, balding and ordinary, came in on cue. His escort of two deputies fanned out at his elbows as they trailed him in: Billy Thomas, almost as old as Gron and a Eunice to Brace's Peter, looking as if he'd barely had time to get his shitcoloured trousers and jacket on over his pyjamas; and Glenys Fylfot, not quite as young and unlovely as Brace, wearing her twopiece blue suit and trademark silk scarf. She looked as if she hadn't been home at all over the weekend and was carrying a sheet of white A4 paper which had clearly just been ironed.

Briefly the barking of the teacher on duty in the corridor outside telling children not to run grew louder till the door was shut.

Brace uttered his usual threat:

'Morning everybody.'

The staff ignored him on principle and chatted with itself more loudly for another nine seconds – Sarah watched them glide on the clockface.

She opened Perrot at the marked page. A new chapter less than a quarter of an inch in. 'Consolidation' it was called. Snappy title, Perrot.

Brace delivered a few okays and rights till the racket reduced swiftly through hubbub to murmur to quiet.

'Daily meetings be buggered' Gron said out of the side of his mouth. He had one hand to his lips not holding the pipestem. 'He on'y does this because of *Hill Street Blues*.'

'You watch too much telly' May said.

'It takes my mind off all the sex and violence in this place. He fancies himself as Daniel J. Travanti. That's what it is. He'll be packing a pistol next, you watch.'

Brace began in his Iamanincrediblyreasonableperson tone of voice:

'Right, I'd just if I may like to flag up one or two –'

Consolidation. It seems likely, almost to the point of certainty, that a concept such as democracy, *as it is now entertained, would have been unintelligible to the late medieval mind, and even a term such as* consensus *would have proved highly problematical outside very rigidly defined circumstances. However*

God. What is it with historians and *however*?

'– and there is an Enterprise meeting this lunchtime, that's right, Ryan? Where is he? There. Yes?'

Shattock's face went tenser than usual and he nodded.

'And that's to brief pupils for the Open Evening tomorrow.'

few would demur at the suggestion that with the accession of Henry VII to the throne of England, the first gleamings of what may with some justice be referred to as the modern age, in which such concepts could begin to take root and develop, began to flicker on the horizon.

'Mrs Sarah Bowen's kindly agreed to help out with the written materials for the pupils' projects.' Mrs Sarah Bowen, who had been told to help out with the pupils' written projects, felt her twin planets tighten harder. 'I think it's fair to say, Ryan –' Brace looked to Ryan as if to check that it was fair to say '– that the Enterprise Project has been a h –' he struggled for a big enough adjective and didn't find one '– howling success.'

Shattock lipbucklingly held back his howl.

'The sixth form Design Technology project in particular is looking good and may even have attracted some sponsorship for us from the factory the boys have been working with –'

Appreciative murmurs from the usual appreciative murmurers.

In this chapter, consideration shall be given –

Perrot, magisterially trailing commas, peacocks serenely and in the passive voice into paragraph two. Breast feathers shall be plumped. Here comes an historical grandee.

'– which may be useful in helping us find a way forward on a number of fronts.'

The ting of the till.

claim to the throne foreign policy domestic the barons centralisation finance

Peacock scratches his marks in the dirt, ties labels to bits of the river, draws up the wafflegrid timetable of his chapter. Flags Things Up. Arrogant. Too important to be a mere *I*. The superiority of a Senior Master equipped with chemical weapons.

She flipped the page. All those pages layered on her, three inch thick Perrot and underneath him the fractured biro of the girl who'd learnt to spell *business*, and then the wafflegrid timetable. Past. Present. Future. Enterprise. Dentist. Phone home. Weeks to view with nothing to view yet bar the parents' evenings and birthdays. Birthday. Shit. Under that the dark tightsmesh stretched over her oozy pink planets.

Two portraits of the dead king looked up at her from the new page. A bland painting and a bland bust made from a lifemask. The slanting light couldn't do anything cruel with the flattened black and white faces. Ordinary and, probably, balding. Counter caster. An unprepossessing, thinfaced man with blackish teeth Perrot parroted somewhere, though there was almost certainly an however and a counterpoise in the other half of the sentence.

Are you happy, Henry? No, I'm dead. Coming top doesn't save you from blackening teeth, death of the firstborn. Must phone home. Ask about Kenny.

She moved her tongue over her front teeth. Crooked as any king's, but not black yet. If they were emulsion paint you'd call them Buttercup Yellow with a hint of Vomit Green. If thy tooth offend thee.

The paler yellow of the shifting sun had angled itself less cruelly. The hill outside was less hazy.

Suddenly there was movement and chairscrape. Shattock and Gron were on their feet, the door was open and some of the staff were emptying into the corridor. Brace had finished scraping his marks in the day's dirt, evidently. She wondered if he'd said anything important. Five unmarked. Perrot unperused. The bell rang. She shovelled her books into her big black shoulderbag and made for the door, intruded her bag into the crush of children in the corridor and let the current drag it and her out. No worksheets yet. Slither.

★

Clint and Dustin sat at the front. They always sat at the front. Each had his fingers plaited across his belly. Each had an almost shaven head except for a tufty forelock. With their heads tilted towards one another and looking coyly up at her they looked like a couple of sentient coconuts.

She smiled and Clint, the darker, fatter and rosier of the two, smiled back.

'You two ought to be twins' she said.

'He can be my twin if he want to' Clint said. 'I en gonna be his.'

Sarah thought about this and then decided to stop thinking about it.

'What we doing today, Miss?' Dustin said.

'You'll find out' she said.

So will I, possibly. Every day a separate item to Clint and Dustin. Mention *last time* to them and a look of concentrated straining comes over them, like Ben on the toilet. Dimly some remembered moment, a sentence or a gesture, will swim up at them out of the cold and murk. That was ages ago, Miss. That was last Thursday, kids. The gleamy, evanescent present enough for them to cope with. You've got to keep catching them on the grids of your reminders, intentions. Keep winding them up like clock-work toys and pointing them in the right direction. Or in some direction, anyway.

It was afternoon and this was 7C. Sixteen girls and fifteen boys so new in secondary school you could still smell the shop on some of their grey sweaters. She had hunkered down and survived the morning, sort of, and sitting at the scarred teacher's desk, teacher scarred as much as the desk, she was rummaging in her bag for the little foil wallet of Disprin Directs. As her hand scrabbled she looked at her week to view on the desk. 7C E for L, it said. E for L? It swam back to her out of the murk.

'We do like you, Miss' Clint said.

'Yeah, I do like English' Dustin said.

'I'm very happy for you' she said. 'Now, Clint.' The class was a bit tired after dinner (sorry, Mel, lunch) and therefore quiet, but they wouldn't last much longer. 'I want you to go downstairs. You know the big wooden cupboard –'

'Oh, Miss, Miss' Dustin said. 'I'll go with him, Miss.' His arm yanked him out of his seat and he rose and fell in rhythmic impatience. Several other children joined in though they didn't know what was being asked.

'No. I only need one person, thank you.' Send two and they take twice as long.

Catastrophe rent Dustin's face. He slapped his hand to his forehead. 'Aw, Miss mun.'

She told Clint about the copies of *English for Life* in the cupboard. Fetch copies up for the class. After the usual reiterations he looked as if he knew what to do. Wound up and directed, he whirred out of the room.

Her hand found the foil wallet.

'Right form one – form seven' she said. 'Carry on reading –' she saw the little sword symbol on the tablet wrapper '– carry on reading from *The Silver Sword* till we get the new books.'

After working out what page they were on and organising shared copies for those who'd forgotten theirs, she sat and tore the foil and placed two tablets on her tongue.

Sweetish fizz. Not much good for the stomach, especially on top of the sherbet lemons breaktime. Womb pain to brain pain. No rest. No stillness. Need something to still the aching gloop in my skull. Wonder if it dissolves tooth enamel as well as sweets do. Sweet disintegration.

The thumping in her head muted, as did the sense of there being a huge crowd somewhere nearby shouting. She looked round, checking the usual suspects. All okay. They'd settled over their books, some of them even reading. Outside on the thread of far road the traffic was thinner and faster. The sky had marbled with cloud. Dove Grey with a hint of Puce. Almost restful.

She swivelled her diary so that its edges were exactly parallel to the edges of the desktop. That's for Mel. She picked up the black biro and checked over the morning.

How to get a headache.

So. After prayers and registration. 9.15. Ding. Round one. 8C books back. She put an ex next to books back. Not books back. When see them next? Wednesday morning. In Wednesday she

20

wrote: 8C books back. Then in Tuesday dinnertime a reminder: Finish 8C books. She'd given them the next piece of work on paper this morning. Stalling. For display, she'd told them. Where, Miss? They'd looked round the bare room used by several dozen different classes and teachers. General Classrooms, General Brace called them. Er, the Library. The Foyer, perhaps. Just get on with it. Finish it off for homework. Why the hell did I say that? After 8C books back under Wednesday she wrote: Collect wk. on ppr. She said it because they fussed, didn't settle. Congratulations, Mrs Bowen. Another direct hit right in the foot with the twelve bore. Ding. 9T lesson two. Still no bloody worksheets. She'd found one crumpled copy in her bag. Technician too busy. Couldn' use the Office photocopier. English Department can't afford. She'd chalked most of the sheet on the blackboard and they'd copied. Spun it out anyway. When next? Tuesday. In Tuesday she wrote: 9T cont. wkst. fin. as hw. When next? Friday. In Friday she wrote: 9T coll hw. Joby wkst. In the little space for Sunday she wrote: Mark 9T wkst. Ha ha. Ding. After break and sherbet lemons she'd reeled into the Physics Lab where, inexplicably, she taught 11E English. Most of the kids already there and Darren and Mark fighting. Nothing serious but it would have got that way. The girls impassive on the stools with their arms folded. Tina never takes her coat off without a dumbly insolent fight. Glad I don' have to teach them PE. Darren redfaced and his collar more awry than usual, Mark snorting, built like Desperate Dan only hairier. Sorry, Miss. He called me a fuckin English bastard and I en fuckin English. So they'd started the oral prac early, sort of. By the time that was sorted out there was only fifteen minutes left. Barely enough to sort the groups and get them talking. Barely time to get round and check the topics. Barely time for Tina to wrap her coat tighter while Sarah was at the far end of the room and mouth the words '– that fuckin cow –'. Ding. And then, when they've gone, go round switching all the gas taps off and then limpjogging the four hundred yards to the far end of C Block with three inch thick Perrot like a housebrick in your bag. 10L reading lesson all I could cope with by then. She checked over 11E's week. Shakespeare, novel, poems. A snip. Essay coming in Thursday. In the little space for Sunday under Mark 9T wkst. she wrote: & 11E ess. Ha bloody ha. But 10L pleasant enough, thank the nonexistent god. Ding. Then ten minutes for dinner. The half eaten cheese and tomato sandwich was still in her bag. Ten minutes before Captain Kirk beamed me up to the Enterprise Meeting. The scummy thirdfull mug of cold coffee still on a staffroom table with her new moon lipprint sticky on the rim. B13 big and cold like a zeppelin hangar. Echoey. Classrooms always seem different dinnertimes. Off duty. As if they're waiting.

The last grit of the aspirin dissolved from her tongue. Nuances of dove grey and puce melted across the windows.

Ryan Shattock standing in his scorched metalworkroom white overalls, chiselly hands clasped across his front unconsciously covering his balls, cropped lip buckling judiciously before the choosing of words.

'Right then, boys –' and afterthinking, '– and girls –'

Sarah checked. Among the twenty one in the meeting, four girls.

And details. Where. Display boards. The logistics of setting up after school tomorrow. Shattock itemised. Of course, Miss Bowen here will be on hand as well as me and the CDT staff. She will? And it's Mrs, prat. Under Tuesday the black biro wrote: 6.00 pm sch. Op. Eve. Tell Mel. Shit. Fifteen minutes of Shattockwaffle before she could go round the groups and look at the written materials for display. It have all been spellchecked, Miss. Darren, smelling of Lynx, stiff with gel, sheepish after the punchup, atoned by showing her his photo display on the garden furniture his group had made. Have you got any idea how much six inch nails do cost, Miss? It's really tight. On'y made two fifty on the chair. Sold it to my gran but she aven got a garden so it's up our back. Sarah looked. Nice, she said, thought she might get a couple for the slabs (sorry, Mel, patio) in the garden.

'Miss.'

Then the rodentfeatured boy in charge of the upper sixth group. Not bad looking really. But the sharp quivery nose, nervous eyes. Hair cropped but somehow infinitely respectable. Clean like a sixties American crewcut. Aye aye, Cap'n. Sort of male teenage equivalent of a blue rinse. His group's stuff for presentation immaculate too. Complicated machine plans. Arcs and straight lines and specifications, lists of figures on gridded paper. Photos and folders and leaflets. Some sort of miniature crane.

'Miss.' Dustin's face screwed up. He was shaking his digital watch at her. 'He've been gone ages, Miss. Can I go and have a look for him, Miss, please. I know where the blue cupboard is, Miss.'

She looked at her watch and started. 'Oh dear. Yes, okay then.'

Dustin went out, leaving the door open. The girl who always sat by the door stretched across her desk and shut it as usual.

We have a lot of material from the factory too, rodent said. And the scale model is ready for us to assemble in the hall tomorrow. Sounded his aitches. His fine hand on the blueprint, his fingers thronged with nerves. Her liner pressed her underneath. Funny how you feel like that after the blood stops.

The class's building murmur was just signalling she should do something when Dustin hurled himself through the door.

'Miss, Miss. Clint've fallen down the stairs.'

A squirt of acid in the stomach.

'Okay. You lot stay where you are. Tammy, you're in charge.'

She ran along the corridor to the stairhead and half way down the first flight, black biro still in her hand. Dustin, following her, talked long sentences mainly composed of the word Miss.

'Shut up, Dustin' she said and then regretted it.

Clint was lying on his back on the landing with his hands under his head, waiting for her. He looked a bit dazed and very pleased. She imagined tiny winged coconuts tweeting in a circle round his head.

Splashed on every part of the stairs and landing and hanging from the handrails were ruffled copies of *English for Life*. An awful lot of them.

She bent over Clint and looked at his eyes. They were clear.

'Are you all right?'

He smiled uncertainly and gave a minimal nod.

'What day is it?'

'Don' know, Miss.'

'No, why should you. What's your name?'

'Clint?' He answered as if it might be a trick question.

'Can you get up?'

Another minimal nod.

'Come on then. Dustin, you start helping with the books.'

Clint staggered and shook his head and blinked his eyes like he'd seen in cartoons as he got to his feet. The three of them gathered the copies. An awful lot of them. Far more than there were children in 7C.

'Cli-int?' she said.

'Yes, Miss?'

How many copies did you try to bring?' As she said this she could see him, as in a film, the shot taken from over his fat right

23

shoulder, opening the double doors of the big blue cupboard and there in tight stacks are one hundred and ninety seven fat copies of *English for Life.*

'All of em, Miss.'

She closed her eyes. Clint teetering down the corridor unsighted by the wobbly stack. Then bobbling up the first flight and round the landing, part way up the second flight. Breakpoint. Something happens. The stack snaps and there's the bookfountain, book-slither. Uncontrollable pagegush.

She opened her eyes and there was Clint smiling and the sub Mondrian grid of squares patterning the book cover. *English for Life.* Like a prison sentence. Grit on my teeth. Poor Eileen.

★

Outside, a serious faced girl was fiddling with something made of wood and paper. She was holding it up and trying to untangle the yards of string that hung from it. Sarah watched her through the Geography Room window.

Last double of the day. The headache was bound and gagged but still twitching. She was nearly five minutes late for the lower sixth double History but none of the lower sixth had shown up yet. Just as well as she had to get the key to the room from the head of Geography, who kept order in his kingdom by keeping its borders closed. It meant he could leave a slide projector and screen out permanently, and the door of the stockroom in one corner open. The blackout blinds, which were literally black, and all the arcane paraphernalia of his subject were more or less undamaged.

Two kids had come to see her in the ten minute afternoon break. Clint, ostensibly to apologise, but mainly to smile at her and say hello and how much he liked doing English, mainly because they could use biros, not like in the old school where Miss Turner made them use cartridge pens and he never got the hang of them. And a small boy from 8C with his exercise book. Sorry it's late, Miss. I been away. On'y come back this dinner time. Then she stole a few extra minutes after the bell rang to contemplate Perrot. Stood in the toilet by the coatstand and the scrolly wall in the pissstink. *In this chapter, consideration shall be given.* More boring than god. And outside, May's voice. The smell is *terrible*, Mr Brace. Terrible

terrible. I won't hang my coat in there any more. Right, May, well inform Glenys Fylfot. She's Fabric. Mr Brace, come in and see for – No, well, look I'll tell Glenys myself. You're quite right. It must be dealt with.

'I wonder what she's doing.'

Sarah looked round. The first of the sixth formers was standing next to her, looking out at girl with wood and paper. Sarah couldn't remember the sixth former's name. One of the keen quiet girls, selfconscious, shrinking, who wrote down everything you said in unsure inflated handwriting.

'No idea' Sarah said. It hadn't occurred to her to wonder what girl with wood and paper was doing. Too tired.

The cast of the lower sixth group assembled itself in the usual series of shambling entrances with coats and bags and grating chairlegs. Thirteen of them. Count how many in a day. Take some doing. How can you know so many, and how count? Ding. Seconds away, round – what number? The last for today, anyway. She gathered her energy and put on a show of being more or less conscious for the last hour and a bit.

'Right –' she said, sitting at the desk where she'd spread diary, mark book, Perrot.

'Oo, it's a gloomy old room this.' Steve, the usual last late arrival, stumbled in. He had no bag and no coat, a flimsy pocket notebook in his hand. He flicked the fluttering striplights on. 'I don' know. This is what they call cross curricular is it. History in the Geography Room. What next? Synchronised swimming in the car park? Sorry, Mrs Bowen.' He wasn't. 'Was I interrupting something?' He sat at the front next to Mandy under the black globe that hung close to the ceiling.

What was that for? A black globe with the continents in white lines, and the nets of latitude and longitude in finer white lines. Degrees, minutes, seconds. A little pulley to lower it for lessons. A fine dusting of chalk on the north pole making an educational arctic. They had one of those glasstopped desks too, at the back under the window, with a light inside so you could trace maps.

'Right –' she said again.

'Can we keep our coats on? It's cold.'

'Yes okay.'

'I en cold' Steve said.

'Well you don' ave to keep you coat on.'

'He aven got a coat with him.'

'That's a' right then.'

The voices came too fast for her to follow who was speaking.

'I don' believe in coats' Steve said. 'They're a bourgeois concept.'

Mandy rolled her eyes upward. 'Aye. Like washing.'

Steve looked at her and pouted. She had dazzling blue eyes and breasts which defied the law of gravity. Sarah felt her own dugs hanging from her like a bloodhound's flews.

'Oo, you're lovely when you're angry' Steve said. 'But you have trouble with irony. Sorry if it just gets a bit too post-modern and beyond you.'

'Fuck off' Mandy said.

'Er, I'm with you in spirit, Mandy' Sarah said, too tired to muster the conventional anger, 'but praps you could have expressed it better.' Though I doubt it. 'Right, for the third time. This afternoon I'm going to talk for a bit about the years of Henry VII's reign and the ways in which he consolidated his power from what was initially really quite a tenuous position.'

Tenuous. Nice. Where'd that come from? Snakish. Slithering. That's where from. Slither. Henry hissing like a snake. Slowly silently now the moon. Tenuous to tenacious. Gripping stuff.

'He – he strengthened his grip on –'

Through the windows behind the class, on the strip of grass under the blind wall of the school hall, she could see girl with wood and paper running back and forth, gripping the string. A kite! There was almost no wind. The wood and paper kite wrote a tight spiral in the running girl's wake.

'Grip on what, Miss?' Shrinking writers had paused as she did. The poised biros.

'On – things.'

'Mrs Waters never let us put a *thing* in history essays last year' Mandy said, without irony.

'This isn't an. Oh all right. Just strengthened his grip.' Spare me the thing jokes, kids, please.

Mike at the back, his chair tilted dangerously against the glasstopped desk, half raised a hand. 'Miss, is it okay if I put my thing –'

'No thank you, Michael.'

Some of them laughed. Really, it was going better than usual.

'But –' Steve said.

'Nor she wouldn' let us start a sentence with a *but*' Mandy said.

'But' Steve said, concentrating, 'you have to grip on something.'

'No you don't' Mike said. 'You can just strengthen your grip, like an exercise. You know. Like, just strengthening your grip.' He exercised his fist on the air.

'Yeah, but in this case –'

'How do you spell *tenebrous*, Miss?' One of the selfconscious shrinkers.

'– in this case' Steve said, 'it's got to be on something. I mean it's not like an exercise.'

'Tenebrous?' Sarah said. 'Tenuous. Tee ee en – look you don't have to write down every word.'

'Is it? Not just an exercise?' Steve said. He was looking at Sarah with his eyebrows raised, asking for her agreement. She suddenly realised he was serious. No irony. He had long eyelashes and green eyes.

'No, okay' she said. 'Yes, he had to strengthen his grip on something. It was his grip on – on –'

'Power' Mike said, and his fist closed and shook in the air.

Girl with kite entered windowsquare left of frame, fists closed on the string, trailing the twirling paper and wood and exited right of frame. A few seconds later she charged back the other way. About year nine, probably. She had stubby legs and her socks had come down.

'Yes' Sarah said. 'That's right.' A lot better than usual. Better than the silence last Friday. But then, Friday afternoon I ought to be grateful they turned up at all. Steve didn't. Good turn out really, but dismal lesson. Giving me a chance today. They always give you some sort of chance. Not much maybe. 'So, let's get on shall we? The relevant chapter in Peacock is page sixty eight. "Consolidation".'

'Peacock?' Mandy twisted her mouth in a pantomime of suppressing a laugh.

'Perrot. Perrot. It's page sixty eight.'

Only half of them had their copies. Steve slid Mandy's copy into the middle of the desk to share it with her and Mandy pulled it away again. Steve looked round for another copy to borrow, saw none nearby and sat back.

'Can you please bring your copies' Sarah said. Sometimes she got a whole minute and a half out of elaborating this point, but today she was too tired.

Working her eyes more or less furtively between Perrot and her hasty notes, she began to build a confused, fumbling story of

Henry VII's purposefulness. Occasionally she looked at the gridded page of her mark book for the list of sixth formers' names to ask a question. There was only the list of names there so far. No marks yet. Have to do something about that. She asked a question when she wasn't sure what the answer was herself and tried to aim it at people with copies so that they might have the chance of seeing some answer in Perrot which she'd missed. Claim to the throne. The barons. Finance. In the film in her head, Henry was played by Brace in a Lulu wig. Staying in his office. Doing accounts. Daily meetings with clerkish underlings.

'Miss, was he York or Lancaster?' One of the shrinkers.

'Well, he united the two houses and the Tudor rose was the emblem of the new peace.'

'But which was he?'

'Well, he married Elizabeth of – of –'

'Lancaster' Mandy said decisively.

'That's right. Elizabeth of Lancaster.'

'No no' Mandy said. 'Henry was Lancaster. He married Elizabeth of York.'

Sarah and Mandy looked at one another. Mandy's breasts pointed outward and upward victoriously.

If I'm going to feel humiliated now's the time. But I don't feel anything particularly, except that the bound and gagged hostage in my head has worked a foot loose and is thumping a heel against the inside of my skull.

'So who married Elizabeth of Lancaster?' Mike said.

Mandy looked round at him and mimed a sarcastic laugh.

'Fuh-nee.'

'I tell you another thing I don' get, Miss' Mike said. He untilted himself from the glass desk so that all four of his chairlegs were on the floor. He sat forward. 'What I don' get is, like, Henry was Welsh, right. Right?' He looked round to check there was agreement. From his seat at the back he could see everybody. Most skewed round halfheartedly to look at him. Some of the shrinkers looked at their intimate pages, where they'd written nothing since they crossed out Elizabeth of Lancaster. 'Right. So, if he was Welsh, okay, and he landed in Milford Haven and all that, how come, how come he was of Lancaster? How come he was that then, 'cause that's like England.' He sat back.

'Well' Sarah said slowly, after the pause, 'Perrot hasn't got a lot to say about –'

'I mean, was it like Jonathan Davies going north?'

Groans.

'No' Mike said. 'I just want to understand that's all. I don' get it.'

'He came back though' Mandy said. 'Jonathan Davies.'

'Old Jon's a good boy' Mike said. 'Not like Henry. He was a bit of a sod I reckon. Do you think it should've stayed amateur, though? Okay. Sorry, Miss. I'll shut up.' He gently launched his chair back against the glass desk again.

There was silence. It would have been ideal for Mandy to titter, but she didn't.

Instead she said, 'Miss, do you enjoy teaching this?'

Sarah stared at her.

Regroup. Make something happen. Suddenly Henry wasn't so Bracelike. He was Jonathan Davies in a Lulu wig. Mud and blood on him after the game. Out of breath and heroic. A bit puzzled by the chaos of it all, the fury and mire, and unassuming, but standing there when the smoke clears, gripping the serpent by the throat. Making the next thing happen.

She cleared her throat. 'Well look, there are things to discuss there. To be honest I'm not absolutely clear about the background to all that, Michael. Perhaps we can come back to it another time.'

To be honest. And I nearly was for a fraction of a second, but still managed to make it fudgy. Gloop.

The shrinkers looked relieved. Mandy, Mike and Steve looked blank, especially Steve. He sat back with his head on one side. His lips, thickish and really quite – well, his lips were pressed to a line. He always wore the same black sweater, crewnecked so high you couldn't see whether he was wearing a tie or not. Black trousers, too. His long thin legs stuck out under the desk. Even his trainers were black. He looked like a piece of dark that had got up and walked away.

'But what I really want to come on to' she said, 'is the broad picture that Perrot touches on in places in this chapter.'

She talked on. Here it comes. Modern or medieval.

'1500 is often given as a convenient date to mark the end of the medieval period and the beginning of what's often called the modern period.' What's often called. The peacock passive stalks my talk. Helmets shall be doffed. On with the floppy hats. End of a period what I feel is randy. 'But really for the purposes of this study, the date of the Battle of Bosworth could be a more appropriate marker.' Henry, taking his gumshield out, wipes the mud from his forehead, has a shower, chooses a sharp suit. And marker. Yes. Counting. Tie our labels to the stream.

She talked on. It was easy. The sweephand on her wristwatch accelerated. Modern and medieval. Henry the Turning Point. Crux. Cusp. Fulcrum. The plop point at which what was one thing becomes something else. Henry the Node. It started to make a kind of sense.

Steve, still linelipped, sat with each hand stuck under the opposite arm, his crumpled notebook unopened on the desk.

'So the big issue' she said, kept going so they wouldn't talk about the magazine, 'the big issue so far as we're concerned is to grapple with those broad concepts and look at how they apply in – your first History essay for A level.'

Some of the shrinkers froze in midscribble. There were exchanged looks. Steve was motionless under the dark planet.

'Henry made a lot of things happen' she said. 'Was he a modern or a medieval king?'

There. The gauntlet thrown down, or a foppish renaissance kid glove.

'And that's the topic I want you to write about. Was Henry VII a modern or a medieval king?'

There was a pause of her making. Her mark.

'You mean, like, homework' Mike said.

Girl with kite careered across the window, gripping the fluttering string and paper serpent. Voices asked for the title again. Deadline. References. (Shrinkers.) Mrs Waters used to show us videos. (Mandy.) Mrs Eileen Waters is waters under the bridge. Sorry.

And I have made this happen.

She looked at her watch. Twelve minutes left. Collect Ben by quarter past. Pay the two weeks. What's in the freezer? Cuppa first. Have to leave it another hour plus before I can retie the hostage. Try Migra-leve this time, praps. How hang on for the twelve minutes?

'Right' she said, 'there's a quarter of an hour or so left, so I'd like you to use this time to look over your notes and Perrot and start roughing out an essay plan. On –' she couldn't remember what day their next lesson was '– in our next session we'll talk the plans over.' Save much planning for the next one. Really has gone better than usual.

She looked at them. Some slumped a little further over their books. All our spines curling forward slower than we can see. Mike kicked himself forward decisively and flourished his pen. All yielding a little to gravity, except pert Mandy, who made her notes sitting bolt upright, and Steve, still laid back, literally, dark arms crossed and head atilt. Sarah looked from his unopened notebook to his face as if to invite him to join in. Slowly his lips unrolled themselves from the tight line they'd been and opened so she could see part of his teeth. Nice teeth. His hair was straight and dark, not too long, a bit ruffled.

'But' he said, 'the end of a period.'

His head straightened and hers cocked, questioning.

'Yes?' she said.

'Well, the end of one period and the beginning of another. It en tha' simple is it? Like one man. It en like that. I mean like one person imposing their will. It en simple like that.'

Outside, the kite had thumped silently against the grass. The socksdown year niner was leaning forwards, hands on knees, her shoulders and chest heaving.

'It'd better be simple if I'm doing an essay on it' Mike said without looking up.

'I mean' Steve said, 'oo, let's face it, hasn' it really got more to do with – or just as much to do – or, no – more to do with the fall of Constantinople and, say, the Silk Road, instead of being down to some bloke with a funny haircut?'

His hands had freed themselves and were gesturing above the desk. Long fingers. Nervethronged. He looked straight at her.

'The fall of Constantinople?' she said, shifting her eyes away a little too slow.

'Yeah. Or even before that when the Turks were starting to expand. And the Silk Road because of gunpowder, see.' He made a noise to imitate an explosion and made a blossoming explosion gesture with the long fingers. 'Bet that made all the difference, brightened things up a bit.'

Mandy, who'd been miming irritation as she tried to make her notes, looked up. 'What are you on?'

Steve turned his pout on her. 'Oo, I know what I'd like to be on.'

'In your dreams, stickman' Mike said without looking up.

'But you take my point though?' Steve looked back to Sarah, wideeyed and asking approval.

She nodded in a kind of circle, trying at the same time to see if his pupils were any more dilated than usual. She didn't think they were.

'Well I think I –' she said, '– well no, not entirely.'

'The thing about it is, see, in ancient times the Greeks, they spread all over the place and they had libraries and scientists and things. Oops. Sorry. There's another thing. And the Babylonians were good astronomers. Did you know our numbers are Arabic, by the way?'

Steve talked and outside the socksdown girl looked at her watch and started to wind up the string on her kite.

Sarah stared at his wide green eyes and the shadowy furze coming on his jaw.

If it wasn't for the hostage drumming his heel. No.

Somebody had turned the volume down. Or she'd sunk in some enveloping murk and the talking face had become bobbly, soundless jelly. Then you surface from wherever it is and the volume goes up again, the face comes cinematically back into focus, like coming to.

'– so really almost any date would do, you could choose another if you wanted to.' Steve came back into sound and clear picture, looking to one side of her, off in his own gloop. 'Oo, let's see. Fourteen fifty something it was for Constantinople. But in fact there'd been a braindrain out of there for years before that, like I said. It en just like one bloke or one moment. There's all sorts of factors going on.'

'You could say that about anything' Mandy said.

'True' Steve said, as though that conceded nothing. 'Tha' don' make it any less so. Actually I think it's a really important point.'

Most of the others were pokerfaced. They'd shut their books. Sarah looked at her watch. Five minutes. Girl with kite had gone. Cod in butter sauce in freezer. Do Ben.

Steve looked round the room.

'Well?' he said. 'What do you think?' And looking back at her: 'What do you think? Mrs Bowen?'

He never called her Miss, for which she was grateful. But he always managed to make *Mrs Bowen* sound ironic. Anyway she never quite believed the sound of her married name. Another bit of god's novel that failed to convince.

'Well' she said, 'give me the broad thrust of it again.' Christ. The broad thrust of it.

But Steve was too preoccupied for the usual innuendoes. His mouth opened and closed like a fish as he gagged on the logjam of ideas, details.

'Well, look' he said at last. 'Oo, this is difficult. I mean, how about if – the title's Was Henry VII a modern or medieval king, right? How about if when we go over the essay plans I'll go over it then. I tell you what I do. If I can have a bit of latitude in how I interpret the question I can do a proper job on it in sentences and all that. Okay?'

'Okay' Sarah said. Mike was packing his books into his huge Adidas bag. She flipped her diary to the timetable. 'That sounds interesting. Well let's say everybody else gets a rough plan ready for next session – Wednesday morning. And Steven.' She looked up. 'Yours is a bit special and you'll need a bit more time. You can do your presentation on Friday afternoon.'

A smile dawned on Mandy's face. 'Sussed' she said.

But Steve seemed untroubled by the thought of having to come to school on a Friday.

'A pleasure, Mrs Bowen' he said.

'So, everybody' Sarah said, 'I'd like you to be ready to give a brief talk, no more than five minutes, on your essay plan on Wednesday. Work independently till then and that'll make it more interesting. And we'll follow it up with discussion and Steve'll do his presentation on Friday. Got it? Make a note.' Sum up. Signpost. Very nearly good technique.

She looked round. A few shrinkers made notes. Steve picked up his pocket notebook – his equivalent of packing his bag. As usual he had no pen. The others moved books bagwards. When the bell rang they made the usual break for it. Hauled bags pushed tables askew.

She wrote under Wednesday: L6D. Hist.ess.pl.pres.&disc.; and under Friday: L6D.Hist.Steve pres.&disc.

Two shrinkers talked as they passed her desk.

'I en gonna do it. You gonna do it?'

'Go on mun. I' can' be any worst.'

Good stuff really. Two doubles more or less sorted. Bound to be overspill speakers or absentees on Wednesday to run on into Friday and fill it up. Two doubles pretty well sorted. Get to know them, they learn something, and not even any marking yet. Could even impression grade em like an oral. Good technique.

'Mrs Bowen.' Steve was standing in the doorway, his notebook rolled like a little telescope, the last to leave. 'I think that's a really excellent idea you had then. Really good. Thanks. You won' regret it.' He went, awkwardly.

She looked at the slither of papers on her desk. They didn' look as if they'd all fit back in her bag, but she would fit them in. The head of Geography would come in in the morning and precisely realign the desks like a Mondrian of educational furnishing.

Children and the occasional member of staff were streaming past outside the window. Gron with his briefcase and, at last, his pipe, his odd, undulating walk. One grey rope of his Zero Mostel was unfurled and dangling back.

*

In the television, thousands of curiously shaped fish shimmered and darted. They were metallic blues and reds, largeeyed, miraculously sharply focussed. Next to them the oblong of window was starting to darken, dovegrey going leaden.

She switched the light on and her ghost appeared in the sky, wearing owlish discs of glasses, the hand raised to the lightswitch, a fuzzy double image in the double glazing. She held the pose, and Ben, looking up from his almost empty plate, froze staring at the window. The ghost tableau stared back at them, but only it stayed still. No escape. The sky kept slowly melting. A light came on in the Jenkinses' across the close and their curtains twitched shut. There were the trickle and gush sound effects of the nature documentary on television.

She willed it to freeze but Ben slid from his chair to the floor, the dirty fork still in his hand, to where his scatter of toy cars waited. Baggy sweater. The blancmange unnetted and rebagged in leggings. Like some nightmare double Dutch interior, only not holding a lute or pointing to some map, just switching the light on.

Free first tomorrow so sort the day out then. But it's 10L second, then 11E for a double, then food. Finish 8C's books then. Or no. I could do them in the free or tonight. Look for the worksheets in the free. Have dinner dinnertime. A novelty. Then after dinner (sorry) double 9E and double 9T. What the hell was I doing with 9E last week? Enterbloodyprise. Tell Mel.

She moved, thinking to get her diary, then saw the butter sauce smirched fork on the carpet. She picked it up and gathered Ben's plate and beaker.

'Thank you, mummy' she said.

'Thank you, mummy' Ben said, interrupting his traffic noises.

And now the bit in the striplit kitchen with chromegleam and the plastic bowl and squirt and swish and the bubbles with hundreds of striplights in them. My overlapped selves projected on the dark window. Come on, god. Sun makes a grand entrance then skulks offstage after doing sod all while we watch telly. Where's your sense of dramatic structure? Just my bit of earth turning its face away. Soon, Mel's return and the usual conversation. Where is he? A bit late. Won' be able to see his garden. Odour of. Every scene bathetically buggered up. Yes. How about something a bit Lawrentian? A knock at the door and a man with quarry dust on his face, wringing his daicap in his hands. The man's clothes and his hair and his face were covered in the grey stone dust of the quarry, covered in stone dust so that he himself was like a statue, save for the gleam of his eyes and the small, diffident, inchoate movements of the cap. The dark haired boy stopped his inchoate whittling and watched the man with dark, suspicious eyes. When he saw the woman looking at him he retreated a little further into the semi dark at the far side of the hearth. Her face lost some of its aristocratic severity as she looked back to her visitor and tenderly wiped the dough from her palm upon a fold of pinafore. We thought the area was clear when we charged up the shots, Mrs Bowen. Charged up the shots. Sounds like the right sort of phrase. We sounded the hooter like always. Not a mark on his face. Then Mel's broken body brought in on a stretcher. Curious neighbours eager for vicarious grief, hesitating on doorsteps. Wearing monochrome shawls. Come on.

She slid plates and cutlery into the hot water. Through the half open door to the other room she could hear the television mixed with Ben's voice. His stockinged foot showed around the door, moving slightly as he played with the cars. Water sounds and water music. A voice. The rich anodyne voice of the programme's narrator. Pauses timed in sync with images she couldn't see. It was warm. Warm routines. A red sock. A warm voice. That's okay. Nice, even.

She came to. The fractured ghost of her face swam at her through the dark glass. I'm tired.

'What did you say, mummy?'

'Nothing, lovely.' Must have said it out loud. I am tired.

She plunged her hands in the washing up bowl, felt, unseen through the web of bubbles, the greasy plate against her fingertips.

'Meanwhile' the voice said, 'in the calmer waters of the under-bank, females lay their festoons of beaded spawn.'

And a hand was reaching across her pulling the curtains shut. The knuckles brushed the flutes into alignment.

'I didn' hear you come in' she said.

'You're on display like a goldfish bowl' Mel said. He pulled off his coat.

'I'm knackered' she said. 'It's in the oven.'

'You eaten?'

'Aye.' The other half of the cheese and tomato sandwich, Migraleve and a pint of coffee. Had to retrieve one slice of tomato out of the bottom of my bag. Hang on. Diary.

She went into the hall and took her diary out of her bag, realised her hands were wet and carried it back into the kitchen under her arm, groping for a tea towel.

'We could get a dishwasher' Mel said, scouring the plates and putting them on the drainer. She never got them properly clean for him.

'There's bourgeois.' She surprised herself with a new word in the routine.

'Not very green either, I suppose' Mel said. 'They use a lot of water.'

'How was work?'

'Blew up a bit more mountain and sold it to the English.' He yawned as he shook his hands and took the tea towel from her. Temporary pit gaping in the garden. He unyawned and looked at her. 'You tired?'

'Knackered. I said.'

'Me too.' He ovengloved the lasagna from the oven and carried it into the other room, past the red sock. 'Any tea made?'

'No.'

'Bugger off then. You had lunch today?'

'Yes. I said.'

'Cor, fishies. Fishies, Ben.'

'No they ent, daddy. They're cars.'

She heard Mel drawing the curtains in the livingroom. Keeping his eating a private act. She looked at the diary and couldn't remember why she was looking at it.

'So how are things in the ivory tower?' Mel said through lasagna.

'You bugger off. I got a meeting tomorrow. In for six. Open evening. You'll have to be back for me to have the car.'

'Right.'

Come on. Why not the dusty corpse on the shagpile?

She heard Mel zap the channel and the anodyne voice gave way to the anodyne music of a soap opera. No. You work till you can't stand up and your brains turn to mashed potato and you watch drivel and talk ballocks.

Sponging the dust from the marble face. Intense silence. Everything sculpted into meaning.

★

After Mel had put Ben to bed Sarah sat at the bottom of the stairs and made a phonecall. (We could get a cordless, Mel said.)

'Hello?'

'Hello, mam.'

'Hello, Sarah.' Always the same tone of huge surprise. 'How are you, love?'

'Very good.'

'You do sound tired.'

'I'm a' right.'

'How's Mal?'

'Mel. He's a' right.'

Through the bottleglass panels in the door to the livingroom she could see Mel, shoes off, headphones on (The stereo's even better through these), head back, corpselike but unmarble, unheroic.

'He's tired too I expect.'

'He's a' right.'

'He've got a hard job, fair play. You do both work too hard.' Pause. 'And how's my Benny boy?'

'He's a' right. He's in bed.'

'Love him. He's tired I expect.'

'Ye-es.'

'What's a matter, love?'

'Nothing. I'm a' right.'

'It's a pity I don' live a bit nearer.' Pause. 'I could have him instead o' that old minder.'

Thirteen miles. She thought of home. The word. Got no further. Change course, head her off.

'How's dad?'

'Oh, bloody hopeless. He's tired. He's by here looking at me. Yes you are. He is. He've put the deckchairs up the attic and he's buggered up now. He'll talk to you in a bit if you like.'

'In a bit. Listen, mam.' What was it? She should have made a list of points. 'Listen, we'll come up this Saturday.'

'Oh, lovely. We don' see you very often. Now listen, now. Tha reminds me. Your birthdy Fridy.'

'Aye.'

'Now I got you a card. Do you want money or what?'

'Whatever, mam. It don' matter.'

'Yes it do. How old are you now. Thirty three.'

'Five.'

'Thirty five. Thirty six Fridy. Good god.'

'Thirty five Friday.'

'Thirty five Fridy. That's right. Good god. Where've it gone? You're catching me up, gell.'

'Half way.' You were this age when you had me.

Sarah put her hand on her belly, gripped a rolling fold of it through her sweater. Gripped. Dug a thumbnail in. Gripped.

'And Mal's?'

'He's forty.'

'Forty. That's right. Same as our Ken. He'll be forty one January. Is it forty one?'

The other item on my list. 'How is he?'

'Who?'

'Ken.' Pause. Remember? My libidinous brother, out of whose arse the sun always shone. Length of pause proportional to his familial entanglements.

'Oh, a' right. He's okay. That bloody old job do get him down. They do make him do a lot o weekends when he 'ouldn' go if he had the choice. The same time they're looking to sack people.'

Pause. Sarah gripped the fold. Go on. Tell me about him and Sandra.

'He used to like it over the works when it was going' her mother said. 'Tha bloody factory. It's a bloody hole.'

Bloody hole. Yes. Her fingers clutched tighter. 'How's Sandra?'

'Huh. A' right. We don' see em very often. Them girls are growing up.' So back with her or not? Ask dad next time. Not now. Too tired.

'It's work do worry him' her mother said. 'There's always talk about layoffs. But listen.' The tiny voice bubbled in the earpiece.

Sarah felt herself sink back, water closing over her face. Sometimes bubbles broke from her mouth as she spoke but she had no sense of what she was saying.

'– so there's no news from you then' her mother was saying from hundreds of miles away.

'Sorry' Sarah said, coming to. 'Mam, I got to go. I'm falling asleep.'

'Aw. There. I knew you was tired.'

Shit. Shouldn've said. 'No, I'm a' right. But I'll see you Saturday, right?'

They went through the elongated courtesies of ringing off.

Afterwards she sat on the stairs with one hand on the phone and the other still clutching her side. Why did I ring? A list of points like a business call or an essay plan. But it isn' like that. Things are gloop. So much effort to manage to say anything.

She went through the livingroom and the dining area to the kitchen. Mel didn't stir. She didn't turn the light on in the kitchen but opened the fridge so it threw its yellow rectangle of light across the floor like a perverse fireplace. Inside, various things given to rotting were arranged in glass bowls.

Unfinished business of the day: a few 8C books left to mark. Unsolved mysteries: The Case of the Reeking Toilet; The Case of the Vanishing Worksheets; The Girl with the Kite Mystery. Mistakes of the day – Christ, how long have you got?

There was an improbably large bar of chocolate and a bottle of Kronenbourg. Supper.

Lighthearted, heartwarming moment with which to regale colleagues in perpetuity: The Great Coconut Disaster.

She took the chocolate and lager and shut the fridge so that the cold green light of the digital clock of the microwave shone harder.

All this enumerating. Really there's the electron stream. Doesn' matter much if you dock and mow and tidy up and do the accounts, work your broom against the tide of blancmange.

Her side hurt where her thumbnail had dug. There'd be a pleasing little blood moon there the shape of her nail.

She went to the door and looked at Mel. His head was back, eyes shut, mouth gaping, spoiling his garden.

Really there's the bookslither, things flowing or drying up. Blood. Hair. Gron's gummed down coiffure unpeeling from his scalp. Bed soon. Get up tomorrow and do it all again. Come on, god. Make it stand or make it run. Enter, a messenger wringing his daicap. Charlton Heston with the tablets. The tablets' sweetish fizz. Or come, sugar, black my teeth, help me rot. Come on. Something nodal. Come on. Something fucking significant.

MAWRTH

It had been snowing in Ermland. Sergeant Lothar pulled off a blue chainmail glove and drew his hand wearily across his face. In spite of the cold, his handiwork had made him warm. But now it was finished and the village was gripped by a white silence. A sardonic leer twisted his face as he and his men remounted their horses. There were only eight of them, but it was enough for such work.

"Good work, men!" he cried. "The next dwelling lies but two leagues westward. Let's to it, in the name of the Grand Master and a full purse!"

But as the band of mercenaries rode from that silent, smoking place, they were met by two strangers on horseback.

Gunther of the Axe immediately raised the weapon after which he was named above his head and made to spur the sides of his horse.

"Hold, Gunther!" cried Sergeant Lothar. "Let us hear their business first."

Unwilling but obedient, Gunther put up his weapon.

The first of the two was a young man of lowly rank judging by his clothes, his poor mount, and the numerous burdens hung about it.

"What business have you here?" cried Lothar.

"Ask my master," the young man replied in Polish.

The sergeant approached the other man. He was wrapped in a long black cloak of some quality, and the soldier noted beneath the hood the dark skull-cap which had flaps to cover the ears. This was a man well on in years, perhaps in his mid forties, the sergeant surmised. The distinguished man's face was sallow and beardless, deeply graven.

"Well?" sneered Lothar. He could see no sign of sword or bow about the man.

"I am Canon Nicholas of the Frauenberg Chapter," replied the swordless man, calmly. Suddenly two piercing eyes burned at the sergeant from beneath the hood.

So this was the great magician of whom he had heard the peasants speak.

Lothar betrayed nothing in his face, though his horse twitched its head a little as his hands tightened on the reins.

I have killed better men than this, the soldier thought.

"And?" he said, curtly.

Without moving his burning eyes from the sergeant, Canon Nicholas drew a document from his scrip and offered it.

Lothar took the single sheet and unfolded it. The strangely crabbed black shapes upon the page were like trees against the winter sky. He knew that you must run your eye along them and tried it once or twice, but no meanings came to him.

"That," said Canon Nicholas, "is my guarantee of safe conduct. I have been on a mission to seek terms between your Master and King Sigismund."

Sergeant Lothar no longer needed to continue his pretence of reading. He understood well enough the great red disc like the blood on the snow that weighted the document. It was the the seal of Albrecht von Hohenzollern Ansbach himself, The Grand Master of the Teutonic Knights. The great magician was a messenger-boy!

He handed back the letter.

"You have failed, Father," the sergeant said. "And the result is work for us."

Canon Nicholas looked towards the smoking village.

"So I see," he said. "And I must continue to keep the church accounts." The burning eyes turned back to the soldier. "You know. Make lists, inventories, such things as that."

Sergeant Lothar stared at him wonderingly a moment and then smiled slowly.

"Our Grand Master Albrecht," he said, "is a great force, a great energy in the world, and our work will be done. Some of us are fated to *do*, and some of us, Canon Nicholas, must merely observe. Bless our doing, Father."

With that he spurred his impatient horse and rode on.

Canon Nicholas smiled wanly after the eight horsemen as they galloped away. He folded the letter carefully and put it back in his scrip.

"*Merely* observe," he muttered. "There were at least two mistakes our friend made," he said in Polish to his servant.

"What were they, Master?"

"First, of course, I'm not a priest, not that he would get my blessing anyway; and second this letter is extremely old and no longer valid."

The servant's eyes grew larger. "You mean..."

"Yes, boy. They could have slaughtered us here and now without fear of retribution. I surmised the oaf would be unlettered. And of course the missive is in Latin."

"Wisdom is strong armour, Master," the servant averred.

"Then we are not wise enough yet," Nicholas replied.

The servant looked from his master to the huddle of ruined houses, and understood.

Two surmiseds. Oo, bad. And what happened to Lothar's glove? He took it off. Did he put it back on or what? Was he wearing it when he took the letter? How was he gripping the reins tighter if. Well, it's sortable. Sardonic. A sardonic leer. Yeah. Have to look up sardonic. And sallow.

Smoking silently, Steve looked into the Canon's burning eyes.

Canon Nicholas looked southward into the wintry light across the unbroken plain of snow. He observed how it curved upward almost indetectably towards its centre, and smiled.

Indetectably? Undetectably?

and smiled. He could see the shape of the earth herself.

But Steve saw the Canon's face thin and vanish against his bedroom curtain.

Look that up too. They're always fiddly, ins and uns.

He took the breakfast cigarette from his mouth and blew the smoke expertly from round his head. The usual strained grey light blotched by the pattern on the thin curtain material. The second hand of the little plastic clock by the bed made a synthetic ticking noise. Electric really. No escapement in there. He didn't look at it. Instead he looked at the length of the dogend on the cigarette. His mother had gone to work ages ago. He'd heard the door slam and rolled over for a bit.

the earth herself. Beyond the icy expanses and the gloomy northern

cities, beyond the huge and stunning snowlocked mountains, lay
Italy.

Nicholas thought of Padua dreaming in the mellow autumn sun.
The sallow autumn sun. The mellow autumn sun. Another world,
but a mere ten degrees away on the planet. Nicholas had measured
the sun and the earth and understood these things. What worms
we are, he thought. His servant watched him patiently and thought
of food. He knew none of this. For him, endless waters still
plunged off the world's rim into the dark.

How do I get them into the village? Servant needs a name too.
Polish name. Find some. Igor? Oh shit. Prepare the potion, Igor.
Who knows. Maybe he knew more than his boss.

Steve sprang from the bed scattering dogends and opened the
curtains.

Down in the road, Waz nextdoor with his baseball cap back to
front was doing something drastic to the jacked up front end of his
Datsun. Steve observed him doing.

Rags of mist were shredding upward from the pine plantation on
the opposite slope of the valley. Everything's folded here so you
can see it. Down the bottom, beyond the tumble of estate houses,
was the main road and the corrugated oblongs of the factories and
stores and the rocky little groove where the river ran. If it was here,
Nicholas might be able to watch the soldiers for ages, even to the
next village. Even up to town, to the left. Sometimes he imagined
Frauenberg as town, with the school on the hill behind like a
citadel. It wasn' too far fetched if you took away the mountain
behind that and had a harbour instead of the bypass and the river.

He looked southward across the wintry flatness of Ermland,
observing how it curved upward almost imperceptibly (yes)
towards the centre. To his right, the Vistula wormed north towards
the dead grey Baltic. Before him, beyond the icy expanses and the
gloomy northern cities, beyond the huge and stunning snowlocked
mountains, lay Italy. He thought of.

Aye, then that bit. What worms we are. Oops. Two worms. Vistula
worming what worms. Wormland. But how do I get them into the
fucking village?

Steve blew out smoke as he looked north across his folded
landscape. Waz had removed a wheel and rolled it against the

gatepost and was levering with a spanner at some revealed bit of brake or something.

At last, Canon Nicholas tore his mind away from the wheel of heaven and bestirred himself.

"Come, Lech," he said. "Let us go into the village."

Lech? Fucking hell. And how would they react? Well how would you? Walk into that.

He drew the final pull on the cigarette. It had almost overpowered the stale metallic taste of last night's lager.

Lech all upset and Nicholas unmoved, maybe. He's a cool dude. Unmoved.

Steve moved. He stubbed the fagend on the fake cutglass ashtray his mother put strategically on the windowsill, hopped round the room putting his jeans on without bothering to change the pants and teeshirt he'd slept in.

He looked at the top of his white contiboard chest of drawers. The usual rubble – empty Embassy packet, Nintendo cartridges. Spent biros, calculator, Collins Gem Guide to the Night Sky, Bic lighter, ashfouled saucer. Two straying videos out of their boxes – the Eddie Izzard and *Indecent Proposal*. That was her idea of a joke, an eighteen certificate for his seventeenth birthday. The planisphere, some books – an Iain Banks, Armitage's *Sun Stand Thou Still*, and on top of the stack, Perrot, covered in graffitied brown paper so old it was going furry. But no roll-on.

Didn' matter. He wasn' going out. He only had a double physics and a form tutorial on Tuesdays. He liked the sixth form and so far had made a point of turning up at least twice a week. He tasted his tongue and rubbed his palm on his chest. No. Today wasn' the day for breaking records and attempting two days on the trot. Stay in and stink.

"No, do not stare so, Lech. Delay is bootless. We must go and see. Take stock of what has happened."

"But my brother lives there, Master."

Lech saw the burning eyes of the great magician soften a little.

"Come, boy," said Canon Nicholas, gently. "Let us go to this place. It must not be avoided."

He took the copy of Perrot to the window and leafed through it.

Excited, he'd taken it to the Exservicemen's Club the night before so she wouldn' pester him all evening about eating. Made two pints of Black Label last ages while he read, sitting in the corner where Gransh used to sit farting and talking politics to keep the frivolous away. The blokes playing don on the next table looked at one another and nodded in his direction. Fuck me, Jean-Paul, one of them said to him. Couldn' you find a thicker book? Steve said, aye I got one two foot thick outside in the wheelbarrow but I couldn' get it up the steps, and they had a chat about it and then it was quiet till Pod with his Adidas bag and all the boys came in after training. Fucking hell, Stick, he said, you fucking poser. You can' do your fucking homework in the club, mun. No pose, Pod, it's interesting, Steve said. Pod said, You got till Friday, mun. Trying to impress Mandy is it, or Baggy? Oo, the two together'd be nice, Steve said. Pod said, At least you *talk* normal, and he didn' bother trying to take the piss at all after that.

But this Henry Seven was seriously into being a bastard. Hard to imagine him going down the club for a game of don and an evening of sustained irony at the expense of life's absurdities. Wouldn' make much of Eddie Izzard. The court jester must have slit his wrists when he saw Henry moving in. But then, what did that matter. He was nothing. A negligible speck in some bigger thing. Probably not half so in control as he looks from this distance. Praps he didn' know what the fuck was going on, like the rest of us. As the chess grand master said, I think I'll just move this pretty horseshaped one.

Down in the road, Waz was reassembling the wheel. His wife, their baby daughter on her arm, was spectating at the gate. Waz was nineteen. Steve could remember him in school when he still had all his teeth and a Mars bar in his hand. All the rusty Datsun seemed to jerk as he armwrestled the wheelbrace, hardening down the nuts. Suddenly he saw Sergeant Lothar as Waz, pulling off the glove, wiping his face. Blood on his face instead of oil.

Downstairs, the tea was long cold.

Won' use much of Perrot in the talk, because like I said, other things were happening. Some twat with a naff haircut wins a battle and gets to be kinglet. Nothing. Meanwhile, the universe changes shape. Really you could get all sorts of things into it. Gunpowder. The Turks. Babylonian mathematics. It all adds up. (Boom boom.) Or probably. Just got to read up a bit. Baggy'll enjoy it. She can just sit back and listen.

She hadn' even bothered to empty the pot. He made tea with a bag in his Thunderbirds mug. She'd left the telly on with the sound down, like always. To keep the room company, she said. Cooking programme so about half ten, quarter to eleven. He didn't look at the clock on the video.

He imagined himself speaking with extraordinary lucidity. Fielding the odd comment from Pod and Mandy like a standup adlibbing to the hecklers. Baggy sitting there with her markbook and huge bag, pushing the big glasses back up onto the bridge of her nose and fiddling with her wristwatch like she do. On a door in the boys' bogs somebody had written *baggy bowen* in thick black felt tip with the loops of the doubleyou in *bowen* droopily distended, a stupendous rivetlike nipple felted in at the bottom of each loop. Another hand had added a Y the appropriate distance below in blue biro crosshatched with pubic hair like barbed wire. All their faces looking up. Tricia and Melanie and that lot that like points and sideheadings wondering whether they should write it all down or not. Go on, be bold. Just listen. If they start writing put some gags in to throw them. One liners. Don' matter if they en funny. Some things work no matter what. Goths, wanking, synchronised swimming. She 'ouldn' regret it. Might even learn something.

We can undoubtedly see Henry as a Man of Action. He seized the crown when Richard had been there a mere two years. Yeah. Something like that. *But to see him as a modernising force is to mistake the symptom for the cause.* Yes. *He grasped the. The.* Something. *Initiative. Delivered the. Was, if you like, a kind of midwife at the birth of.* Bum. *He wielded the forceps of destiny.* Fuck. It's gone all Terry Pratchett. *Some men, perhaps, are doers.* And Henry did it all over Richard. Keep that. *But.* But. There've got to be a but, butt. *However, symptom for cause* et cetera. Henry got boring and all we could do was wait for the next one to come along, and then we were for it. Henry Eight. Intellectuals with pricks are always trouble. No. *However, to call Henry VII the fountainhead of the modern period* (oo!) *is rather like saying Sid Vicious was the originator of the self-parodic post-modern sensibility.* Trouble is, maybe he was. *I want to argue that Henry was a man of his time, a medieval chieftain.* Not chieftain. *A medieval* something, *a part of what was being made rather than a, well, a maker.* Burst of applause. Puzzled boredom from Tricia and Melanie. The suedecropped top of Pod's head pointing at me. Pursed lips and narrowed eyes from Mandy. Oo, unman me, Mandy.

Above the telly through the back window he could see the houses in the top street, whose gardens backed onto theirs. Somebody up there still had their curtains drawn.

All a bit obvious, though. Really ought to take it from somewhere completely different. The startling start. When it all connect it's easy. You can start anywhere. Although, finding your way back to the bit you wanted can be a bugger. Gransh had a phrase he used to throw up like a screen so he could jump from one place to another behind it when he got lost in the maze, in the Exy, keeping the frivolous away. The thing about it is this, he'd say, and tap his finger on the edge of his pint, or flick his thumb across the tail of his fagend so ash fell like punctuation marks. And switch back to the point. The thing about it is this. Flick. Start where, though?

He thought of the ash falling endlessly on Gransh's black trousers. The dead grey Baltic.

No fags on the contiboard. She'll have taken hers to work.

The cookery had given way to a black and white film. He looked at the hairstyles, the shape of the women, the lustre of the print. No pointy shoulderpads yet. Not the daring floppy braless stuff like the early thirties – good to wank to, those – but not those kind of cast iron military brassieres they got a bit later. 1937? Eight? He'd check it against TV Quick later. Everybody putting their armour on. Getting ready for the war. Smoking villages. Gransh would have been about sixteenish, seventeen. My age. Working a couple, three years already.

Outside, Waz hammered something metal on something metal.

Steve found a fiver and some coppers in the jam jar on the fridge. Man of action. He slipped his bare feet into the trainers which didn't have laces, and went out for fags.

Master and servant rode slowly towards the thatched cluster of houses. The cluster of thatched houses. As the buildings loomed, Lech was overtaken by a growing sense of dread. Why were there no children running out to greet them? Where were his brother's daughters with bread and milk for him?

By the gate, Waz was leaning against the Datsun's radiator, staring down under the open bonnet.

'Stick-o' he said when he saw Steve coming.

'A'right' Steve said.

'Know anything about cars?'

'Tha' bit's the engine en it?'

Waz nearly smiled. 'Rust held together wi cobwebs and willpower. Can your mam get us a selfgrips on discount in the shop?'

Steve wondered what a selfgrips was. Sounded good material for a wank gag.

'Probly' he said. 'I'll ask her.'

Waz's gloveless fist was closed round the end of an oily spanner. Lothar, doing things but not quite knowing why.

All the mist had been drawn from the pines and the sun was rubbing at the clouds. Mellowish. It was the dead bit of the morning and the main road at the bottom of the valley was quiet. There was the squared pattern of cars in the carpark next to the corrugated oblong of the DIY store where she worked. The stony course of the river running to the confluence of the two valleys.

Could keep it really short and strong.

It had been snowing in Ermland. When they went into the silent village, Canon Nicholas and his servant made a list of the dead. Lech found the body of his niece by the frozen water trough and he wept quietly. As he rolled corpses over and brushed the snow from their faces, Canon Nicholas thought of the lost tithes and sighed. Cold bit him to the bone. And he thought of Mistress Anna, alive and warm in his bed at Frauenberg. She was so vital. Ermland! Ermland! This war would have to be lost and won before his work could be completed.

'Winning then, Waz?'

'Persevering' Waz said.

Or maybe Waz wasn' Lothar or Gunther. Maybe he was one of the village men lying in the snow. Car mechanics instead of scratching the earth. Or he was both, either, depending where the current took him.

Steve glanced at Waz's wife to say hello as he passed, but she was teasing a swollen reddish disc of nipple between the baby's gums. He looked away.

Lech approached the great magician carrying the dead child, the tears standing in his eyes.

"What wisdom have you for this, Master?" he wailed.

Nicholas looked up at him and then about abstractedly, at the smouldering ruins and at the crimson medallions of blood on the white snow. He had to keep calm. He had to calm Lech so that he could give him the names for his list. The Canon turned his eyes up to the cloudy vault above. And when all this is done, he thought, if I could but understand the perturbations in the courses of the moon and Mars, the universe would be within my grasp.

Steve gripped the crumpled fiver.

Not half bad. Frozen water trough's a nice touch. Might even write it down one day.

★ ★

'Shouldn't you be interfacing with the clients, Mrs Bowen?'

Sarah had thought she was alone in the staffroom. She was staring at the huge rack of oblong slots of the staffroom pigeon-holes. They went from the floor to as high as she could reach and they were wider than she could stretch out her arms. If you stared at them for long enough their geometry danced backwards and forwards like an optical illusion in an old children's annual. She realised, as she snapped out of it, that she'd been observing this effect for some time.

She reached up for her pigeonhole near the top left as if that was what she'd been doing all along. She didn't look round at Peter, who was standing next to her, as she pulled out the three slips of paper. Peter suffered from acute, possibly terminal, irony.

'Morning, Mr Carrick' she said. 'No. I'm happy to be able to tell you that I'm currently in a non-contact situation *vis à vis* the clientele.' So piss off. She looked round and smiled. 'And you?'

'Upper six' he said. 'Sorry. Year thirteen. They're milling some floss.'

'Ah, Mr George Eliot.' Christ. It's catching.

'Indeed. Much more of a man than his son, young T.S., I always thought. They're doing an exam practice essay. I wanted to do *Joseph Andrews* so I could set them the famous cricket question: How would you position Henry Fielding? But it was not to be.' He reached for his slot near hers. 'So I thought I'd just take this opportunity to throughput some paperwork.'

You can identify people by the look of their pigeonholes, like you can read character in discarded shoes. Gron left a pipe and his tin of Erinmore in his slot so that, even when they were covered in memos, the papers slid and tilted at characteristic angles. The pigeonhole belonging to one of the new young members of staff contained a half eaten Snickers bar and a copy of *Mountainbiking UK*. The head of Geography kept his half full and neatly stacked, graded by size, with largest items at the bottom. Some people let their mail collect with no thought of public opinion so that their slots bulged and gagged dangerously. Narky little memos from people whose earlier memos had been ignored were ignored along with the earlier memos. Peter's pigeonhole was like that, but then he did have the licence of being head of English. Sometimes it got so full it lifted the shelf of the slot above. It would be nice not to have a slot at all, no letterbox through which people had a look at you daily without your knowing. Some people didn't seem to mind. Either completely unselfconscious or amazingly bigheaded. Some people fart in lifts too. Sarah kept her slot empty.

She sat in one of the institutional armchairs with the window on her right.

The shoulder of mountain was wearing a cold drape of mist which the sun hadn't started to lift. Peter fetched a metal wastebin and sat at the table where Gron and May had sat the day before. He placed his mail on the table and the bin between his feet as if he expected to be sick. He'd taken about a quarter of the papers from the pigeonhole. Kept it deliberately and impressively full. Like potatoes. Like Mam peeling the potatoes. The bucket and an upright chair. Only she sits with her ankles crossed and one knee lolling. The bucket to one side and the newspaper with the peelings on her lap. Keep them for the ponies. Dropping the tatoes. Gloop. Sinking with a bubble, the starch turning the water a bit milky. Just a bit. Bevelled from the knife. Spud diamonds.

'This is the initial phase of the prioritisation process' Peter said, shuffling through the mail and dropping two out of three items into the bin.

The sound of the water heating in the urn rose as the thermostat switched on. It reached its small crescendo, the silver lid rattled, and it died back. Small processes. Preparing, making. Morning things. Warming and waking. Dad with the paper and firewood and the early cool flames. Stretching a double page of the *Western Mail* across the fireplace to get a good draw and the flare of orange backlighting the newsprint, the smell of it starting to scorch. The whiff of the steam evaporating out of the damp hankie stretched over a shirt under the flatiron. Patient things. For Ben it'll be – what? Ironing, still, but not much else. Emptying the crumb tray out of the toaster, the long voice of the fan oven on Sunday mornings, gentle voice on a telly documentary, that sort of thing. But the sun drawing mist out of trees. Yes. Curling off like a huge woodshaving. At some point a process turns into an event, or tricks you into thinking it does.

'It's peaceful' she said.

'What?' Peter said. He licked a finger and disposed of another sheet of A4. 'Binning bumf can be very therapeutic.' He stopped and looked at her and widened his eyes. 'But peaceful. No. The peace is an illusion. You've been taken out of the front line for rest and recuperation. Elsewhere as we speak there is carnage at a thousand blackboards.' He glanced at his watch. 'Which is where I ought to be come to think of it.'

She looked at moonface. There were twenty minutes of her free period left.

Peter carried on binning, a little more quickly.

He was slightly older than Sarah, tall and thin, and always dressed in the sober autumns of the confirmed male teacher. But he indicated that it was camouflage rather than substance by wearing dayglo fluffy socks, occasionally a different colour on each foot. Bilious pink had happened. Today was kermit green. They glowed in subversive neon between his chunky cords and sensible brown shoes. They sometimes led her to speculate on the possibly Hawaiian garishness of his underwear.

His eyes slid in her direction. 'You all right?' he said.

She started as if she'd been woken and made as if she'd been reading the three slips of paper. The first was a reminder from Shattock about the Enterprise Open Evening. Tonight. (Shit.)

'Lusting after my socks again. Caught you.'

'Well, they're. They're. Socks.'

'Don't pull my leg about my socks. You don't know where it might lead. Okay for tomorrow, by the way?'

She looked up. 'What?'

Peter had one index finger thrust under an envelope flap trying to use it as a letteropener. Suddenly she imagined him in only his socks. Camouflage gone. No. No socks. Stripped of irony too. That's just camouflage for the camouflage. Sort of strong and a bit tanned underneath. Reliable enough, fundamentally, under all the shit. Firm.

He was looking straight at her, his eyebrows slightly raised, as his finger snapped through the buff paper and she came to. Her cheeks felt hot. He was looking at them. Don't say anything, Peter, please.

'Tomorrow. You know. The in service evening. Four till six.'

Thank you. 'Yes. Of course.' She missed only a fraction of a beat. Her cheeks cooled.

She flipped open her diary and there it was under Wednesday. 4 pm Eng. Inset. ass. Ass?

'What's it on?' she said. 'Just English is it?'

'Yeah. Some panjandrum from County Hall. One of the Advisory Team, what's left of it. There's blood on the walls there too. Some of the primary teachers are coming.' He raised his letter opener for emphasis and resumed normal irony. 'The Cycle of Assessment. That will be interesting, won't it children?' And he stared at the bin full of bumf.

'You can understand how Eileen felt can't you?' Sarah said.

Peter looked at her then back to the bin.

She wondered if she had a sherbet lemon left in her bag and simultaneously knew that she didn't. Only the Disprin Directs, but she hadn't got the headache, yet. Sweetish fizz.

The second piece of paper on her lap was a timetable blank. Staff are requested. Rebloodyquested. To complete the following. Please include class designation, location, subject or nature of activity, pupil numbers for male and female separately, in each teaching session. NB, total contact time should not include attendance at assembly, registration, and breaktime or bus duties. This information must be accurate as it forms the basis for Welsh Office statistics. (Fuck.)

'Fuck' she said.

'Yeah' Peter said, still staring at the floor.

'No. This flaming timetable I mean. Honest. Words.' She was going to say *fail me* but failed.

'Oh, that.'

Less than fifteen minutes left. 10L then double 11E after break. Could fill most of it in now. Leave the numbers out. Get them from markbook later.

She started writing and got as far as second lesson Monday. 9T. Worksheets. Double 9T the end of today, her diary said. Cont. wkst. fin. as hw. Did she get all the worksheet on the board yesterday? She scrabbled in her bag for the one copy she'd turned up. It wasn't there.

'Peter.'

He'd finished his bin therapy and stood up decisively, as if the sixth form had milled enough floss.

'Yesser.' He sat down again, pleased.

'Have you seen my *Joby* worksheets?'

He looked blank.

'They're sort of on blue paper. You know.'

'*Joby*. Nice book. Good old Stan Barstow. Yeah, you showed me the sheet.'

'No, I mean –'

'Is Northern Realism significant, or is it a load of old cobbles?'

'– I can't find it.'

'Oh, right. No. Sorry. I meant to get a copy from you for the Scheme of Work. Goes well with the kids that one. I use the TV script myself. Have you tried that? Good for comparing genres.'

He got up again and picked up his bundle of papers and books.

'It's all right' she said. Trouble is you have to concentrate so hard on the class you can't enjoy the words.

It was right for Peter's accent. She could imagine him reading it well, if he could manage to play it straight.

'Nice historical detail' he said. 'The little boy playing with Dinky cars and sex and war looming. His mother hurt in the breast.'

Ben had come into bed with her again that morning and pressed against her. Time he didn't know about pouring across the ceiling.

'But sorry. I haven't seen it' he said. He stood again and moved to the open door. 'Praps Eunice picked it up. But the telly script is good material. The opening scene is beautifully constructed. Everything's to the point. Not a line wasted.'

'Unlike life.'

'What?'

'Beautifully constructed, unlike life.'

It was an opportunity to waste a little more time absorbing this so he took it.

Meanwhile Sarah looked at the third slip of paper. A memo in Glenys Fylfot's spiky handwriting.

Sarah – Can I have a quick "word" with you some time tomorrow or Thurs? Please call me to arrange a time. Glenys.

An expert at pointless quotation marks. Or no. Vaguely threatening quotation marks in this case. A Word. So what have I done now? The Clint incident? He really did brain himself and his parents have rung? (.)

'All right?' Peter was watching her from the door.

'Mm.'

'You're okay for tomorrow evening then.' The good head of
dept. marshalling his troops. 'Let me know if there's a problem.'
He paused, looking in some pointed way, then seemed to wipe a
thought away. 'It's pretty convincing, I think, *Joby*. A bit old fashioned, but that's in its nature. It's a –' ironic gearchange into mock
academic voice '– Well Made Piece.' And out again. 'It deals in
things the kids can recognise.'

Sarah nodded. Go away, Peter, or the kids won't recognise you.

'Besides' he said, 'I'd say it matched up to real life –'

The phone rang. Peter crossed to where it was mounted on the
wall.

'Staffroom.' He listened and looked round the room pointlessly.
'No he isn't – No I'm afraid I can't, I'm just on my way to teach
– I'd try about ten fortyish if I were you – Right – Thanks – Yes
– Sorry then. Bye.' He hung up and went back to the door.

'I mean' he said, 'if you didn't shape things you'd go stark staring. Anyway it matches up pretty well to what happens I'd say.' He
looked at his watch. 'Bloody hell. After the eerie silence the NCO
has blown his whistle. Good luck, Bowen old chap. Promise you'll
visit my old mother in Halifax if you get back to Blighty. Once
more unto the brats, dear friend.'

The door slammed behind him, wafting a nostrilful of women's
bogs at her. The grid of pigeonholes measured the air where he'd
stood.

Two words had ruffled him, thrown a stone into what he
believed. Unlike life. She felt proud and guilty of her succinctness.
Although he was a generation or so away from the book, it might
have wobbled his picture of himself. The rock gone jelly. The auto-
biography in your head that you revise a little daily, the secret
curriculum vitae for when you apply to yourself for confirmation
of your decency, your worthwhileness, the wellmadeness of your
life, as if it ought to have a plot and a moral. Looking back and
tidying the stacked events, seeing patterns and connections. That's
why stories really belong in the past tense even if some smartarse
does otherwise now and again. God, for instance.

Funny the words bothered him and the phonecall didn't. If this
was a well made scene the phone would have meant something, but
it didn't. Somebody else's thread or nonthread arbitrarily intersected
with his, that's all. You just edit it out otherwise you'd go stark
staring.

She stared at the bin, which he hadn't put back.

But then, the tatoes in the bucket are real enough. Knifesculpted and hazy under the starchblurry water. And the lovely orange flare through the newspaper. Sometimes it singed to burnt toast colour then flowered into fire itself and dad would feed the burning paper up the chimney with miraculous calm. But not a story though. Moments that swim back. What were parts of warm routines become occasions. Minnow lyrics. Somehow they escape, leak through the net. Ben's foot and the warm voice. The airbrushed lath.

The silvered urn played its drumroll. The mist arched upward. Normal melting etc. has been resumed. Or it could be cannon-smoke. Distant drums and artillery pounding rocks. Mountains shattering somewhere just out of sight.

It was time. She stuffed the three slips in her bag.

What's Glenys after, though? Ten ell far end of C Block. Give myself four minutes at least to get there. Fill the timetable break-time, leven ee double after that, dinner (sorry), look for worksheet. Nine ee double, then nine tee. What was I doing with ten ell?

★

Bloody poetry. Ted fucking Hughes. Perfect poet in all parts.

With the anthology from her locker stowed in her bag she made her way down the empty corridor rubbed by the tidemark of shoulders past the doors of the Men's Staff and the pisswiffy curly-painted Women's Staff to the English stockroom, retrieved a stack of copies of the poem, on past classrooms where through wired panes in doors she saw staff mouthing and looking at their watches, past the year tutors' office. Through the open door she saw May pursing her lips, Gwil Evans red in the face, eyes bulging, leaning towards a boy about four feet tall. 'That was *not* a nice thing to say to Mrs Davies.' The boy was looking past him through the window. And on by Glenys's office. She slowed. The door was half open, a wedge of her plush blue carpet visible. The monitor on Glenys's computer stared like an idol in a shrine. On the screen, a complicated geometrical shape made of a net of white lines was revolving noiselessly in virtual space. Could have a word now. She took a few more steps and could see round the edge of the door

Glenys in her blue squareshouldered suit, her arms across her midriff. She wore shoes which attempted the compromise between looking high and being sensible. She was talking to a sixth form girl who had her back to the door. You can always tell sixth form girls by their tights. A bit taller that Glenys. The conversation was inaudibly low. Sarah could still hear Gwil not quite shouting next door. 'Right, Dane my boy, I think you owe Mrs Davies.' Glenys was looking earnestly at the blonde head, nodding minimally. Suddenly she looked past the head and saw Sarah. The head turned and Mandy's dazzling eyes looked emptily at her for a moment. A corner of the girl's mouth twitched and she turned back so that her hair lifted a little, like the twirl of a pleated skirt. Sarah turned and walked on quickly.

The succession of tableaux. An illusion of instants, freezframes, when really there are other people's processes. People cut in and out of one another's story and get an impression of fixity and purpose in the other. Meaning. Really there's only fluid. Fixity's a trick played on the passing eye. Peter's graven face. Mam and the tatoes. Really there's just dribble. Ooze.

She swam down the murky corridor to the stairhead which smelt of cheese and onion crisps with hint of stale sweat.

A thin stream from a tap not quite turned off. Even Mandy, with her meticulously crinkled blonde cascade, her enamel prefect badge solid and permanent as the sign for a London Underground station on the upper slope of her impertinent ski jump tit, eyebrows plucked into taut arches. Prefect Mand in all parts. You can smirk and carry clecs as much as you like, my girl. You're still just gloop in disguise. A lot of water and a little electricity slishing about. Badges and shrines and power dressing all flotsam on that. A Martian passing in the corridor would see the processes and not read the signals.

She imagined a thin red being with three eyes and a quaint fifties raygun. His weird eyes seeing through it all, knowing it for gloop. His language without concrete nouns, composed entirely of verbs and a few abstract nouns. Seeing not things and things happening, but the fact of happening. Would see through, with the third eye. Could smear all the furniture and windowframes and shoulderpads away as if they were wet paint. Through tweed clothes and neon socks to the chambers and pools and capillaries whispering with fluids. Submarine delicacy and horror.

Martian. Could use that. Craig Raine meets Ted Hughes. A

worksheet for ten ell. In this poem, Hughes. Imagine you are a. Shit. Worksheets.

As she walked outside under the cliffface of C Block she prepared the poetry lesson in her head. A bell rang and complicated tides of children washed around her.

★

Some simmer. Some bubble. Some boil and spit continuously. With boilers, like 11E, you come out flayed raw every time. That noise just at the edge of human audibility is the lobstersqueal of teachers being boiled alive in vats of steaming children. But 10L – let's arbitrarily mix our metaphors – was one of the ones that are educational equivalents of the three toed sloth. Strange to the point of being terrifying, and implacably slowmoving.

God the boring author in a rare moment of whimsy hung 10L by its peculiar claws, its head on upside down, from its metaphorical branch in the grey room at the end of C Block, and melted smiling into the ether as Sarah came in.

She thought she heard a hiss that sounded like *effbee! effbee!* and the knock and scrape of chairs as people darted to seats, but when she looked the collective upside down head stared at her from the grid of desks.

She did the theatre of a businesslike entrance, placing diary, anthology etc. on desk, and stared it in the eye a moment.

'What's the matter with you lot?' she said.

'Just had maths' a figure slumped at the front said.

'Oh I see. Fair enough in that case. Right then. So you'll definitely be in the mood for. Poetry.'

She paused for effect. There wasn't any. They stared as at a cloudy sky, even the nice ones, Barry Getley and Gabriella Simon.

'Okay. Try to contain yourselves.'

They did.

And *effbee*? What the hell was that? She shook the thought off, stared at the odd upsidedownthing. *Go on*, it said. *Do something. Or don't. Who cares.* She felt her face warm as it stared – second blush this morning almost makes you feel young – its three eyes x-raying her bundles of bloodfilled tubes stiffening with the surge of blood. Not a blush really.

She flipped her diary open. More businesslike business.

'Well, I enjoy these little chats enormously, but it's only a single lesson and we've only got' – a glance at her watch – 'thirty three minutes left till break and we can't exchange pleasantries all day. So. Poetry. Let's pop another masterpiece in the killing jar.'

She was talking like Peter. The rocklike ironic carapace.

She looked around, worried that somebody might ask what a killing jar was and then she'd be up a blind alley to do with metaphors that would waste twenty minutes. Almost a good idea. Nobody spoke.

'So. The plan is' – good technique. Set the agenda then review later. No matter if there isn't one. Give the impression there is one and people go away convinced of an event rather than mere ooze. Not a blush really. It was adrenalin or something. Adrenal. Some tide runs in the blood and unbidden the plasma firms into something momentarily definite. You become someone of a different kidney. Sorry. Summon up the blood. 'The plan is.' What was the plan, or semblance of? Barry Getley broke ranks, leaning forward and registering in his face something close to interest. Thank you, Barry. Admittedly the kind of interest you might see in the face of a person watching a tightrope walker who suddenly starts to wobble. But at least the face of a human. The rest were still the Martian three eyed sloth inscrutably watching a wobbly monkey about to tumble from the highest branches and atomise itself on the forest floor. 'The plan is we have a first look at this poem and discuss it, and on' – a glance at her diary – 'Thursday, in that lesson, you can start a worksheet on it, and possibly another poem to compare. And that could be the basis of a piece of coursework for GCSE.' Christ, I'm on form today.

The highwire steadied under her feet. She looked at Barry, who actually looked pleased, bless him. The sloth was unmoved.

'Could you give these out, please.'

Slumped Figure stayed slumped in spite of the stack of smudgy photocopies presented to it.

'Preferably today.'

Slumped Figure unslumped in slowmo and in slowmo obliged.

A susurration of paper and minute hissing voices. The tiny movements of hands and eyes. That's better.

'That's better.'

Some looked up from their copies wondering what she meant.

'Sometimes it's like trying to kickstart a plank with you lot.'

They were still wondering.

'Right. Turn the poems face down for a minute.' Hands together. Look round. 'Okay. Don't peep just yet.'

Slumped figure had sat back down and was reading. It wouldn't have been reading without the instruction not to read. So far so good.

'I said no peeping. Here I am. Thank you. Yes. Face down. Right. I want you to think of –' what do I want them to think of? I said worksheet didn' I? Shit. 'I want you to think about the way we look at things.'

'Easy. With our eyes.'

'Well done, Barry. Very astute. I mean how we often look without seeing, and when we do look *and* see for a change, how surprising it can be.' She glanced at her watch. Thirty one minutes. Fill timetable breaktime. Fit in doing a worksheet somewhere. Didn' say for Thursday did I? Where was I? 'For instance.'

The Martian sloth and Barry waited, watched her, waiting for the for instance. Wobble wobble. Splattered monkey for tea.

'By the way' she said, 'did I say Thursday for the worksheet?'

'What worksheet, Miss?' Slumped Figure looked straight at her with three clear, sincere eyes.

'You didn' mention no worksheets, Miss.' A freshly broken voice from the back.

'She did' Gabriella said.

'Did-unt.'

'She did.'

'Well I didn' hear her' Slumped Figure said.

'She *did*. You leave her alone. Ignore em, Miss. They're all thick in this class.'

'Eil bloody Itler' the broken voice muttered.

Gabriella's tightcurled head spun round. 'Shut up' she said.

Sarah noted the emphatic aspiration after the tee and pee, the glottal punctuation mark, the clenched teeth.

The head turned back to her, the voice softened. 'Ignore em, Miss. Thursday you said.'

'Right. Thank you, Gabby.' Now there's no way out of having to write the fucking thing. 'Now then.' Where was I? Wobbling. For instance. A for instance of what? It was all right before you decided to help.

'Looking at things, Miss' Gabby said.

'What?'

'You were talking about looking at things.'

Did I say out loud where was I? Thought I just thought it. She's telepathic or I'm losing my. 'Yes. Thanks. Looking and seeing.' Grip. Toehold. Here we go again. 'When I taught some of you in form three, sorry, year nine, you might remember we talked a bit about this. We use our eyes all the time but we don't always use them well. We get used to things and stop looking hard. Then sometimes we can tell something's changed but we can't always tell what it is. Like if somebody's redecorated, or moved the furniture round, or if they've shaved their moustache off and you don' know what's different at first, or sometimes you don't even notice anything's changed at all. Our eyes and our minds get lazy. Like Sherlock Holmes said to Watson, you see but you do not observe. So sometimes we have to remind ourselves to see. To really see. We have to jog ourselves to look hard. Like, how many of you can remember the colour of the outside of the classroom door? Or the colour of the eyes of the person sitting next to you. See what I mean. There we are, we use the word "see" all the time for all sorts of things. See what I mean. See you tomorrow. Seeing a thing through. But we don't actually see all that well for a lot of the time.' What the hell am I talking about? 'So. But it isn't only to do with observation, with what you notice. It isn't only to do with factual things. With facts about things. Like the outside of the classroom door's red –'

'It's grey, Miss.'

'Or so-and-so's got blue eyes. It's also to do with. With.' Wobble. Barry and Gabriella looked anxious.

'Not just with facts. With other things. With, well, feelings.' Shit. 'Atmosphere. The whole feel of a – a – thing.' Oh shit. Too many things. Mandy's twirling skirt of hair and her admonitory look. 'Like when you're describing a – an object or a place, when you're describing some, some thing, being vague is no good.' Too bloody true. But wobbling less. 'The atmosphere, the feel, is made out of detail and you've got to put that in to make it work, and you can't put the detail in unless you've observed it first.' By god I've very nearly made a point. Not the one I was aiming at but never mind. 'So if you want to write, you've got to observe.' A road opened in her mind about observation, a familiar track of lessons about observation, the senses, memory games, finding the words, being exact. But that wasn't it yet. What was the other thing? The strangeness of it. The three eyed upsidedownness of other. That was it. 'But there's something else too. When you look hard enough at things. Things. When you look hard enough at anything it becomes strange. Like a folded coat or a roomful of people, or the hair growing on the back of somebody's neck, or a fish.' Jesus Christ. She listened helplessly as she talked and talked.

'Like my nan's teeth' Barry said.

Gabriella looked a scornful question mark at him, but perhaps he was throwing a lifeline.

'How do you mean, Barry?' Sarah said.

'His nan've got weird teeth' Slumped Figure said.

'No. Well, yeah' Barry conceded. 'But not that. I mean one day she looked all different and I couldn' tell what it was and it turned out she had new teeth.'

'Right.'

'Made her look like Jimmy Hill.'

''Cept he shaved his moustache off' Slumped Figure said.

'Thank you, Barry.' Yes, thank you, Barry. 'But like I said, I'm not just talking about noticing details, but how noticing the details makes a whole.'

'A hole in what?' Slumped Figure. It was starting to fancy itself as Martian wit.

'A whole picture. A complete picture.'

'Oh. A hool.'

'Hool, yeah. And that hool picture can often suddenly seem very strange. Like. Like.' The hairs on Mel's razored nape. Your mind tears off like a lawnmower with the throttle stuck open and you hang onto the handles while it knocks all the formality shitless out of your formal garden. Like your reflection in the doubleglazing. strange like that. Wait. 'You know those little shaving mirrors that magnify your face.'

About a third of the class had softened into something recognisable, had its head on the right way up and just the two eyes. They signalled they'd seen such mirrors and made noises of disapproval and disgust.

'Yes. You know what I mean. Even your own face is a strange place in one of those mirrors.' Five minutes ago that would have got a laugh or at best slothdisdain, but you know. You know. You're all looking at yourselves through the loophole in your self-esteem, and there's the alien gloop looking back with three eyes. Everything's alien if you look at it hard enough. You can see those greasy craters and faulted plains of another planet, every morning when you think about sex and smear yourselves with Clearasil. Swift's trick. Just change the scale a bit to show how strange it is. 'Everything is alien if you look at it hard enough.'

She stopped. The children looked at her and she looked at them. Slumped Figure – she recalled his name, Gavin – had a red nose and half closed eyes.

'Got a cold?' she said to him, very quietly.

He nodded minimally, mimed the word 'Headache.'

In her head she sat at the back next to the boy with the broken voice and saw herself standing at the front. Short and tubby and strawhaired and looking at her watch and talking for far too long. She kept still. Perhaps you *could* hold it, like yesterday morning. Have the flux resolve into some perfected lyric, like the tatoes, the fireplace, put it in the Hall of Moments. Call it *interfacing*, Peter. Three eyed upsidedownness of other is what makes us recognisable to one another. Hold it like this.

No.

'My lawnmower's hit a wall' she whispered.

Gavin showed no sign of surprise. Perhaps it was his cold.

My lawnmower's crashed through the wall and dragged me into a lovely bit of wilderness, ungeometrical as you can get. A still pond among the trees and people sitting quietly, reflecting.

Pallid sunlight strengthened on the screen of the back wall above the children's heads. She glanced over her shoulder through the window. Beyond the beaten up demountable classrooms and above the tiled ridge of A Block the cannonsmoke was curling upward. In the classrooms figures were moving. The earth was still revolving. The gush of electrons.

So how do I get from the pond and the trees back to the bloody poem? This is the bit I'm supposed to be good at. Words.

'And if you're going to write' she said, 'you need to look hard. Be aware of what all your senses are telling you.' Pause. 'We're going to read a poem about something pretty ordinary at first glance, pretty everyday, but the writer's looked very hard and felt very deep so that he can write something very strong. I'm going to read the poem to you first, then you're going to read it to one another and discuss it in pairs.' Oh, the technique of it. A roll on the drums. 'Turn your sheets over.' Susurrous shuffling. A fanfare. 'It's by Ted Hughes, and it's called.' Pause. '"Pike".' Silence.

She looked at her copy and began to wonder whether it might turn out to have anything to do with what she'd said.

She read it aloud anyway. Badly. Those two long sentences at the end. Some crap about England. What was that about?

On the last word, '"watching"' she looked at her watch. Ten nineteen. Sixteen minutes till break and fill that bloody thing in. Just enough to get through what they have to get through. Another six sessions like this to go today and hardly any headache yet, unlike Gavin. Go on, god. Do a jump cut. Fast forward. I should cocoa.

'Right then. Into pairs.'

Shuffle and scrape. Give them a minute. Even number. Stroke of luck.

'Okay.' She flourished chalk. 'Jot these questions on your copies for points to discuss after you've read it through a couple of times.'

She turned and saw for the first time a large and detailed diagram of a uterus on the blackboard. Most of the sloth had been staring at this for most of the lesson. She erased it and started to write.

What general impressions of the pike do you get from Hughes's poem? How does the poem create these impressions? (Choose words, images and details for comment when you discuss this.)

She stepped back from the blackboard then forward again and underlined *How*. Technique, technique, Mrs Bowen. The how question leads them to the literature. There. Pick the fishbones out of that.

'Right. When you've copied that down, carry on.'

She sat at the front, took the blank timetable out of her bag, and looked hawkishly around before settling to fill it in.

Go round in five minutes and see how they're getting on. The pratting about will have started by then. Add this to the inner CV. Made a halfway decent attempt, heroic but foolish, to overcome the gloopness of gloop in collaboration with a group of comatose fourteen year old three toed sloths. Decorated for keeping on talking in the face of overwhelming odds. Almost seemed to convert the messy flow into a Moment on that very nearly memorable Tuesday morning. Who's fooled? That's only past tense stuff. Died of metaphors shortly before her thirty fifth birthday. Will be fondly remembered for her inexplicable references to lawnmowers and rattling the head of English with the possibility that present experience may be formless. Leaves behind a doting young son and a beige husband with headphones. Wait a minute. CV? Once again the diamond stylus of imagination skips uncontrollably across the scratched vinyl grooves of metaphor. Nothing vitae about it. Obituary.

★ ★

Steve, gripping the fiver as he walked to Maggie's shop, thought of Padua dreaming in the mellow autumn sun. He'd never been to Padua. He went to Majorca once but he couldn't remember much about it, except for having an erection on the beach and wriggling around facedown on his towel till he came, to get rid of it. Presemen days, of course. As far as Nicholas ever went, or possibly came. Then, he did have to cross the Alps without the aid of flying machines. Draw a wheel with its centre on Brynhelyg Housing Estate and its rim touching the Beach of the Wanking Innocent in Majorca and there's my universe, so far. Probably swallows Padua, if not Rome. He did go to Rome too. Further than Henry Seven ever went, probably. Went to Brittany. Did he ever get any further than that? You never know. Prospective kings were forever dropping by at the Pope's place. How much did he know? Endless waters plunging into the darkness his picture, probably. Stuck to Brittany and talked Welsh with the locals, Shw mae, mon frere, smoking Gitanes and shrugging a lot. So further than him I should think. Pity I only got the wank out of it really. Ground the grains a bit smaller. But then, look at it positively. I marked my furthest south by shagging the planet. Suffer, baby.

The unmellow early autumn sun over Brynhelyg, a little paler than a new pound coin, had its face marred by the mist unpeeling from the pines.

A hearse bumped past him on the Estate hill. There was one pothole by Maggie's shop you could keep ducks in. Steve waited for the hearse to hit it. There was the familiar jolt but the coffin didn't bounce out of place.

In comedies and horror films they did. Jumped out into roads and burst open and then the corpse came back to life. But there are those clamp things that hold them in place really. He remembered them. Sandwiches. Mam in proper shoes instead of trainers. Relatives you don' know who don' know what to say to you and you sort of watch them suffer.

All the other cars with people in second best clothes followed, skirting the pothole. Must be somebody from the top street, in the box.

Maggie's shop was a lockup. It was on its own on the wrong side of the road, the side where the mountain fell away. If you passed in a car, which Steve rarely did, the shop looked as if it stood on nothing at the far edge of the pavement, its small front flush with the black railings. It was like suddenly seeing somebody peering at you over the edge of a cliff. From further down the hill, when you doubled back on the hairpin and passed under the back of the shop, you could see how it stood uncertainly on some rubbly spoil-heap, built up to the road's level on cementdrenched breezeblocks. The only window at the back was a small frosted one. Maggie's lockup bog, he assumed. It was a blind tower that seemed to prefer not to look at the huge space at its back. The nearest thing to an architectural folly on Brynhelyg, unless you counted the Estate itself. On the front rusty grills were fixed over the windows, though it didn't get much trouble, being stranded on the wrong side of the road. When it was shut, Maggie kept an eye on it from her council house opposite.

Through the grill Steve could see Maggie talking to Tricia Henneghan, who was her niece. Next to Maggie, who was a dead ringer for Obi Wan Kenobe cropped white hair and all, Tricia looked good. He stooped his shoulders a bit more than usual and went in.

'Trish.'

'Hiya, Steve.' She never called him Stick.

'Hiya, Stick, butt' Maggie said. She sounded like Sylvester Stallone, except for the accent.

'Twenty Embassy Regal and a sherbet fountain, please.' He stooped his shoulders further still, studied the fiver as he uncrumpled it. He was aware of his soiled, extremely cheap laceless trainers in the distance, and his bony sockless ankles. Tricia had looked at them. She was leaning against the lolly freezer, her arms loosely folded. Whatever the conversation had been, it had stopped.

'Sherbet fountain ey? Wow.' She wore her mouth a little sideways.

'Oo, yeah' Steve said. 'Me and my teddy bear snort the white powder up the licorice tube.' It don' matter what you say. You just got to be fast. 'And why en you in school?'

Her sideways mouth didn't move.

'Twenty emby reegs and sherby fount' Maggie said.

'That's a good one' Tricia said. 'Done your talk?'

'I started it. Just thinking about it now, as a matter of fact.' He paid and took the goods, looked at her. She was slight and dark with long straight hair. One of those people who always seemed to be dressed a bit old fashioned, sensible. Grey jeans and pale green top. How do some of them manage to look so clean? 'You?' he said. 'Yours is tomorrow.'

'Yeah. I started too. I'm finishing it this afternoon. Look, I aven got any lessons on Tuesday, right. I can't work in that Common Room. But then, I'm only doing ten minutes. Some of us get a whole session.' Her arms didn't move. Her mouth slid up to the side as she finished speaking.

'Well, yeah yeah.' He picked up his change. If he crouched a bit his jeans might hide his ankles. 'It's interesting stuff, you know. Trying to think what made a bloke tick back then.' Back then. The selfconscious Americanism grated as he said it. 'In those days. Trying to see what handle they had on things.' He dropped a coin.

'You can do mine if you like' Tricia said.

He looked at her as he picked the coin up. She was looking at Maggie with a suppressed smile. She looked back to him and wiped the expression. She had the knack of snootiness even with Maggie as her auntie. She worked hard and made notes. Numbered points and all. She wanted it tidy and divorced from events.

'I'll just come and listen to yours tomorrow' Steve said. 'Then I can pinch your brilliant ideas, Miss Henneghan.' He could just see her as a teacher. Standing like that with her arms folded and keeping a straight face. Boiling things down to numbered points.

He put the fags and money in his pocket. He'd have to carry the sherbet fountain in his hand and look a twat.

'Somehow I don' think you will, Steven.'

'Oo. Irony already.'

'Who started it?'

'You did.'

Maggie made minute adjustments to a sparse display of stacked tins. Her arse wasn't made for a puce shellsuit.

Steve stood awkwardly long turning the sherbet fountain in his hand and then shifted a little towards the door.

'I mean' Tricia said, 'there won' be anything brilliant enough for you. I'm cobbling something together. Think Baggy'll care?'

He stopped and and almost looked her in the face. The pale top was made of some fine ribbed stuff and had short closefitting sleeves. She had small breasts. Looked as though she'd just washed her white elbows. He imagined her holding her arms up to a mirror by a front door. Checking they were right before she went out. And she didn' get it. Genuinely didn't. To her it was just a hoop you had to jump through. About passing. About getting past Baggy.

'I think it's interesting' he said. 'It's about things that happened. People.' The hearse bumped through his mind. 'People who lived. Their bones are in the ground somewhere.' The endless rain of dead ash. 'It's.' He clutched the sherbet fountain like a stick of dynamite. 'Real.'

Her arms hadn't moved from her midriff. She was looking absently at the stick of dynamite. 'Yeah. But Baggy still don' care.'

Steve stopped himself from saying *so what*? The clunking unreality of *real* was still weighing on him. A lot worse than back then, even. *Real*. Jesus. He tried to think of something to say that wouldn't sound pretentious. There was nothing.

She looked at him with her sideways smile.

'How's your mother, Stick?' Maggie said.

'Okay' Steve said. 'Same as ever, really.'

'You look after her.'

Steve looked at Maggie. She seemed serious. Then back to Trish.

'See you in the morning then' he said.

'Oh aye' she said, casting doubt.

Snoot.

He made a mess of getting out of the shop. Too many arms and legs. A step where there shouldn't be one, and his laceless, unbearably cheap trainers slapping the soles of his feet. Through the grills covering the grimy window he saw them resume their conversation among the shelves and fridges as if he'd never been in. At the blind back wall of their tower, fifty fathoms of air fell down to the valley floor.

★ ★

The sexy rodent with the crewcut and his crew of sixth formers twitched around his stand. The display table was neatly covered with buff, or possibly beige, ricepaper. On it were the photographs and meticulous technical drawings enbalmed in clear plastic booklets, and in the centre, lying in state like a dead king on a catafalque was the steel, aluminium and perspex model of the rodent's sponsorship-winning design. There were more drawings and photos on display boards behind it, and on a gleaming aluminium frame above them, the logo and name of the factory the boys had been working with. It was professionally printed in heavy serifless block letters, black and a little italicised to give an impression of movement.

Sarah recognised the name. A factory twelve miles away, close to her parents. Where there used to be moorland and header ponds for the steelworks, now there was a nonplace sliced by overlit roads, a shedscape of windowless superstores with their carparks, and windowless factories. Ken.

In the windowless school hall the light was still pinkish. When the low energy tubes strengthened, it would whiten and harden, turning eyesockets and upper lips almost black with shadows like a scene from *Dr Strangelove*.

The three other displays of Enterprise Projects ranged at the back of the hall looked nicely ordinary next to the rodent's palace. Darren's group had set up a garden bench and table and put a plant pot next to them. With luck nobody would bother reading the group's accounts of their work on the display boards. Darren stood gelled and nervous, occasionally moving the felttipped pricetag which stood on the bench as if there was one position that would solve everything. He was actually wearing a school blazer.

Some parents were arriving early, blinking in the odd light and uncertain where to go. A sixth form boy and Mandy, crinkleheaded and glittering, sat at a dining table placed near the doors and gave the incomers leaflets and advice. Probably what she was talking to Glenys about this morning. Yes. Surely. That. Brace greeted people and shook hands with people who looked as though they weren't used to having their hands shaken. He smiled and talked and looked at his watch a lot.

Sarah looked around being observant, because after the Martian sloth that morning looking and seeing worked its way into every lesson – 11E, 9E, even 9T. I didn't *see* where I put the worksheets so now I have to *look* for them. A merry quip 9T chose to ignore. And 11E mucked up or quietened down depending how you look at it, because seven or eight of them were off helping Shattock preparing the hall, allegedly.

He was standing at the front, conferring seriously with a parent and glancing round to check arrivals. He was nervous and wearing a suit to prove it. Even under the pink light his face was the colour of lead.

Because when you're knackered you can't control the filters. All that stuff gushing in through your eyes like a firehose. Beating you senseless with your senses. God doesn't know how to select the significant detail. You just get the lot. All the crap. The hairgel and the beany aftersmell of school dinners and the pinkish, whiteturning light that fails to signify anything.

She was sitting on one of the red plastic hall chairs, the only one sitting, apart from a few people testing Darren's bench, because of her feet and her head. No time for a bath after feeding Ben. The Disprins, some roll-on, a clean blouse and the keys from Mel and out. Seventy chairs, four big displays, three DT rooms opened with staff and kids working for parents to see. Two staff on the tea urn and biscuits in the serving hatch, her and Ryan here, with Brace as god himself looking on his works and his wristwatch and smiling. A Big Production.

At last the parents assembled and sat and Brace, sitting at the front with Ryan, stood and made Opening Remarks nobody needed to hear. He made some obscure financial references. Enterprise Allowance. He talked matily about the Professional Team which had put the whole package together as if he and they had dedicated their lives to this evening, as if everybody knew about it, as though the press had followed it for months as a tabloid soap. The man from the *Gazette,* who looked fifteen and consumptive and pissed off with having to wear a tie, sat near Sarah with his notebook open and unmarked. Brace mentioned people she'd never heard of. He was Talking It Up. Somewhere on his desk was the draft memo in which all this was an Outcome to justify a sum of money he'd got from somewhere. The Sixth Form Design Technology Project in particular has been a h – highly successful venture. Sponsorship may. Industry and Education hand in hand. Of course we mustn't forget Year Eleven's sterling efforts with their furniture. The prices are. She watched his balding dome glinting unreally.

The blood twitched in her calf muscles. The plastic of the chair was unkind to the post natal haemorrhoids. Shoulders aching too. Why shoulders? Need bath. Is this what it's like from the halfway mark? Selfknowledge through subtle or unsubtle pain in every inch of self. And full tomorrow. Or one free? Can't remember. Lower six double hist to start. Yes, sorted, if they're gentle with me. 8C. Did I finish the books? Shit. Check. Finish. Record. Tonight, have to be. Books back and and collect in the stuff on paper. Them again on Friday. Mark for Friday? No. Back to books if need be. The paper stuff for Friday. Then 7C. See if Clint's got a bandaged head. After grub – what was it? And something after school again. Years ago this morning Peter said. Inset. Christ. Wednesday. The sump of the week.

Domegleam was replaced by leadfaced Shattock. He was looking at the parents as if they were a three toed sloth. She heard the words 'our Enterprise Coordinator' from Brace as he did a stooping run towards the door, like a man in the trenches and not used to it, looked at his watch, and slipped past Mandy out of the hall.

Sarah looked at her watch. He'd spoken for less than five minutes. Straight to his office to put the finishing touches to his memo. Writing it in to an application for money from somebody else. No, come on. Just a cup of tea. Even counter casters have to live.

The leadenness of Shattock's face paled as the unnatural light hardened. Corpse White with a hint of Terrified Yellow. She felt the air go tense. A wobbly tightrope.

Shattock eyed the sloth and then looked down to the tiny piece of card he'd placed on the table in front of him. She felt him feeling selfconscious. Like when you've been to the dentist. Dentist. Shit. And had a cocaine injection and your face feels numb and a mile wide.

'Thank you, Mr Brace' he said, to the door, which had closed noiselessly on its sprung piston. His moustache looked like a stain. He looked down and touched the card, like Darren shifting the pricetag. It was a punctuation mark in the silence. 'I won't talk for long –'

In a film now the shot would melt into the next important bit. But the best you get is the recession into murk and you still have to live through all the minutes. Your calves twitch and Shattock stands with his hands clasped covering his balls, the black noseshadow disfiguring his hairy lip.

'– The occasion this evening is to mark –'

All you can do is float along with every nonmoment. Let the overlit gush of pointless detail drench you. Occasion?

Suddenly everybody was laughing. A real laugh, not just polite.

Shattock had managed some sort of joke. His face cracked in a relieved smile. He loosened, gestured towards the displays as he spoke, named some pupils and staff, gestured to the hatch and urn and platters of biscuits, gestured towards Sarah. People looked round at her. Fathers with earrings who looked far too young to be fathers and others who might be grandparents. She smiled. What had he said? She kept smiling and hoped whatever it was it didn't mean she was expected to respond.

Tomorrow afternoon was, yes, double 9E and then 10L. No, one free then 10L last. Free last on Thursday, because that's why dentist Thursday.

But a laugh though. Had that been a Moment? A Something to shore up against etc., and I missed it. But 10L last. 10L. Ted fucking Hughes again. Thought they weren't till Thursday. Where's my.

She looked to the floor by her feet but her bag, with her diary in it, was at home.

Get the worksheet done in the free but do something else with em tomorrow. Reading. Back to worksheet Thursday. If I can get it copied. There. That'll do. Stop thinking about that now. I said stop.

One of the parents who looked like he might be a grandparent had cleared his throat and was asking Shattock a question. Looked about fifty and had long grey hair. Hands big with work. A baggy dirty green coat fussy with zips and flaps and toggles.

Come on, god. Think of Chaucer. Significant detail. If you had any taste you'd do this scene in black and white anyway. But you mustn' expect to live up to Ingmar B. or Stanley K.

She listened to the man selfconsciously sounding the odd aitch. Reasonable though plaintive. Don't you feel, Mr Shattock, that given the? Isn't the thinking behind the whole?

Ryan nodding and pursing his lips, rocking back and fore as he stands, hands still clasped across his balls, respectfully waiting to make sure the question's finished. Well, actually, Mr Morgan, I'm very sympathetic to what you've said. We have been through some difficult. But now I believe we can use the situation to our. On the positive side. Mr Brace has already pointed out. And the experience gained by the pupils. Worthwhile. Practical skills. Fulfilling. I realise this may not be fully. Does that go some way towards?

The hands unclasped, gesturing a question, inviting the end of the exchange. Mr Morgan nodded ritually.

Shattock said last words, inviting people to circulate and talk. Tea was being served. Eunice and the secretary at the urn started filling cups. The babble and break of chairs moving.

You could ask something about the structure of it. Discuss the structure of Ted Hughes's 'Pike'. No. Discuss the narrative structure of. No. Come on, it's 10L. It jumps from moment to moment. Pike snapshots. Themed pictures. Stepping stones, jumps across, rather than in the gush of it. Theme of Nature red in tooth etc. Lyrics with attitude. Far from minnowish. How could you phrase it?

She realised she was the only one sitting again and got up.

'Any sales?' she said to Darren.

He was red in the face in spite of the white light. 'Naw. Nobody got any money.'

Like visiting royalty she said polite things about the furniture.

Darren enthused. He got technical about hammer and nail carpentry, started pointing out tricky cuts and corners. Sarah nodded and smiled, not listening.

'Trouble is see, Miss, up somewhere like Brynhelyg this stuff 'ouldn' last ten minutes.' He said it like a middle aged man. Phrases he'd learnt.

She'd been brought up on an estate rougher than Brynhelyg. She looked up at his big red washed face, the points of spiked hair pointlessly shining.

'You think so?' she said. She sensed him sensing that she disagreed.

'My auntie do live up there.'

She looked at the bench and back at Darren. 'They're pretty heavy.'

He knew what she meant. 'You'd have to nail em down where she live.' He looked at the bench so as not to look at her. 'It's like Bosnia or somewhere.'

Darren's parents approached with cups of tea.

'Lovely.' His mother sank onto the bench, cup in hand. 'Oh, we're so proud, Mrs Bowen. It's a real achievement. We're *so* proud.'

Darren's father got interested in a speck of nothing on the armrest and Darren looked at his mother as if he might drive a six inch nail through her forehead.

Sarah left them on the seat in the sterile garden with its pot plant. She imagined the bench, smashed in the stony river among the upended shopping trolleys.

But then, dad's garden was safe enough. The back garden, anyway. Even had a swing, once. Rough bit of mountain twenty five years ago shaved green as baize now. A little flag of care. The only thing that ever got nicked was the gnome his sister bought him, and he'd left that out the front deliberately to get rid of it. Keep a lock on the coal cot and you're all right. People are people, even if they go incognito as three toed sloths on Tuesdays. Or rodents.

The rodent and his crew were still twitchingly purposeful around their display. She pretended to look at some inept glossy brochures the factory had given them and browsed the display boards. The group of pupils had produced a near booklength folder on the project complete with contents list and index. Among the displays there were some photos they'd taken in the factory. Windowless, unpainted breezeblock walls and undramatic bits of assemblyline machinery. All the pictures looked botched, as if the shutter had opened too early or too late. Wonder if Ken. Mam on the phone. Should've listened. No. Only the one figure in all the photos, in the one picture. A woman in nylon overalls at the edge of the frame, turning her head away so that only her ear and cheek were visible, as if her face had been removed.

'You've done very well' she said to Rodent.

'The pictures are the weakest part' he said. 'They kept strict control on what we could photograph.'

'Why?'

He shrugged in an almost human way. She imagined melancholy under his efficient surface.

'Weren't they welcoming?' she said.

Rodent looked at a colleague and then at her. 'The senior engineer who –' he hesitated fractionally, '– dealt with us was very busy. But he was helpful, considering.'

He paused. She looked at him.

'As welcoming as he could be in the circumstances' he said.

He paused again. She looked at him again. He had nice teeth, though not as nice as Steve's. His lips shut over them and opened once more.

'Let's say' he said, 'they didn't entirely encourage us to pursue careers in engineering.' He looked at his colleague and back at Sarah and came close to smiling.

She made do with that. A bright boy. Could get a diploma for diplomacy. Probably would. She felt recruited to the game. The visiting royal asking inane questions about Targets and Outputs. She looked at the cranething model and touched a pearly aluminium plate. Parts slid and hinged sections opened.

'It's a splendid looking thing' she said. Splendid. Christ. 'What does it do?'

Mr Morgan, the man with the unnecessary green coat, stood gazing at the squared blueprint at the other end of the table.

'Well' Rodent said, 'as the label says, it's a lateral transfer system for disc brake assemblies. It takes the disc brake housings off the lines and transfers them sideways across the factory to the next process or storage. Lateral means sideways.'

You don't say. 'Oh.'

'Up till now the operatives, like the woman in the picture, have had to manhandle the housings off the line into the boxes on pallets and have a forklift to move them. But this would cut all that out and make it quicker.'

A woman manhandling. 'Are they going to make it?'

Mr Morgan ran his huge hand along the perspex ridge of the lateral transfer system for disc brake assemblies. 'Aye' he said, looking at her. 'So Rob do tell me. Right, Rob?'

'Yes' Rodent said.

She looked from Rodent to Mr Morgan. The light had reached its hardest so that they looked bleached, but she could see a resemblance around the nose and mouth. Other than that, father and son looked as if they might have come from different planets. They watched her make the connection.

'Thank you for helping the boys out' Mr Morgan said.

His monumental hand closed on hers. She imagined the whitepink blancmange of her flesh squidging out between his stone fingers.

'This group didn' need my help at all' she said. You must be very proud, Mr Morgan. It's a real achievement.'

'Oh they done a good job. No doubt about that. I got my doubts about the whole waddycall of it, though. The politics.' He said the word apologetically. 'I dare say you guessed that from me asking Shattock that. You got to ask yourself about the.' He looked down at the photograph. 'But no, fair play. The boys have done a good job. I'm pleased with em. Aye.' He nodded.

Rodent cast his eyes down on the perspex, steel and aluminium. He kept very still and didn't say anything.

Mr Morgan's eyes were chlorine blue. The same helpless melancholy. 'It's what you got to do nowadays to get a crust.'

She turned to the model and tinkered with its wheels and hinges. 'But it's quite an –'

'It's excellent, isn't it?' Brace was back, holding his cup of tea in both hands. 'Hello, Sarah, Mr Morgan. I don't mean to embarrass Robert, but the Industry Link segment of the project has been –'

He intoned the praises, raised the cup enthusiastically as he spoke.

Mr Morgan nodded and more or less smiled and his eyes didn't change. Sarah tried to take her hand from the model and couldn't. Some moving part had decided to stop moving and her fingers were stuck. She tugged but a felt a spike of metal scurf digging into the side of her index finger. She looked around. Nobody had seen. Mr Morgan was making his excuses and leaving. Rodent and his crew were at the far end of the table. Brace, stranded cup in hand, turned to her. She acted as if she was leaning casually on the machine.

'This Robert, you know' he said. 'I think he'll go far. Mathematician. I don't think his father realises it, but he could well be Oxbridge material. In fact it might have been better for him if we'd made him Head Boy.'

In his head, Brace would be composing a paragraph for the local paper about Valleys State School Oxbridge Success. If I wasn' so tired I'd puke. Without looking from him she subtly tried to free her fingers.

'And how are you?' he said. He leaned towards her over his cup, earnestly solicitous. 'Are you all right? I appreciate the way you've helped out with the History Department.' He looked away absently at the photo of the operative. 'Gron's mentioned how manfully you've been coping. It's been difficult for all of us –'

As she tugged her hand free she felt the scurfspike cutting a furrow along her index finger. She bit the side of the finger along the cut and sucked. Salt blood. Christ. A drink.

'– and really, Eileen's – tragedy – was so unfortunate. You can never tell about people's private lives can you. And of course it hasn't done us any favours at all –'

He looked round but seemed to notice nothing, or took the fingerbiting as an attempt to suppress emotion which he'd better ignore.

Private lives, you bastard. It was this place.

'– but it had to be managed. So we do understand, and appreciate it.'

Strong on regal plurality and the evasive if not peacock passive.

She thought he was going to pat her on the head, but he didn't. In Bracespeak this might even qualify as an apology of some sort.

Parents were leaving. Through the hatch she could see Eunice and the secretary loading crockery into the Heath-Robinson school dishwasher. Ryan had two boys starting to stack chairs and, out of sight of Brace, was waggling his hand to Sarah to indicate a drink. She knew he'd walked to school and wanted a lift to the pub.

'So' Brace said, 'you're all right.'

My legs ache, my feet hurt, my shoulders are stiff, I'm knackered, my finger's bleeding and my arse is sore.

She bled into her own mouth and nodded.

★

The Drovers wasn't noted for its crowds on Tuesday nights. Its big advantage was that the landlord seldom served kids, so you didn't get a year niner staring at you as he lit his cigarette and looking pityingly at your choice of lager. There was just the gambling machine flashing its signals to no one, and a few regulars on stools by the bar not even bothering to banter, looking at their beer bellies and the curling out of date calendar.

Ryan had an argument with Eunice about the second round. He'd already got the first. It was the kind of argument you're genetically programmed to start having when you get to early middle age in which both parties insist on paying in certain ritualized gestures and broken sentences and wave money at one another. At last the loser backs down, putting the money away with the dull eyes of one whose spirit has been broken.

'You bully' Eunice said putting the tenner away.

'Right, I'll get you a double for that.'

'You will not. Cliff'll skin me if I go home squiffy.'

Shattock pointed expertly at optics and pumps, itemized, gave instructions. He looked over his shoulder to the bay where Sarah was sitting. Same again? he mouthed. She raised a thumb. Her handkerchief was wound round her injured finger.

The chemical tang of the first half was already numbing her mouth. She used the toe of one shoe to lever the other off. She could feel the imprint of the stitching on her skin. Wiggle your toes and you pop back into shape like a cartoon figure getting up after the steamroller. Something to do with squashed veins reinflating, the flow coming back. Gritty toes inside the tightsmesh.

Eunice and Shattock came back with the drinks. The tweedy windsor knot in Shattock's tie was loosened and so were the wrinkles in his face. They'd opened to show they were quite shallow. He looked younger. She took her glasses off and he went into soft focus. A bit younger still. Nice to unbutton and flow. Accept gloopness of process and melt gracelessly.

The other Design Technology teachers had had one and left – Sarah suspected for the Rugby Club – so he slid along the upholstered bench next to her. They spent every breaktime with him in the windowless bolthole which was the nervecentre of DT kingdom complete with DT kettle and a special dispensation for smokers, so they'd have to spend the rest of the term with Shattock, being debriefed about How Well the Night had Gone.

'Yes' Ryan said. 'Went off well in the end.'

Fourth time you've said, Ryan. Why am I counting? 'Yes.'

'It went off very well, Ryan' Eunice said. 'I liked the one about Captain Kirk.'

The joke. 'What did you say, Ryan?' Her own voice sounded far away.

He looked at her.

'Sorry' she said. 'I missed it. I was too tired.'

He shrugged. 'I was getting my retaliation in first.'

'He said' Eunice said, 'that the pupils have started calling him Captain Kirk. I suppose with a surname like mine I've got to be grateful for small mercies.' She laughed and lifted her gin and tonic. 'You're very honest, Ryan.'

Shattock fought off a smirk, looked down. No, it was nothing really. Rehearsed repartee.

He was glowing a little, fanned by Eunice's compliments. Men are like that. Boyish half concealers of sulks and glowy pride. And Eunice, pushing into the wrong end of her sixth decade, at the age of perpetual praise, a preener of anyone who looks younger than she is. Everybody's auntie. Peter called her Auntie Yune sometimes. Occupational hazard to praise indiscriminately. Some vestigial flirt there too, perhaps. Ankles of a slim sixteen year old, sod her. Mandy ankles. Those black knitted blouses with glittery bits and two tiny diamonds in that ring. No fold of fat on her finger to bury it. A Smart Woman, mam would say. Shame on her, batting her eyelids at a boy like that. No. Come off it. The auntie syndrome, that's all. Hardly a toyboy with his forelock vanished and the stained buckielip. Still, from her angle. No.

It struck her as she picked up her glass that their drinks looked like them. Earlier we were our own pigeonholes. Now this is us. Eunice the straightsided gin and tonic, without tint or taste. Getting ready to be old. White as old man's hair, papery and withered and bleached. Getting ready to be a corpse. White and crabbed like last year's spider, albino dangling in the shed window. Ryan a brunette pint bulging towards the top. Flakes of yeast winding floorward noiselessly inside the lit cylinder. What could they be? Dandruff. Dead skin. The rain of bits wiped from the memory at the day's end. What's shed. Snakeselves. Flakes of dead soul. And me the blond lager. Spherical glass. Hm.

She bit into the lager, felt it cold on her teeth. The gush of blond light.

When she surfaced Eunice was saying, '– all over now though, Ry.'

Shattock's face reclenched, the nose shifting up a little as the lip did its buckling. It was hard to swallow beer against an awkward thought.

'Well, no' he said. 'I'm in at eight tomorrow to finish off clearing up. I promised the caretaker. And I've still got a few trips to the factory with the upper six boys. And girls. You wouldn' believe the driving I've done back and fore to that godforsaken place.' He glanced at his watch.

'That's where I'm from. In fact my brother.' Sarah stopped. 'Get that Rob to build you a teleporter. Beam me up, Ratty.' She heard herself laugh.

He looked up at her and smiled.

'God, don' talk to me about tomorrow' Eunice said.

He looked young again. One of those people it's hard to place. She sometimes met people she used to teach who looked older than she did. One on the checkout in Leo's Friday evenings. Left a year ago and somehow accelerated straight into her late forties. The stream running faster in shallow places. No. Nasty thing to say. Besides, that would make Eunice profound on account of her ankles. Hardly. Oh you bitch. It seemed to happen more to boys. Freshfaced kids and then eighteen months later, a beerpot and gaps in the teeth, the look of tragic boredom.

'How old are you, Ryan?' she heard herself saying.

By this time he had unclenched again. He looked at her.

'I've got double 9R first thing' Eunice said. 'That bloody Gethin Devereux. I could swing for him.'

'Thirty eight. Who's counting?'

'There's thirty three in that group. Thirty three. I've told Peter. I know there's a bulge in year eight, but a bulge with Gethin Devereux in it's another thing.'

So, youngish, really. Yesterday in cruel Mondaylight you could have put him at fifty.

The blond rim of lager eclipsed him as she bit again. No toothpain this time. His face stretched pleasingly around the foamdrenched screen of glass. Everything bobbles round in the gloop. She shrugged.

'It's the battle of the bulge' Eunice said. She sipped her drink for punctuation. 'And did I tell you? Brace's asked to see me.'

'Oh dear, Eunice. What've you done now?' Sarah said. Her voice was a little too loud and she couldn't get the volume down. 'Haven' been too nasty to Gethin have you?'

'No, I tell you, it's not funny' Eunice said.

'Come to think of it I've been summoned too' Sarah said.

'What, to see Brace?'

'Yes. No. Glenys. Had a "note" off her today. One her "notes". I think it was today.' She cast a net back into the tenebrous gloop. The gleamy present with its row of shiny pumps and bored barman enough. Too much, even. This morning? Think so. Yes. The blue carpet. Mandy's twirling hair.

'Oh well, she's all right. I get on with Glenys.' Eunice sipped her gee and tee. 'What about?'

'I don' –'

'Brace doesn' like me. I tell you, Sarah –' she dropped her voice and leaned forward so as to exclude Shattock '– he'll have me out if he gets the chance. My age I earn too much for him.'

'I'd go like a shot' Sarah said, too loud.

Eunice mimed a 'sh' and said, 'No you wouldn't.'

'No. You're right. I wouldn't.'

'I knew from the minute he swung it with the governors to appoint Peter. No disrespect to Peter, of course. Younger see, and a man. That's natural. But still.'

She was warming up for a familiar speech, this time spiced with the worry of the appointment with Brace.

Sarah looked round at Ryan, who had been sipping his pint and trying not to look left out.

'These women' she said. His face stretched around the screen of glass again.

'And how old are you?' he said. Finding a way back in but, given the subject, shutting Eunice out.

'Thirty four point nine nine recurring.' She put her empty glass down. 'On the cusp of. Something.' Beginning of the middle. No. The middle is a point without extension. Beginning of the second half.

'You young whippersnappers' Eunice said.

'Yeah, but who's got the whip and who's going to snap?' Sarah said. 'My round.'

She got up and brushed past Eunice before anybody could start the No I'll Get It ritual. She was at the bar and ordering before she realised she was limping.

The barman struggled to wrench his head away from his hand and took the glasses from her without looking at her. The barstoolers glanced at her and then looked at one another.

'Not for me, barman' Eunice called, outwitting the courtesy game at the last second. 'I've got to go.' She elaborately retrieved a handbag, approached the bar, looked Sarah up and down, dropped her voice in the worldexcluding manner as she got close. 'Will you be all right with –' the voice disappeared and turned to mime '– *him?*' Her eyes moved Shattockward.

Sarah nodded.

And resuming normal volume, 'See you tomorrow then, Sarah. Bye, Ry.' A sudden smile at him and she was gone.

Shattock watched Sarah as she fetched the drinks. She stood with the blond globe in one hand and the yeasty beer in the other and saw herself, as she'd seen herself with 10L that morning. Only no sun to move it all along. The slumped barstoolers with their bellies, and the tobaccogunged striplights. And her. Eyeless in the Drovers with her gashed hand and one shoe off. Old people in hospitals must stand like this, seeing themselves with terrible lucidity, wondering whether to bother moving time and making the next thing happen. Eventually you don't. Eventually wherever you are your teeth blacken and the Jenkinses shut their curtains and you just stop.

'Oh' she said. 'My shoe' and limped back to Shattock with the drinks.

You could make a moment like that. Make a nothing. Moments leak through unwilled mostly and sometimes they're too naked to bear. If you could will them. If you could make a Nothing. Perhaps that's what Eileen was doing. Making a lyric. Being creative.

Shattock said cheers and sipped. He looked at her and then didn't look at her. Things had turned fractionally awkward.

She tried to eclipse him with the blond rim again but the glass, being full, didn't want to tilt that far. Her mouth was full of the cold lager and she spluttered as she put the drink down. He was looking at her mouth. She cuffed the wet away.

'Sorry. I'm tired. This's gone straight to my head.'

'You all right to drive?'

'Oh yes.'

'It's a bit strong that. They make it strong these days. You know, some of the ciders nowadays are eight per cent and more.'

He talked knowledgeably about percentages, pointing to the lager and beer alternately. Proportions. Two of those would make three of these, strengthwise.

'It's a bit like war really' she said. She heard herself laughing, still too loud.

Shattock didn't oblige with the feed line.

'Well' she said, sipped. 'Ask me why.'

'Why what?'

'Why is it like a war.'

'Why is it like a war, Sarah?'

'Oo-oo.' She reacted to show she'd noted his attempt at irony. 'Because of all the care and expertise and things.' She held up her glass. Must have been that stuff talking to Peter this morning. Carnage at a thousand blackboards. Mist like cannonsmoke. She waggled the glass. 'All the planning and finesse and mathematics to calculate the blowing off of heads.'

Ryan seemed not to have heard. She stared at him, not, at first, realising she was staring at him because she was pissedtired.

He looked at her, away, and back and reached for words to mask the fractional awkwardness.

'Thanks for helping out' he said. 'Tonight and everything.'

She lifted her drink and and he lifted his.

Fancy Eunice asking that. Her mind *was* working that way. What do you expect with ankles like that? Get ready, Cliff.

'No problem, Ry.'

She looked at him and smiled as she put her drink down. His pint was two thirds empty. He looked studiously at nothing. He'd run a mile. Shy Ry.

No. No.

He sipped again, or it seemed like a sip, but the last third was gone. Foam islands slid and wheeled down the inside of the empty glass. A hint.

'Shall I take you home then?' she said. And that didn' come out right either. Or praps it was okay. Innuendo is in the ear of the listener.

She was standing, noticing the missing shoe, cramming the reexpanded foot back into it, trying to. The foot resisted and throbbed. She swayed and waggled till it recorseted itself.

'Oh, tight fit' she said, and heard herself giggle. 'Innuendo is in the eye of the beholder. Listener. The ear of the.'

'Don't you want that?'

Her glass was still half full.

'Better not, thanks.' Good girl. 'I'm a good girl.' That wrong too.

He put the glasses on the bar, which elicited a somnolent maty nod from the barman, and they left.

Outside it was dark.

Bunch the wrapped hankie into palm. Purse. Keys. The fumbling armfuls of the constantly hustled.

She opened the passenger door first, chivalrously held it for him to fold himself in. The forelockless head and stained lip dipping, colours transformed under the orange streetlights. Reds blacken. Greens wash to some neutral grey. The air gone cold, promising autumn.

She listened astonished as the engine fired, held her foot a fraction too hard on the accelerator fractionally too long. She glanced at Ryan, underlit by the glow of the dashboard. He would be clocking that. A man who knows his beer strengths to one tenth of one per cent will measure all judgments and misjudgments, but he showed nothing as the car slid away. The wrinkles were harder, restored to their usual stoniness.

She spectated, still astonished, as she drove. She seemed to be controlling the car but didn't feel as though she was. Ryan's hand was clamped a little too tight on his knee near her hand on the gearstick, which shifted up the gears without her volition. His fingertips flexed a little. Streets and lampposts fell past the windscreen, flickering dim orange. He stared ahead. His house lay between the school and Sarah's, that was all, never mind the male beer and smoke smell or the end of day cocktail of deodorant and stale sweat overwhelming the car's little plastic airfreshener and the whiff of boiled sweets dissolving in the doorpockets. Yesterday's planettightening. The moistness.

'There's that dickhead Leyshon' Shattock said suddenly.

She touched the brake.

'Look at him' Shattock said. 'No sign of him in registration again today.'

Momentarily she saw Steve, the sixth former, walking towards them on the pavement's edge. Shoulders hunched, head down, the furious neon bud of an almost spent cigarette brightening in his drawn face, his hands in pockets, and under one arm a familiar, bashed, housebricksized book. He glanced blankly into the windscreen of the braking car. Saw two middleaged teachers. Pair of glasses. Moustache. Granite and blancmange. Exhaustion, if only he knew it. And gone.

Shattock had put a hand against the glovebox.

'Sorry' she said.

'No problem.' But said as if there was one. The hand returned to his knee. 'You know he got held back a year? God, he's a superior little turd.'

He was already in tomorrow's registration. Marking them in and doing totals. The herringbone pattern of attendances spoilt by the string of zeros against Steve's name. The pubby fun gone already.

Astonished, she watched herself tap his clenching hand.

'Relax, Ryan' somebody said.

His hand tensed even harder. She took hers away.

'You okay driving?' he said. 'Do you want me to drive?'

'I'm all right.' Suddenly she was in control.

'Won't –' His voice was gone. He cleared his throat and tried again. 'Won't see that bugger five to nine tomorrow morning.'

'Actually, he works pretty well for me when he turns up.' Oh, smug half truth.

Ryan said nothing.

Tomorrow. The tunnel of road swallowed them. Wednesday. The U bend of the week. Just hold your breath and go under and wait for the gush to wash you through it. Her black school bag and diary and timetable were at home. Full or one free? What had just seized Ryan got hold of her. Oh yes, in fucking set. Lower six double hist first. Yes, the housebrick. Steve actually interested.

'Next left' Shattock said.

She watched herself steer proficiently up a steep hill past a few

terraces, where his close of chimneyless seventies bungalows bloss-
omed on a cul de sac.

He paused fractionally too long when they stopped before
opening the door. He looked at her.

'Well, thanks.'

Mrs Shattock, frizzyhaired and pretty, appeared in the lighted
livingroom window and raised an arm to yank the curtains shut.

Ryan got out quickly.

★ ★

"This," declared Bishop Fabian von Lossainen, "will not do!"

He pressed the silken handkerchief to his moist lips and regarded
the Chapter with a rheumy eye.

The hooded figures did not move. The only motion was in the
breath that formed on the chilly air and the fitful flickering of
shadows as the lamps' flames stirred.

Canon Nicholas, standing before the Prince-Bishop's throne,
could barely disguise his contempt. He looked down so that Bishop
Fabian should not read his feelings in his eyes. Things had been so
different when his Uncle Lucas had sat in that chair.

"It will not do!" the Bishop repeated, though no one had
disagreed. "So the Grand Master will not call off his dogs unless
we swear an oath of allegiance!"

Nicholas's lip curled. Lech had long stabled the horses. Mistress
Anna would be in the tower waiting.

"That is why I made no reply to the Grand Master's demand, My
Lord," Nicholas said, evenly. "I knew that this would be... difficult."

"Difficult!" cried Fabian. "Difficult! You have a talent for
understatement, sir. Either that or your abstruse studies have
softened your brain. Your late uncle, the last Bishop, indulged you
too much with all those holidays in the south. We all know how
little your strange ideas have to do with the Real World! We face
annihilation, Master Copernicus!" He sat back exhausted and
wiped his mouth once more.

Nicholas wondered if he should offer physic to the Bishop, but
decided to remain quiet.

"My intention," murmured the Prince Bishop. He cleared his
throat, sat up, and started once more: "My intention is to... to

make no reply. We cannot accede to such a demand from such barbarians as these. Not until we can see who of the Teutonic Knights and King Sigismund is like to win the issue, at least."

Nicholas struggled to suppress a smile.

The Prince Bishop did not notice.

"Your Grace speaks wisely," Nicholas said.

"Had you been a better emissary, there might have been no need of further wisdom on my part." Fabian looked down at Canon Nicholas, pleased with his own wit.

But the magician's eyes burned with a strange intensity. What mystery was suggested there! Fabian sensed that this enigmatic and charismatic black-clad figure could see and touch some universal nerve beyond his, the Prince Bishop's, comprehension. He felt his own spirit quail.

In his room in the tower, Nicholas knew, Lech had banked up the fire and spread furs before it. There were his books and his instruments. Anna's children would be asleep. The Bishop's word – *annihilation* – rang through his head.

"We have had word from other quarters," the Prince Bishop continued, nervously, awkwardly, over-explanatorily, his face ghastlier white even than was usual, "that Grand Master Albrecht is moving his war-engines and cannon here, to Frauenberg!" The picture of his own end was written in his face as he stared at Nicholas. "We shall remove the major part of our court, ourselves and our retinue, to our estate at Allenstein, and thence to any other secure place that is required. Though the limbs be hacked, the head and heart must be protected!"

Nicholas nodded. His ale would be warmed, the candles ready for him to sit and read. She would have swept the snow from the platform on the tower from which he measured heaven. She would be standing demure with the jug of ale.

"You, Master Nicholas, shall stay here and oversee all matters of the Cathedral as my proxy. You, who have your head in the clouds, shall face the fires of the earth! Shall face reality!"

He sidestepped a bit of sick on the pavement.

Fabian stared at him as he gave this instruction, but the magician's gaze did not waver.

"Yes, my lord," said Nicholas.

And guns. Aye. Gunpowder. Not much longer for walls and things, really. So old Aitch Seven was pushed by technology. The writing on the wall for castles (boom boom), though they'd hang on for a bit. But really that was it. Like machine guns changing the shape of battles, only bigger than that. The invention of the stirrup smashing nations. Gunpowder. Seriously big shit. Though, Nick knew the walls of Frauenberg were too thick for a while yet.

Demure with the jug. Oh, Anna, Anna. With this fool out of the way, Nicholas knew he could continue his investigations into the true geometry of nature.

Then a car whirling past. He felt himself annihilated in the glare of the headlights. Two small boys in baseball caps framed in the square of dirty yellow light of the chip shop window paused in their eating from the paper, flicked vees at the going taillights.

'Oy. Miss mun, Baggy' they called. 'Miss mun.' 'Gi's a bit.' 'Have a bite o' my chip.'

The fatter of the two threw a chip out into the road.

Steve hunched, sucked on the fagend grownuply as he passed.

Crossing the wintry courtyard of the fortified Cathedral grounds, Nicholas saw servants slithering along in pairs carrying chests of valuables to carts. The Bishop's plans were already in hand. There were whispers among them in Polish. They would have heard of Fabian's intemperate words and, packing for the fleeing canons, would be close to panic, even mutiny.

Hang on. Canons and cannon. Tricky. Cannon in canons out. An unwelcome pun. Exploit it or avoid it? Can a canon carry on considering the cannon? Guns. His war engines and guns here. Enough.

Brynhelyg bulged black above him straining against its fret of orange streetlights. He climbed the dogleg and saw Maggie's blind tower silhouetted.

He wrapped his black cloak tighter and strode to the little door at the base of the massive square tower in which he had his apartments. He looked up to the upper windows lit by the flickering of candles and the flames of the fire, and hurried in.

Past the shop, he saw the swell of his own street and the top one behind it. In the top street in a back window of the house that had had its curtains drawn that morning, a candle seemed to be flickering. Somebody cut off, perhaps. The livingroom window of his own house was filled with bluish shifting underlight from the television.

He climbed the steps in the front garden.

Master Copernicus, clad in black, stood in the narrow lancet doorway of the top chamber of his tower. He shook the flecks of snow and ice from his cloak and they vanished like meteors.

There was the coiling red light of the huge log fire licking across the furs spread before it; his astrolabe and triquetrum, his library of arcane knowledge, his half completed self-portrait still standing upon its easel – and in his painted hand, like a bauble, an image of the sun upon a stick enclosed in a circle. He smiled.

And there, sitting against the edge of his table, was Mistress Anna. She did not approach him, though she unfolded her arms from her midriff, placed her hands on the table's edge, and leant her shoulders towards him in an attitude of anticipation.

He did not speak but dropped the cloak from his shoulders as he moved forward.

Gently she turned and lay back upon the table. Her free raven-black ringlets fell upon the pages of an opened book. It was the Almagest of Ptolemy opened to the image of the universe. Her head rested upon the earth itself, and she wore the planets like haloes.

"And how goes the world, Master Nicholas?" she asked quietly.

His eyes burned into her as he thought of the ransacked barns and the deadstrewn villages.

"It goes as it ever did," he said, "but not the people in it. Tomorrow, the Prince Bishop will be gone, and I will be in charge, and Frauenberg, outside these walls, will be on fire." He shrugged and pulled slowly at the laces of her fine-ribbed gown. "Nothing is fixed, not even the earth."

In the livingroom shifting with cold television light, Steve looked down at his sleeping mother.

The sound was off on the telly. The male and female leads of an American film were emoting at one another in some distraught silent conversation. They were doing a lot of work with their lips.

Their eyes looked away a lot and then straight at one another glittering with wet, as the scene cut from shot to shot.

His mother had dropped the channel zapper on the carpet next to the smoking ashtray. Her head was wedged awkward against the settee's armrest, trapping the copy of *TV Quick*. Her mouth was open and she was snoring lightly. The flap of skin under her chops, not really enough to call a double chin, not yet, hung the same way as her mouth. She was wearing her black work trousers, some kind of nylon, that made her pot look bigger and showed the fag ash. Her feet were bare. He touched her big toe gently, where it was hardened and gone like ageing Cheddar cheese. She didn' move.

Manless and past it, pretty well.

Feeling safe, he stroked the cheesehard ball of her foot.

Upstairs in the cold bedrooms clothes were hanging in the wardrobes. Her dresses all nicely out of date. Men's clothes some of them were. In the real wood wardrobe, Gransh's trousers were hanging, blown through with minute fragments of ash. Some magician there ought to be.

Her foot twitched and she made a sucking noise as if she'd been dribbling, though she hadn't. Salivary glands slow down when you kip. GCSE Biol.

He stopped stroking. She hadn't woken. Totally fucked. Not recently of course.

Afterwards, as Anna slept, Nicholas pulled on his cloak and looked towards the door, the door that opened onto nothing, onto fifty fathoms of air. He slid the bolt and opened it, and stepped into the icy night upon his observatory platform. Under the bloodshot eye of wayward Mars the town was starting to gleam with many fires.

Nicholas observed.

Yeah. Some magician. He opens a door or a window and there everything is, and he reads it. All.

The kitchen door was open and she hadn't shut the kitchen curtains. He could see at the top of the steep back garden the candle still flickering in someone's bedroom window. The old lady. Funny, the one that had had the curtains drawn, but they were wide open now, shadows ruffling the ceiling. Window open too. The orange glare from the streetlights beyond made it so you couldn't see the sky, but it was cloudy anyway.

Some magician. But not a fucking astrologer. Don' want to give the wrong picture. He only did that to keep the bosses happy, but really he could see past all that shit. Bloke with cloak who keeps the frivolous away. Sees through the smoke.

He closed the door once more and turned back to Anna where she lay by the fire. The pink discs of her nipples had hardened and roughened in the draught. Had hard.

Had hard. Oo. He moved towards the stairs.

Hers weren't bad, considering. You could see the bumps through the DIY shop teeshirt. Just floppy enough really. Pity. Wasted on a mother, those.

It was cold on the dark landing and there was the stale smell of hanging clothes.

Some magician. Bloke with cloak there ought to be, who knows how everything works. Star scatterer. Man with the sun on a stick. Wand burning with extraordinary truth.

★ ★

'Sare?'

He always said it like that, so that it rhymed with wear, but with the arr slightly rolled.

'Sare? Are you awake?'

As he slid under the duvet he wrapped his beigeness around the curve of her back.

'Sare?'

'Ruh.'

'What?'

She mumbled in the right sleepy way to put him off.

His right hand crept round to her front and twiddled about among the folds of her nightie. The bobbly dink squashed itself against the crack of her backside. He tried and failed to kiss the back of her neck and fidgeted because there was nowhere to put his left arm. He tried squeezing it under her but couldn't.

'You came to bed early' he said.

'I know.'

'Course you do. Sorry.' Pause. 'We've had a busy day in work too.'

He talked about work. A battle to do with extending the quarry. Three to four years' deep quarrying left, so if we don't extend, the jobs'll. There were houses, an estate perched on the northern lip.

When she met him, when she was twenty-four and he was half a stone lighter and they were both more or less defying gravity and he even wore a teeshirt with a fake coat of arms and Idontgoto University written underneath – though he had been – and she asked what he did, he looked straight at her and said I'm in hardcore, then waited a bit but not long enough for it to get cruel and said about geology. She said so that's why you've got tiger's eyes, meaning the stone, because that's what they were like, a bit transparent, with striations of dark and light brown and brilliant orange when you looked close, but he didn't understand at first, thinking of a real tiger, so it sounded far more like the come on that it was than it should have. And that was it. Click.

The mountain was hollowed like a drilled tooth. He'd moved from the west when some quarry there was worked out, bringing an accent that was ever so slightly other, the vowels slightly shorter and the arrs slightly rolled. And now this one was coming to an end. The rounded south face of the mountain with its scrubby trees and glimpses of steep weathered rocks looked firm and ancient when you drove up that valley on the main road, but as you drew alongside the flank of hill you could see part of the gouged limestone amphitheatre, and the quarry had been cut back and back southward until the hill was just a grassy filmset. One good push, a smallish detonation in the wrong part of the cliffface, and it would all go. Fall of dust. So they could only go north, where the houses were. We are always at war with ourselves. The hanging stonedust blurred the air there sometimes like smoke. Make a good lesson, maybe. Have the kids roleplaying locals against quarry bosses. Year nine. Split the class. Locals, owners, workers, press, mayor and corporation and let them argue it out.

He was warmer against her back. His talk got quieter, jumbling with her thinking, then sporadic, then he stopped.

She squeezed from him and turned so that she lay flat, looking up. Her eyes were wide open. The dark had a grain to it like iron filings. Year nine. Nine ee for a double after dinner (sorry) tomorrow. How was it? Lower six double hist first, but sorted. Eight see seven see dinner then double nine ee one free and top off with the three toed sloth then inset for a delightful little extra. So, work backwards. Sloth is pike so free before'll be time to prepare the worksheet, just, or dinnertime I could prepare it and I might get copies for last lesson. So nine ee nine ee. What were they? Shit. Diary. Could do the quarry thing. Morning then. First thing double hist oh death. Mandy'll say, What's that plaster on your finger miss? But sorted. They do the talking. And eight see. Eight see were. Shit. On paper. Working on paper and books back tomorrow. Did I?

She switched the light on. It was quarter to one. Mel blinked and squinted. She pushed the duvet back and got up.

Not replacing it or switching the light off, she went downstairs to check if she'd finished marking 8C's books.

MERCHER

When Steve walked into registration before Shattock had arrived, there was a moment's silence from the fourteen other sixth formers and then he got a round of applause. Pod led it with obscure shouts of approval, flung back in his chair and beating his hands together slowly above his head. Most of the others joined in in half-hearted irony.

Steve put one hand on an imaginary belt and raised the other in the air, elbow bent, the palm held stiff and opened, waved slightly as he swaggered in, thinking of Saddam Hussein.

'My people' he said.

But the couple standing pelvis to pelvis and staring at one another at the end of the bookcase paid no attention, and the knot of girls cwtshing to the radiator didn't break their conversation or unfold their arms from across their midriffs. Why do women do that, the loosefolded arms like Tricia in the shop? Worried about their tits dropping or something. Well, not her, praps. But quite like em dangly myself. Leonardo was onto something with Mona. Accurate observation. The essential gift for the Renaissance Man and the stand up comic.

'Who're you then?' Mandy said as he swaggered by her.

'Saddam Hussein. What do you think?'

'I thought it was the queen' Pod said.

'Just bloody sad I'd say' Mandy said.

He kept demonstrating so she'd get it, but she seemed not to and carried on with some homework.

He felt a bit awkward, still parading and waving after the ovation stopped but he wasn't sure how to get out of it, so he still had his arm in the air when Shattock rushed in and yanked the blue register open.

Steve shot his arm straight up as if tugging the sleeve clear and looked at an imaginary wristwatch.

Shattock, standing bent over the register with his pen poised, stared at Steve. They watched one another for a moment and everyone except the snoggers and the radiator girls watched them. Steve realised this wasn't the right move.

'Oo, I'll have to get a watch put on this wrist' he said, and moved over to the bookcase.

Lower Six Two registered in the Sixth Form Library, so called because it had stained carpet tiles, curtains, and one glassfronted bookcase, locked.

Shattock looked at his own watch and started calling the names and pencilling in attendances. He sounded pissed off.

Steve scanned the spines of the books. All sorts of odds and ends in no sort of order, and lots of gaps. Hymnbooks that had strayed from the shelves in the Hall, out of date dictionaries, a book which must be called *The Pleasure of Ruins* but the dustjacket was ripped so it looked like *asure of Ruins*. Some stuff in Welsh. Old Everymans. And there, next to an unpromising volume about industrial decline in south Wales, was a thin book by Fred Hoyle called *Nicolaus Copernicus*.

Steve stared at it. It was as black as his sweater, and the lettering of the magician's name was coppercoloured. He looked round the door of the bookcase to see how he could get into it. He tugged at a corner to check it was locked.

The pelvic pair were moving away. Registration was finished.

'Steven.' Shattock was sliding the pencil into his breast pocket. The other sixth formers were leaving the room.

Steve gestured at the bookcase. 'Mr Shattock, how can I –'

'Come here a second.' He looked at the register and then up at Steve. 'Look, it's –'

'How can I borrow a –'

'Hang on, now. Let's sort something out.' Shattock paused and watched the last of the other sixth formers leave the room. 'Now it's very pleasant to see you here this morning and all that, but tell me,' – he looked straight at Steve's face – 'where have you been?'

Steve toyed with the idea of something ironic here, treating this either as a profound questioning of the nature of experience or the cautious speech of a coy lover. But he just said, 'How do you mean?'

'I mean, like, attendance.' Pause. 'Where have you been?'

Shattock let the silence bite. Steve stared at his check shirt and the weirdly symmetrical knot in his tie. He smelt of soap and Germolene.

'Sorry, Mr Shattock. I'll, like, bring a –'

'See, Steven, we haven't seen you since, let's see –' he looked down '- last Thursday.'

Steve thought back. 'I was here, like, Monday.' He knew he was copying Shattock saying like and he couldn't stop himself.

'Oh indeed? Not in registration though.'

'But I went to lessons Monday.'

'That's very obliging of you.'

'You can ask –'

'So, come to registration. Sooner or later you've got get down to it, and frankly my lad, you've made a pretty pathetic start to the year. You've got to get your head out of the clouds and be realistic.'

Steve looked at the dusty wallmounted lights. They had naff sixties frosted shades and weren't even switched on, when they should have been smoking torches. He stopped himself smiling.

'Look, I've got to keep accounts for the likes of you.' Shattock paused again and did a funny bulging shape with his upper lip and breathed through his nose.

'Sorry. Sir.' Steve hadn't called anybody sir since form three, but it seemed the right thing to say.

Shattock asked him where he'd been on each day in turn and Steve responded with a blend of truth, lies and silence. Then Shattock went into some long spiel about registration and the law. Apparently the Minister of Education came round and personally threw the switch on the electric chair for teachers who cacked up their registers. Sounded tempting. Steve made various promises, nodding and staring at the scary knot.

When Shattock had finished and actually shut the register, Steve tried again.

'Mr Shattock, this bookcase –'

Shattock, turning for the door, stopped and looked back.

'The thing about it is, there's this book, like, I'd like to borrow it.'

'Okay.'

'On'y the cupboard's locked and all – how can I –'

'How the hell should I know? Look, Steven, I'm late.'

'It's astronomy, see, like –'

'Ask the secretary or Mrs Fylfot or something. But get to

assembly pronto.' Shattock looked at his watch and ran out of the room.

'– like history and physics.' Steve's fingers meshed to try to show what he meant. 'That's, oo, everything.'

Wherever Shattock was going it wasn't assembly because he went the wrong way down the corridor. Extra tea worked in before before next lesson maybe. Lazy sod.

Steve changed his fingers to the explosion gesture and then the splitfingered Star Trek salute.

'Aye aye, Captain.'

The fool out of the way, he could continue his investigations. He looked round at the bookcase.

★ ★

A new metaphor. The day's lessons waiting to be done are aeroplanes circling above the airport, stacked. And I'm air traffic control, sweating and looking at smudges on the gridded radar screen and if I get it wrong –

She stood outside the locked Geography Room and realised it was Wednesday, not Monday or Friday. L6 Hist in Room C9 on Wednesday, twp. She headed back up the corridor, occasionally barking at a kid to keep left and walk. Her overloaded bag hampered her.

– if I get it wrong whole roomloads of children will fall out of the sky, and something –

Across the carpark between buildings in pearly morning light among the kids crisscrossing to lessons. The thin cloudveil glowing, promising to rub away to sun.

– will fall out of the sky and something terrible will happen. The fire engines and the slides and ambulances and little figures in helmets milling, shouting in tiny voices.

As she walked into C9 she considered the stack of planes to be landed that day. Stacked like the marked 8C books waiting to be returned. She smiled at that. A small victory.

C9 was a room with bare white walls and bright with striplights. Like being in a fridge with the light on, except one of the lights was buzzing a bit. She laid out markbook, diary and Perrotbrick on her desk as the lower sixth cast assembled shamblingly. A couple of them rushed her with the usual quiet, urgent excuses for not doing their presentations today and I'll be ready Friday, Miss. The trick was to put a good one up first, she knew from all the oral lessons she did in English, but she didn't know many of these well enough to tell yet. Only early October. All the marking just cranking up to full power and half the kids still strangers. Kids? Another unconvincing word in god's novel. Children. Pupils. Students. Young people? Oh dear. People. Steady on. A bit radical to admit that. So it would have to be randomish. Hope there aren't many shrinkers in the first batch. Mandy first, perhaps? She'd think I was picking on her, which I possibly would be. Her head twirling and Glenys's Note. Can I have a quick "word". If she's complained, I'll do something – something terrible. See Glenys today, maybe.

She counted the class.

Eleven, so three missing. Using her markbook she took a register.

Mike muttered to one of the shrinkers, 'What's she doing that for?'

Steve, of course, was among the absentees. Ryan had been right. She noted the names of the other two under Friday in her diary. They'd do their presentations then. That's why, Mike.

'Right' she said. Remind, summarize, explain purpose of task, define task, they do it, assess. 'Remember on Monday you had some qualms about the essay I've set, so this session is to help you with essay planning. So remember you've all got to do a presentation outlining how you intend your essay might go, showing the line of argument you take and the conclusion you draw on whether Henry VII was a modern or medieval king. So we're literally comparing notes in quite a formal way. So when your turn comes I want you to stand at the front and speak nice and clearly.' Oh technique. She half listened to herself. It was a familiar chain of words from many lessons. She perhaps should change the tone a bit for the sixth form. Pitching it a bit condescending maybe.

'Miss, do we aff to stand?'

You're reading my mind, whatsyourname, but it's said now.

'Yes' she said. 'If you stand it's easier for people' – people! – 'to see and hear you.'

She announced the order they were to speak in to stock expressions of horror and resignation. She put Mike first as he at least spoke clearly.

Sarah shifted to the back of the room and sat. Mike stood in front of the rollerboard, which was rolled to the section squared like graphpaper, and looked at his audience confidently. He flexed his fingers and took some deep breaths as if he was going to play some Rachmaninov.

'Well, I think old Henry was basically more of a medieval sort of a king at first, but then he changed into more of a modern sort of a one, because he had to, like, do it the old fashioned way to start with, because –'

Sarah unfastened her wristwatch as he spoke, laid it on the desk, picked up her biro, and was about to start making some notes, when he finished.

She looked up into the silence.

'That was quick, Mike' she said.

'Oh. Thanks, Miss.'

'Typical of him' Mandy said out of the side of her mouth, and the girls sniggered.

Sarah invited questions and there was the familiar long pause.

'Right? Okay then' Mike said. 'That's me done.'

He waved goodbye to his public as he barged past the table and back to his seat before Sarah had a chance to fabricate a question of her own.

The first double lesson of the day lasted one and a quarter hours. As she graded Mike's talk she calculated that at this rate all the presentations would be finished in slightly more than twenty minutes.

Next up was Melanie, the shrinker who'd watched Girl with Kite with Sarah on Monday.

She put her notes on the desk and stood with her palms pressed either side of them, her elbows locked. She rested one foot on its toe the way a mountain pony does and tipped her head forward so that her long straight hair made a curtain round her face. There was a long pause, the foot balancing on its tip rocked a little, an elbow unlocked and a hand caressed a strand of the curtain to one side, and she started to read in a monotone which wasn't quite loud enough to understand.

Some of the class leaned forward and some stared at their desks. They seemed to be listening. Sarah bent forward and tried to signal her to speak up, but the drape of hair was closed again like the blanket over a murderer's head. Perhaps the class could actually hear her, except for Mike, who was lying back in his chair and scratching sleep from an eyelid. If this was Peter Carrick's lesson he'd be up out of his seat like Dickie Attenborough directing, saying, 'Hit the back wall, love, hit the back wall' and Melanie's face would be going blotchy red and her page would swim. Better sparing her that and not hearing a bloody word.

Sarah looked at her unmarked notepaper and the secondhand of her wristwatch spiralling towards break.

She's written out the whole essay and is going to read the lot. Most gratifying are the ways of the shrinkers. All conspire in this. We can doze while she drones. Education, education, edubloody-cation. Say a word often enough and it turns meaningless. Everything will be all right.

There was a scuffling at the door. It burst open and the handle crunched into the wall.

'Oo, it's nice and bright in here.' Steve stepped in, looking round as if he'd never seen the room before, which he possibly hadn't. His green eyes were glittering.

Melanie twitched her curtain but she kept on reading.

Steve looked round for the teacher, the way they always do when you sit at the back.

'Sorry, Mrs Bowen' he said, when he'd found her. 'I went to the Geography Room by mistake.'

She picked up her watch looking at it pointedly and nodded him towards a seat.

Steve did a music hall doubletake on Melanie and a Tom and Jerry tiptoe to a vacant desk.

At least he'd turned up. Another small victory. Must smirk at Ryan. And he was actually carrying a book. Not Perrot, admittedly, keeps that for carrying around town at night. But still, a book. A thin black hardback.

Steve got up again, Tom and Jerried to the door to shut it, and went back to his seat.

All that unsettled the class. They started to shuffle and snuffle. A few started to whisper. Mike scattered his crumbled sleep oper-atically and coughed the way a seal barks.

Melanie kept on droning like a plane on automatic pilot.

'Er, scuse me.' Steve, nursing his book, was leaning forward.

Melanie cut the engine and Sarah half expected her to wheel into the floor, but she merely caressed some fronds aside and looked up.

'Sorry. Scuse me. Could you speak up a bit, please? Praps it's just me, but I can't hear a thing.'

Mike made some obscure noise of frustration.

Melanie looked at Sarah, who nodded fractionally, raising her eyebrows and smiling a bit to encourage her.

Melanie resumed a little louder, then dropped back to the regulation drone, then interrupted herself:

'Miss, do you want me to read it all, Miss?'

'Er, how much more is there?'

Melanie riffled paper for a long time. 'Fourteen sides, Miss.'

Sarah considered. It would help the controlled descent to break-time. But. Faces watched her.

'Well, you've done very well, Melanie, but you needn't have written it all out yet. This is a planning exercise, see. Can you have a go at just summarizing the rest in a minute or so?'

The faces were disappointed, except for Mike who'd already suffered his ordeal and wanted all the rest to get theirs.

'Hear hear, Miss' he said. 'Quite right.'

Melanie's curtain came down as she thought about this. The class listened to the striplight.

'I'll just read the conclusion' she said at last.

The pages were riffled again and the curtain caressed and there was a beautifully elongated pause until she found the start of the finish.

'Therefore it can be seen that –'

And her voice slipped back onto autopilot just below the intelligibility threshold, then diminished until Sarah couldn't tell whether she'd finished or not. Melanie twitched the curtain aside and looked up to signal she had. The minute hand had moved a few degrees.

'Thanks, Melanie. A bit quiet, but well done. Anybody got a question?'

Another silence in which everybody watched the rocking of Melanie's upended foot.

The sound of a thin black hardback snapping shut.

'Er, yeah. Me' Steve said.

Mike rehearsed the frustration noise.

'So' Steve said, 'I didn' catch it all, but you went on about the Statute of Maintenance and Livery. See, I think –'

There was a communal groan. Mike whispered, 'Shit mun, Stick.'

Sarah watched her watch and Melanie watched Steve, frightened.

'– that was, the Statute of Maintenance and Livery, all right it was a bit of a stroke, like, but I mean, was it really all that innovative?'

Melanie went blotchy and looked down, but there was to be no tense silence. Steve was speaking the rhetorical question that would come at the beginning of an impenetrably argued paragraph.

'Because' he said, 'I think, if you put it right in context, they were pretty legalistically minded sort of thing, back then.' He paused, but not for long. 'In them days. So they would've been well used to the king or whoever trying to tighten his grip –'

The volume went down as she watched the spiralling second-hand. If you could turn the volume down at will. If you could make the point on the spiral move faster. Or stop it altogether. But in this case faster would be better.

The volume came back up. Steve was still talking. A seal barked, scattering more sleep. Must be on the other eyelid by now. The insect buzz of restlessness had grown a little. How long can you let them go on before they start unbuckling their belts and demanding to see the captain?

One of the girls gave her an imploring look.

Sarah nodded.

She waited for something like a convenient pause in Steve's talk – he'd just said something about the court jester slashing his wrists – when she said, 'Thank you very much, Melanie' and nodded her to her seat. 'Thank you, Steve.'

'Oo, right' Steve said.

Sarah wrote a C in her markbook for Melanie, remembered she'd heard almost nothing, and added a minus, then remembered she'd used the word 'conclusion', and crossed the minus out.

By the time Patricia Henneghan got up to speak, almost an hour into the lesson, Sarah felt she was seeing the same person again and again, slightly changed. Long straight hair, lustrous the way it's easy for it to be when you're sixteen or seventeen, and the sixth form variant of the school uniform – shirt with the tie relatively neat, veenecked sweater with prefect badge, grey skirt and black tights. Patricia's variations were the smallness of her breasts and her subtle layer of foundation makeup and undemonstrative eyeliner.

The restlessness Steve had stirred up, by asking awkward questions and then answering them himself after every speaker, continued mutedly, but Patricia spoke clearly as if she were a schoolteacher already. One day, Sarah could tell, she would be. Don't do it, Patricia. A variation, an earlier version of me, but yielding nothing to gravity. Yet.

She finished the businesslike summary of the main points of her essay. B plus in the markbook, no problem.

Sarah had given up inviting questions long since as Steve cut in immediately every speaker finished.

'Mm. Yeah. Thanks' Steve said. 'But don't you think –'

The choric groan went up again.

Mike pressed his hands to his face and said, 'Shshshshsh-shih.'

Patricia stared emptily at Steve, without doing any curtain stroking. She didn't go blotchy either, though her lips rolled closed into a firm line.

'Miss, mun.' Mike's hands slid onto his head as he whispered. 'Stop him. Please.'

'– the thing is, the, like, late Fifteenth Century worldview was pretty dynamic, for a few people anyway. I mean, it may not look like it at first, but it is when you look a bit closer. Perrot's pathetic on that. You mention foreign policy, but see –'

Patricia had gathered her papers and was keeping pokerfaced while he talked on.

'Keep going' Mandy said. It was her turn next.

'– Perrot don' talk about the most important thing, which was the Cabot expedition. I mean I just been reading about the impact of Columbus in Cracow.' He paused dramatically and looked round. 'Cracow!'

'Fffffff-fuh' Mike said.

Mandy was smiling admiringly at Steve and nodding.

'I mean, like, for pretty well everybody the ends of the earth was a place you didn' go back then – in them days – where waters plunged endlessly into space.' He made a waterfall with the fingers of one hand and waved the book with the other. 'So I mean the Cabot thing was probably the most important thing *conceptually*, and in the long term probably *politically* as well.' He stopped as if that made everything clear.

Mike's hands slid from his head. Patricia started to move away from the front.

'How do you mean, Steve?' pert Mandy perted.

Patricia kept moving back to her seat. Steve turned on his chair to face Mandy. She leaned forward, watching him. Her smile and her eyes widened. Steve noticed her and then seemed to become selfabsorbed once more.

'Well see –'

A miasmal sigh passed through the class as he went back over the conceptual and political in turn. But Mandy kept on perting. Her arched eyebrows arched further widening her eyes and she responded with nods and smiles to every appropriate shift in Steve's tone of voice.

'– see, the *tech*nology of it, plus what a few of them knew about the *cos*mology –'

He seemed to be making sense. Something about the inching on of ideas. Sarah could feel him teetering along the line of an argument she didn't quite get, sense his wobbling. He might not resolve it. You could feel that the strand might snap under him. Like Kenny sometimes when he tried to play the piano at mam's house and the tune would clog and he'd break down. Or like doing poetry with year ten. The silent fall through air. But she couldn't quite follow it. He didn't know how to make it clear, perhaps, and when you sit at the back with your markbook you have to follow as much of the subterranean politics of the classroom as you can. The sleepscattering, groinscratching, sealbarking, sighs and whispers. Everything that mucks it up.

And Steve, as far as she could tell, didn't clinch his air paragraph. Instead he stopped and gestured with his book, looking at Mandy.

'So' he said, 'there you are. I can do it properly on Friday.' He smiled. 'But look, it's, like, your turn I think.'

Sarah couldn't tell from where she sat, but she thought Mandy's pertness froze on her. There was a pause and Steve looked to Sarah for adjudication.

Mike was nodding. When Sarah concurred and called her out, Mandy walked to the front only slightly flatfootedly. The look at her watch was understated, and the moue she pulled as she faced them was as subtle as something very late in the career of Alec Guinness.

She had notes ready, at least, and it didn't look like fourteen sides. She ironed them onto the desk as if she were practising to become a Glenys, and started speaking with a theatrically half-concealed sigh.

By this time there were no new points to be made, every syllable of Perrot having been beaten into lifelessness, if it had ever had any life in the first place, in the previous performances. She skipped across some points as efficiently as a stone across a river, while the secondhand did a few more spirals.

There was little time left and Sarah should save some minutes for summing up. She had a page of notes now. Points for the essay and points about how to make the points and points about how to structure making the points and points about presenting the made and structured points. Remind them who's left to speak on Friday. The two missing, two there wouldn't be time for today, and Steve top of the bill. Really it wasn' bad. Keep structures and routines and you keep making it to Friday. What could the something terrible be, anyway?

'Mi-iss.' A coaxing voice gently waking an elderly person.

Sarah looked up from her watch. All the class were watching her. Mandy wasn't quite smiling.

'Miss, you okay?' she said.

Sarah ignored the question. She stared at Mandy.

'Is it your finger?' Mandy said.

I knew you'd say something in the end. 'What's the problem, Mandy?'

Mandy shrugged minimally and looked back at her notes.

Was that a small victory or not? Can't tell. The air was tense.

'Could we leave a bit early, Miss?' Mandy said. 'Mrs Waters used to say when we were in the sixth form we could finish a minute or two early sometimes.'

'Get on with it.'

Mandy's wide eyes widened. Temper temper, they said.

The class spectated. Through the cockpit windscreen Sarah saw the horizon rear. The earth stood flat in front of the plane like a wall. Roads and rivers and cities spun towards her.

'Just thought' Mandy said. 'Thought it'd suit you, Miss.' She was still staring.

Where were the little fire engines?

But Mandy went back to her notes. She read one more very long convoluted sentence in a singsong voice and then said, 'That's that.'

'Thank you, Mandy' Sarah said. 'We're all impressed.' Honest. 'Any questions?'

Everybody looked at Steve. He had slid down in his chair, his legs sticking straight out like black stilts, and was staring at his opened book. Sarah could see the pages from where she sat. There seemed to be geometrical figures and lists of algebraic formulae.

'Uh?' He started when he noticed them watching. 'What? Sorry, this is good stuff. Have you finished then?'

'Any questions' Sarah said again.

Mike started emphatically dropping his books into the gaping Adidas bag. Mandy was eyeballing Steve ferociously. Steve stared back, but only sometimes at her face.

'Yeah, course' Steve said.

But there was a pause as he seemed to try to think what the question might be, or perhaps he was drafting the answer. Mandy's eyebrows tried to say something to him in semaphore. He didn't see that. His mouth opened and shut as he stared at her upwards and outwards.

'Pig' Mandy said suddenly, and she flatfooted fast back to her desk, slapping Steve on the head with her sheaf of notes as she passed him.

'Do you charge any extra for that?' Steve said, as the bell rang and there was the Pavlovian turmoil of packing and pushing furniture aside.

The time. Sarah jumped up and moved to the door to head them off, tried to call them to order, gatekeep. Most of them paused, still on their feet, and looked at her. She announced that there were points to be made which she'd make on Friday, and there were five left to speak, including of course Steven. As they heard her voice drop to conclude the sentence they sidled out. Mandy's face was calm, bar the flared nostrils. She avoided looking at Sarah. Mike was shaking his head more than Stevie Wonder and muttering about Stick. Melanie tugged her curtain aside and smiled at her and said, 'Thanks, Miss.'

At the end of each farce the cast disassembles and perhaps somebody made something happen and perhaps not. There ought to be Lloyd Bridges or Burt Lancaster or somebody standing in a control tower chewing a wet cigar butt that's lasted right to the end of the final reel looking out onto the wintry tarmac and saying, 'What a woman!' and then a closeup on Sarah smiling in the flaw-blown sleet beside the intact plane, the cold wind romantically shifting the dark wings of her Lulu wig. Everything changed utterly. Or perhaps only time had passed.

'Good stuff, Mrs Bowen' Steve said, lingering after the rest had gone. Last in last out. 'I like the way you just get on with it. Not naming anybody, but some people interrupt too much, you know?'

★ ★

After break, Steve stayed in the Common Room for a bit.

Groups of sixth formers sat chatting under walls spread with curling, studenty posters. Nobody was chucking things around yet or playing hand table tennis, but it was early.

Somebody had broken the mug he brought in at the beginning of term and anyway he was threatened with blacklisting from the tea and coffee by some twat from upper sixth with a blazer for non payment of dues. But Trish surprised him by including him in an offer of coffee.

He hung around with her by the kettle while a group of the History lot sat near the lockers. Pod was in the middle of them, with Mandy, who was yawning and stretching with effortless sexiness, but when she looked at him her eyes went hard and he felt obscurely that he ought to keep away.

'Milk and sugar?'

'Black and strong' he said impressively. 'Three sugars.'

'Well, you made it then.'

'Uh?'

'Today. You got here. Helped Baggy spin it out too, poor dab.'

'How do you mean?'

Trish's mouth went up on one side. 'You know.'

There was physics this afternoon but he 'ouldn' stay for that. Matthews had been funny ever since Steve tried to explain chaos theory to him.

He felt for the cigarettes in his breast shirt pocket, remembered where he was and looked round for a concealed corner to light up in, then thought he'd better not.

Besides, there was plenty to think about after History. And the book too. Funny, appearing like that. A Starry Messenger. Have to sit down and think through what to say. It all connects. Unified fields.

'Oh well.' Trish started to load the half dozen mugs on a tray.

He realised she'd been leaning against the sink waiting for conversation.

'Mm, I enjoyed your talk' he said.

'Oh yeah.' She clattered a spoon onto the drainingboard.

'Aye. I did.' He slurped his coffee and hurt his tongue, but kept talking. 'You focussed on foreign policy didn' you. But see, I still think Perrot underplays the Cabot bit. Probly because he don' understand what it means. Because, I mean.' He thought of Cabot on his ship, a rocking little platform in the North Atlantic. They used a quadrant to measure the sun. Never really got lost. Grasped the shape of the planet. 'I mean observation, just looking hard and a bit of brainpower and imagination changed – changed everything really –'

'Steven.' She was leaning towards him, holding the tray ready to go to the lockers. 'Shut up.'

And he was left clutching a mug of coffee made the way he never drank it, except for the sugar. He watched the uprightness of her walk as she balanced the tray and how her sweater clothed the outturn of her hips. Beyond her, the waiting historians looked up and cleared a way for her to the low table. He considered a moment and then turned away. He leant against the crash bar of the emergency door and burst out onto the path that ran along the back of the building.

'Shut it behind you, Leyshon, you dickhead.'

Steve waved his fagpacket and the book at the friendly voice as he went out and heeled the door back, leaving it open half an inch so he could get back in.

He squatted against the windowless wall behind the door and lit up.

Smokers' Alley, a weedgrown path that backed onto a steep grass bank, was deserted. He opened the book. There was a bit about orbital eccentricity.

> In all cases the orbits are nearly circles. Even for Mercury the shorter axis of its orbit is only about 2 per cent less than the larger axis. This was a most fortunate circumstance since it permitted approximate theories to be developed that were based on circles.

The air was still. He watched the smoke making a slow straight filament. The surface of the coffee was still as glass. The sun had scorched away most of the high cloud and it was gleaming palely. Invisible, eccentric Mercury was buzzing about it. He thought of it, amazed. A tiny cartoon firefly with a luminous arse whizzing and singing in a small electronic voice that throbbed in speed and pitch as it dashed round the back of the sun.

IF you SOLVE my MYSterEE
KING of STARmen YOU will BEE.

He tried the voice and chanted:

'I WHIZZ aBOUT from HERE to THERE
I AM the STARry MESSenGER.'

Started sounding like ET going round in a slow tumble dryer and
began turning into Olivier's Richard III. He thought of the video
Carrick showed them in the fourth form and tried the cod scholar's
ballockless nasal whine:

'When NicholUS
CopernicUS
Looked out inTO
The univUS.'

Need another line.

He hunched one shoulder and tried it louder to see if that would
pull the next line through:

'When Nicholas Copernicus
Went striding through the universe –'

But he never cracked Mercury. Thought it was a circle. That
was Kepler. The magician had to bend the figures a bit because of
that. Should have bent the orbits instead. Boom boom.

He Oliviered it up a bit more:

'When, my liege, Nicholarse Copernicarse
Did bestride him so mightily about
The univarse, he – he –'

The cartoon voice came back

'He LOOKED inTO the STARry NIGHT
To CHECK my ARSE was STILL aLIGHT.'

Someone was pushing at the door. It opened and shut again
quickly. There was the farting sound of suppressed laughter. It part
opened again. A hand appeared and then Pod's dark cropped head.
Somebody was pushing him out and then pulling him back.

'Stick, mun' he said. 'Get off will you. A' right, I'm going, I'm
going. Stick, mun. Enjoying youself?'

Steve unhunched his shoulder, pretended to cough, and looked critically at his cigarette. 'Still alight' he said.

'Oi, Stick. Fancy a pint after?' Pod stepped out and pushed the door to, squatted next to him and looked at the bank. 'I could do with one after that fucking lesson' he said. 'Sorry. A' right. Nothing personal.'

'My old girl don' get paid till tomorrow' Steve said. 'Fag?'

'No thanks. I got a game after, too, come to think of it. Tell you what then, I just thought of this. Friday dinnertime. What d'ou think? Before Baggy. Start the weekend early. Sixth formers' perk. Gang of us.'

Steve had shut the book so Pod wouldn't see the formulas. The emergency door was still slightly ajar, but there was no sign of the pullers and pushers.

'Mandy've got her old man's car Friday' Pod said. 'We could go down the Adit. I aven had a good dinnertime on the piss since GCSE results.'

'I never get pissed' Steve said.

Pod looked at him.

'Well, I do obviously. But I've got a theory about it. It's all to do with the rate we metabolize alcohol. See, it takes about an hour to metabolize one unit, they reckon. That's so it completely clears your blood. So I reckon if you're going to equate absorption to time, you ought to calculate your drinking in terms of units metabolized and deduct it from the total number of units you've taken, so the zero case would be, oo, if you took an hour to down one unit you'd have absorbed it as fast as you drank so one from one is nought and you aven had a drink. So one unit's half a pint of beer they reckon, so if you took four hours to drink two pints, actually you've had literally bugger all.'

'Two pints is bugger all anyway' Pod said.

'Yeah exactly.' Steve started to see new depths in his theory. 'You on'y just start going fuzzy then. So I reckon you could do your arithmetic and work out how to keep yourself just nice and gone like, about the three and a half, four pint mark, while drinking continuously. Plus they're bound to build in a safety margin with that one unit per hour bit, like the safe working load on a crane, so you could probly add, oo, at least ten per cent to how much you could take. I aven done the sums, but it'd be pretty easy to work out. You could probly have the first two at normal speed to bring yourself up to the mark and then have your sort of sip rate worked out for the metabolization-versus-getting-totally-stuffed ratio to take you up gradually to your preferred limit, then switch down the zero rate when you think you've had enough.'

'Go on then. Work it out then.'

'Well, say you had the first two pints real quick, say fifteen minutes. Fifteen minutes, that's a quarter of a unit, so that's.' He had to stop and think.

'Eighth of a pint' Pod said.

'Yeah. So you've only actually had one point eight something, say one point eight seven, of a pint. So start to slow it down. Half an hour for the next one is half a unit to deduct so that pint only counts point seven five, so say you do the next one the same, you've only really had an extra one and a half, so one and a half plus one point eight seven is three point, er, three point three, three point three seven.'

'Plus your ten per cent.'

'Yeah. Minus, actually.'

'So are you coming then?'

'So let's work out one more round and deduct the ten per cent at the end. So another pint in half an hour would be another point seven five really, is three point three seven plus point seven five is, well, it's only a spit and a fart over four. Four point one and a bit. So less your ten per cent to eliminate the safe working load is point four oneish, so subtract that is three point sixish, call it three point five. So you've been in the pub less than two hours –'

'Hour and three quarters.'

'– hour and three quarters and you're starting your sixth pint but in real terms you've only had three and a half. So scale your sip rate down from there on and you could keep drinking without going over the four pint mark ad nauseam, and never puke up.' He flicked the tail of his cigarette and the punctuation marks fell.

Pod looked at him and then laughed.

Got him. Steve pulled on his fag so as not to smile. 'It's based on empirical fact, and a bit of brainpower and imagination. Weird science.' He paused. 'There's probly some snag, though.'

'Yeah.' Pod made the money sign with his fingers. 'Plus' he said, 'after the first couple of hours you'd be so fucking wazzled you 'ouldn' be able to do the sums. You'd have to have a co driver like in a rally to navigate for you.'

They looked at the grass bank, which wasn't doing much.

'I reckon, though' Steve said, 'half the blokes down the Exy have already cracked it.'

They thought of the don players and barhangers in the Exy who had perfectly controlled decelerating sip rates. Steve could see them bobbing in the water, numbed, just out of touch with the mainland, but never actually lost, not completely.

'Christ' Pod said. Then after a pause, 'So, you coming then?'

'Uh?'

'Friday. Down the Adit.'

'Yeah. Course.'

Pod sprang up, brushing the seat of his tight school trousers. 'Good man.' He moved to the door. 'So get to the Common Room beginning of dinnertime if you're on for it.'

Somebody started swinging the emergency door open from the inside before Pod touched it. Pod smiled at whoever it was – Steve couldn't see them – and mouthed a 'Yes.' He might have put a thumb up as he stepped in. The door slammed.

There was no handle on this side of it. Steve would either have to knock and look a prat now or walk right round the building and in through the main door and look a prat in a few minutes. The little groups would be sitting and talking in closed circles of low chairs.

No. There was the book, and plenty to think about. He looked at the pale sun where invisible Mercury was reeling and singing. Thanks to parallax, you're going to walk me home.

He dropped the dogend of his cigarette into the black disc of coffee and got up.

★ ★

'Miss, Miss.'

'Hit, hit' she said, looking up from her diary, but Dustin didn't get it.

'Miss, have you seen?' He was standing by the window of the upstairs classroom looking into the sunlit staff carpark.

She thought for a minute it was another slashed tyre and was glad she didn't have the car.

'Miss, it've just parked.' Clint, bandageless and as intellectually intact as he ever had been, was dancing and jabbing a finger at the window.

A fair part of 7C were clustering to the glass.

She considered calling them to order but then looked at her watch. It was last lesson of the morning and there were eleven minutes left to dinner (sorry – no I'm not.) Why shout? It's sunny, sort of. A truce.

'It's a merk, Miss' Dustin said.

One of those gleamy preautumnal days that catches on everything chrome and shiny and puts it into incandescent soft focus.

'Yeah and some nerk just got out' Clint said.

'Yeah, a nerk with a merk.'

She went to the window.

'Oh, a *Merc*' she said.

The silvered Mercedes gleamed milkily, outsized and a little askew in the pattern of oblongs in the carpark. The driver's door was standing open like a wing. The man who'd just got out sleeked the hair at his temples with the palms of his hands and reaching inside fetched out a grey jacket on its hanger.

'Posh' Tammy said.

'Cool' Clint said.

Dustin said his uncle had a Merc. He have. He have. Honest. He told me.

''S like a spaceship' Clint said.

The man had put on the jacket. He seemed to fold the hanger like a carpenter's rule and put it back in the car. A stiffsided black briefcase appeared. The wing clicked expensively shut, loud enough for them to hear. Nerk with Merc approached the main door of A Block.

'So who's the spaceman, Miss?'

'God knows' Sarah said. 'Now then, show over. Back to seats.'

The girls went back to their chairs quite quickly. Boys, living down to the stereotype, talked hushed and urgent about cars. Most of the copies of *English for Life* were shut, their sub Mondrian carpark covers hurting the eye.

She went back to the diary blare where she'd been noting the past and blocking in the future. She flipped the page to next week. It was about a third filled with her tortured knitting pattern notes. And back to this week. Today. Previous lesson: 8C books back. Collect wk on ppr. She put a tick by that. The curly wad of lined A4 sheets was in an envelope in her black bag. On Friday afternoon for her free lesson she could mark 8C's work on paper. But then, it could wait till Sunday. When next for 8C? She flipped to the timetable. First on Monday. Shit, no leeway, still, start Friday and Sunday for what's unfinished. There were two lots booked in for marking on Sunday already. 9T worksheet and 11E essay coming in tomorrow. So those two. Three, three and a half hours if you go like a train. More like four. So better with 8C in frees and dinnertimes (sorr – no, fuck off). So mark today dinnertime and the free this afternoon. Lose the free tomorrow because of the dentist. One free Friday aft. No come on. Won' have enough octane left in the tanks for that. Or this afternoon's free for Pike worksheet. Yes no choice about that, really. No other time for it.

She wrote in for Wednesday afternoon: Fr. Pike wkst. – prepare.

Which means I'll have to get to 8C Friday, glide it on empty.

So in Friday she wrote: Fr. start mark 8C wk. on ppr.

That is always assuming Billy Thomas and his shitty suit don' give me a supervision. And the book to look for. Shit. That.

Putting the marks in her markbook in the small hours for 8C she'd noted the usual two or three exercise books missing, three this time. In the lesson returning the books, forty minutes ago, allowing herself the smile of a small triumph, she'd made the usual inquiry. Why no book? And got the usual answers. But one small boy insistent. I give it in, Miss. I was away Monday morning about my knee and I come and give it in special Monday afternoon breaktime, Miss, remember. By the staffroom, Miss. You took it. She stared at him. She couldn' exactly remember it, but something gleamed at her through all the clutter of detail. A bugger when they hand in late. You never have the right pile handy to add the late ones to.

To Fr. Pike wkst. – prepare, she added, Find missing 8C book.

The 8C boy tiny and delicate, like a primary kid. The outer flesh of his nostrils and ears neat, translucent as porcelain. Made you want to touch it. Benlike.

But really, a moderately successful morning. Another not half bad half day for the inner CV. Lower six double hist to plan, more or less. Most of them had a go at preparing something of some sort. Time on their hands in the Common Room yet. Too early in the term for them to have got much work on. Make a change for Mike from dropkicking coffee mugs over the striplights.

She looked up.

Dustin, who had been making roaring noises while gripping the steering wheel of a Mercedes, crossed his arms and looked at something on the ceiling. She had an impression of figures who had been standing up and happily thumping one another sitting suddenly and bowing their heads. Clint was hunched over a drawing in his rough book. She leant forward and could see the upside down carshaped profile with cartoon vroom lines trailing from it, a cartoon moon in the background, and inside the car, the driver's head squarehelmeted with an aitchshaped aerial sticking from the top.

'Space auto, Miss' Clint said, without looking up. 'My uncle reckon god was an astronaut. He read a book.'

She looked at her watch. The usual countdown in both ticking and the emptinesses of stomachs.

'What do you think, Miss? Was god an astronaut?'

'Oh, that's a tricky one, Dustin.' But no, he was just a nought. Absolute zero. The absolute zero. Ask old Khayam.

'Right then, kids' she said. 'Countdown to dinnertime. Books away.'

A whole morning without headache to self or braindamage to any pupil. Something to be said for the smelly itchy routineness of it all. Good thing about getting tipsy so easy is you don't get the chemical hangover. The lower sixth talks, for instance, and then breaktime, edging into the crammed and buzzing staffroom, making for the silvered urn, past the young man finishing his Snickers bar, inching between Elis Richards, head of RE, purveyor to the children of the nonexistent deity, bulky, like a whale standing on its tailflukes, his grey sideburns lacquered on his cheeks, blazered and talking, reverentially, technically, arcanely, about deficient handling skills causing breakdown during second phase possession in the game on Saturday, and Sarah excusemeing and turning from him to pass because two whales belly to belly and standing on their tails would be more alien and other than the three eyed Martian sloth and anyway embarrassing, and there, turning, she saw his interlocutor was Shattock tired from his early start, clutching a mug of tea, and she remembered about Steve and did her best to smirk but it came out as a mere smile, and in fractional acknowledgement the corners of his mouth twitched under the stain, which, at these close quarters, resolved itself into single sawnoff thick male hairs, some black and some red as those on Mel's sleeping nape, and the pupils of his eyes adjusted to see her, the fractional shift of eyebrows by way of hello, and then the eyes moving fractionally – all these fractions – readjusting to avoid, or merely see past, her to Elis Richards again. And then at the urn with her cup, she watched the milk blossoming a spiral galaxy in her coffee. And was that, in the nounless flowing and buzzing, an almost Moment, something close to nodal and, almost, even, willed? A certain stiffening of tissue around the right nipple (why always that one first?)? A different, more pleasant kind of melting? A close encounter of the thawed kind? Touching the face of the big zero? A real, actual, literal clitoral twinge? That Happened. Miasmally enough for no one ever to know except herself and possibly – though improbably – him. Life made of stuff like that. Minnow lyrics. Some sharp-tasting ones, like the old in hospital, and some, like this, sweetly corrosive, but all of them too fleet for the inner CV to catch. If you could stop one. Stop it dead, or alive, like Monday morning had almost been.

She watched 7C and 7C watched her as the bell rang, some with their arms folded in memory of primary school.

'Right –' she said.

But she didn't hear the end of her sentence as they broke for the door, Dustin purring like a Merc.

★

The Careers Library was flooded with preautumnal light, though half the window was slatted with blinds. There were pastel grey metal shelves around the walls full of organized looking leaflets. The room faced south and the paintwork was relatively unchipped and little of the wood effect formica had been stripped from the tables and it had a carpet and a computer, and there was even an upholstered swivel chair for the computer. The Careers Library was like this because Brace's wife worked as a part time careers adviser, which fitted conveniently with childcare, and Brace himself was the guardian of the key. Only selected sixth formers and occasionally staff were allowed to borrow the key. Whenever there were meetings involving visitors, this was the room Brace insisted they use.

When Sarah arrived at the door for the Inset meeting at four, Eunice was standing with her hand on the handle looking in through the wired glass panel.

She turned when she saw Sarah and mouthed voicelessly, 'Look.'

Inside, the rodent who had designed a lateral transfer system for disc brake assemblies was sitting at the computer monitor in the shady corner by the blind, and with him was Melanie, the curtain-haired historian. His hand was locked on hers on the mouse. Though their backs were to the door, Sarah knew – it was something about the attitudes of their heads – that they were silent, and they were both looking straight at the screen, where the cocked little arrow of the cursor, pointing to some icon, trembled.

Sarah's headache eased. Suddenly she found herself holding back a laugh.

'Bless em' Eunice whispered. 'Modern love.'

'I think they're going to click' Sarah said. And the laugh momentarily broke through.

But the sixth formers didn't hear. Rodent had taken his sweater off. It was draped over the back of his chair, and his white shirt-sleeve was separated from Melanie's arm by a sexually tense fraction of an inch. The sides of their heads closest to one another were rimmed with the electricpale light of the screen. They were still.

Then Sarah saw Melanie's hair shift as her head started to to tilt very slowly towards Rodent.

The two women held their breath. They stood at the door, Sarah's hand on Eunice's on the doorhandle in sympathetic imitation of the young man and woman.

Everything had stopped in their world. The minimal shifting of the cursor on the screen showed them that they were the only two left, and they'd escaped. Sarah hoped they realised it. She thought Rodent's head might be inclining minutely towards the hair curtain, but it was hard to tell.

'Go on, Rob boy' Eunice whispered.

Sarah looked at her and then back to the haloed couple.

Then a third hand, heavy and stony, came on top of hers.

'Oh dear oh dear. Come on, ladies. Wake up.'

And the door was open. Peter pushed between them. His lean tweedy body strained through into the room.

'Come on, you two. No canoodling. There's a meeting in here.'

The rodent and the historian started. Their hands unclamped from the mouse and they jumped up. As Sarah and Eunice went in, Melanie swayed towards the door, her eyes downcast, her hands tugging the two tongues of her hair to her cheeks. Rodent, malely and intensely, leant at the desk, clicking, shutting window after window. Even in the electric screenlight he looked a little pink, if expressionless. The three teachers watched him.

At last the monitor went as blank as his face. He adjusted the cord on the blinds to open the slats. As he left he handed the room key to Peter, who was sucking in his cheeks. Sarah knew he was holding back, just, something facetious.

Melanie had waited for Rodent outside. Sarah imagined them walking away down the corridor, not looking at one another, talking about career opportunities.

'Whew.' Peter rubbed pretend sweat from his forehead. 'Nice and warm in here.'

Sarah's headache came back.

Some of the tables had been pushed back against the shelving and the plastic chairs arranged in a few concentric semicircles. At the opposite end of the room from the monitor was a flipchart and a sleek, pristine overhead projector with its screen.

'Good day?' Eunice said as she and Sarah sat in the back row and waited.

Sarah looked at her and rolled her eyes. They hurt.

'Never mind. They've all gone. It'd be quite a nice place except for the kids. I've –'

Sarah pulled her diary and the brown envelope of 8C's work on paper from her bag to try to get something done before and possibly during the meeting. Eunice talked to her in a hushed, confidential way so as to exclude Peter, who took the cue and sat in the front row.

'– so anyway –'

Sarah flipped the diary open and scanned the entries for that afternoon. No, not good, Yune, not in the end. The morning teetering on the long fall and the afternoon drowning, sort of.

First double of the afternoon, 9E. She hadn't had time to prepare the quarry thing – that to do for next week maybe – so she'd tried to cover the pre Twentieth Century lit requirement. Used the handout she prepared at the end of the summer. In the last departmental meeting Peter had wanted all of them to do 'The Charge of the Light Brigade' with year nine and Eunice had been enthusiastic but Sarah'd refused. Why not? Peter said. Seems suitably daft and lemminglike to me. Serve the National Crapiculum right. Yes, Eunice said, I like Tennyson. Irony wasted. Peter, seeing it was a way of keeping her happy, pursued it. Well, Auntie Yune, would you like to prepare a. I'll help you draft it. Sarah ended up agreeing to do another Tennyson, 'The Kraken'. Hm, nice and short Peter said when she showed him a copy, cheeky bastard. And then he tried to make a haemorrhoid gag –

'– I went breaktime this morning to try to see him, and Justine looked in his appointment book –'

– a haemorrhoid gag out of the line about unnumbered and enormous polypi in the many a wondrous grot and secret cell and the huge seaworms. So this afternoon 9E got twenty five minutes on apostrophes and then the Kraken, because she hadn't lost the worksheet on that. Not a bad one. You can give them research things on myths. Do pictures. Even talk about the words. Some of them love it when they know the hard words. Then you have to stop them putting hath and sleepeth in their own poems.

'– appointment book if you please. It'll have to be tomorrow, Justine said. There's a sixth former with him now and he's got a vip coming in a bit. She says vip for vee eye pee. Anyway –'

Sarah looked earnestly at Eunice, not listening, and then back at her diary.

The room was filling. The nonspecialists who picked up the odd class. The NQT Snickers eater, wearing a sweaty tracksuit and eating a Riesen bar this time. Teachers from other schools nearby. There were almost a dozen altogether.

She made a note in her diary for the following week to collect 9E's work on apostrophes and the Kraken homework. But the real cheeky bastard, end of dinner(sorry)time, was Billy Thomas, coming in the staffroom looking harassed, clutching supervision slips. Present for you, Sarah, he said. Then, Sorry, a bit late. 9R to supervise lesson seven. One of the maths teachers home sick that half hour, so my free down the Swanee. The mockers on getting the Pike worksheet out. 9R for forty minutes with nothing to do. Poor Eunice actually has to try and teach them things. Gethin Devereux with the outsized head in full flow. Forty minutes in the mobile classroom with the damp in one corner and the cloth torn off the rollerboard and all thirty three of 9R. And no phone in there.

Peter was rubbing his eyes. Eunice came to the end of some bout of speaking.

'Yes, quite right' Sarah said.

So for 9R she scrounged some wordsearches from May. Half of them looked disgusted and said, Not another one of them, and a couple set to doing it.

Gethin whooped and clapped. 'Word search, word search' he

said. 'Yip, yip. Good darts, Miss, good darts. Brilly-*unt*. Very educational.'

The panjandrum from County Hall had arrived in the Careers Library and taken his position at the OHP. It was nerk with Merc.

The lesson spent with 9R and trying to outface Gethin Devereux meant the hostage in the head had broken his heels loose again and was drumming them slow and hard against the inside of her skull. And the worksheet would have to be prepared tonight.

She wrote in her diary for that evening. Take Pike home. Wksht!

Eunice was still talking to her, in an urgent whisper now that the inservice meeting was starting, anxious to get out every detail of how she'd failed to see Brace during morning break.

Close up, nerk with Merc's grey suit looked impossibly new and neat. The shoulders came to exactly equal angles. He had a silk, patterned yellow tie. She imagined him judging that one stripe of colour in a mirror. He opened the stiffsided case, placed sheaves of handouts on a table, and, as he had when she'd seen him in the carpark, he sleeked his temples with his palms. The hair there was feathered with silvery grey curves. He wore large glasses, disconcertingly like Sarah's, and a large smile.

Eunice shut up at last when Peter stood up. He looked as though he was made of mud as he stood next to nerk and welcomed the handful of teachers from other schools and said, Look on the bright side, a couple of hours now and that's an afternoon less out of our holidays for inset come half term. Sarah watched nerk's face for signs of registering this slight slight, but there was none.

Gethin's hair was shaved down to about an eighth of an inch and then had some stripes razored into it. He was fat and a bit taller than Sarah and he had sores round his mouth.

'Got a pen?' he said.

She didn't answer because she knew he had the next line ready. She walked to his desk and put a biro on it.

'Where's your report sheet, Gethin?' she said, because he was always on report.

'Yip, yip, bad darts, Miss, bad darts.'

Peter introduced Martin Ayers of the Advisory Team at County Hall. One of the colourcoded handouts was passed round and his name was on it and she saw it was Ayers as in Rock, as opposed to and Graces.

'I didn' know they had an adviser left' Eunice whispered.

Sarah knew the corpses of the careers of most of the advisers were buried in unmarked graves in the political woods. Mr Ayers smiled the smile of the last froglet in the jar who's just devoured his siblings. Another outbreak of metaphors. Stop it.

The fan of the OHP purred just on the borders of audibility as Ayers tested it. It threw its pale trapezium on the screen. Too pale. Ayers looked to the windows but seemed disinclined to pull the blinds, and shut the machine off. As he spoke he took off his jacket and draped it carefully on the back of a chair. His shirt was finely striped like the narrow feint on a maths exercise book, and he was wearing springy silvered armlets to stop his cuffs drooping over his knuckles. The teachers stared at them.

More handouts came round. Sarah tried not to sigh and put her diary and brown envelope back in her bag.

'Well' she said. 'Have you got it or no?'

Gethin shrugged.

'I'll have to tell Mr Thomas' she said. In fact take great pleasure in telling Mr Thomas.

Gethin put his fingers to his mouth and made anxious eyes. 'Oh, I'm so scared' He said. '*Really* bad darts, Miss.'

'Leave him, Miss' one of the girls said. 'He's a mong.'

'Watch who you're calling mong, bitch' Gethin said, kicking the table away.

The soft light gleamed on the big round glasses.

'I've spent a very interesting afternoon with Dave Brace' Mr Ayers was saying, 'in and out of a few classrooms and looking round your campus –'

Eunice pulled a face and mimed to Sarah, '*Campus?*'

'and I have to say, those of you who work here, you're so lucky, so lucky with your situation here, with stunning views, and a real community to serve. And I do feel from what I've seen that you could be quite well up to speed in time for your next inspection.'

Sarah pushed the table back into place with her foot.

'I'll tell him about that too' she said. 'Pick the pen up, there's a good boy.'

She watched the selfsatisfied glowing of the armlets and listened to Ayers' voice. Something about relevant to Key Stages Two and Three. An Outcome from a Working Party. The Cycle of Assessment. Assessment Requirements. Implementation of Requirements. Christ. Implementbloodytation. He spoke in chapter headings, capital letters and all.

Gethin, his huge head tilted forward, looked up at her through his eyebrows like a flickknife. Eunice was going to do 'The Charge of the Light Brigade' with this class. He was sitting at the back near the door, ready for doing a runner and where he could see everybody. He sat at the back of the bus on his way home too. She saw him sometimes on her bus duty days, in the centre seat, the hairless nape and cropped dome looking fragile and unbearably other.

The technique was to move him to the front, deprive him of the power to make others turn his way. But he looked like he might refuse to move and then it would be face off.

'All too often' Ayers was saying, 'we lose sight of assessment as a meaningful part of educational strategy. These new proposals –'

Gethin's hand was creeping across the formica towards the biro with absurdly exaggerated slowness as he looked up at her. He was chanting some rhythmic noise and after a moment she realised it was an attempt at the music from *Jaws*.

Ayers talked about exemplar assessment material. Methods of building assessment into a positive feedback loop. Means of computation that would allow aggregation of achievement across all strands within the level. The teachers were referring to one of the handouts. A gridded white sheet. Sarah unfolded her copy. It looked complicated.

As Gethin's arm moved forward, he slowly pushed up the sleeve with his other hand, until, just above the elbow, she could see tattooed on the flab a blue circlet of barbed wire.

There was a box in the top left hand corner for the pupil's name and form and another in the top right for the teacher's name and the date.

The OHP purred. Ayers was working between the flipchart and the barely visible image of the handout on the screen, defining, pointing out.

Sarah whispered to Eunice, 'Do we do one of these for each kid?'

Eunice nodded.

Gethin's hand suddenly darted onto the pen. The sleeve was back and he moved normally, like a film suddenly freed from slow motion. He pulled the wordsearch closer and studied it.

'*Right* you are, Miss' he said, a bit too loud. He flourished the pen. '*Orff* we jolly well go.'

She risked turning her back on him and walked to the front. Her headache boomed.

She looked at the latticed sheet. The lines felt like crisscrossed cheesewire cutting her retinas. She pushed her fingers under her glasses and rubbed her eyes. The negative image of the page was still there. Things print themselves on you.

She thought she could hear Gethin muttering something, something too low to pick out, repeated like a train rhythm.

You couldn't move him to the front anyway, not with a full room like that, not without moving somebody else and causing another problem. She'd already sent two kids to borrow chairs from another room. The technique now was to ignore the subliminal message, try not to strain to work out what it was, because that was what he wanted. His next move is to escalate it or give up. For now all you can do is hope for the latter. Just keep airborne that long. Only another half hour. Most of the kids probably thinking the same thing. Just survive. But things print themselves. Or change the metaphor. Everything shaves its piece off you. After, you can't be as you were. Cuts. Cuts a template in your memory. What was he muttering? Sounded like *cream of the month, cream of the month*, but that couldn't be it.

When she opened her eyes˙she saw her left fist had tightened on the sheet. Her fingernails were digging little moons into her palm and the finger with the plaster was stinging. She let the paper go and smoothed it against her thigh.

Ayers' voice came back to the surface. 'So, once per half term for this exercise would be a reasonable way of tracking progress.'

A couple of primary teachers near her gasped.

She looked at the assessment sheet again.

Even when you'd worked out what the hell it meant you'd need perhaps twenty minutes to fill it in. Seven see eight see nine tee nine ee and some of May's eight ess en, assuming you don't do it for year ten or eleven. How long?

'Got a calculator, Eunice?' she said.

Eunice shook her head.

Sarah groped in her bag and found her own. There was some makeup caked on the LCD but it was still readable.

Call it a hundred and thirty kids conservative estimate and twenty minutes each.

She pressed the buttons. She looked at the answer and redid it to check. Then checked again allowing fifteen minutes for each kid. She looked up at Ayers. He had taken his glasses off. Their arms had flicked his silvery feathers into little points. His eyes were small as currants and he was still smiling.

Cream of the month, cream of the month, tumpetty tumpetty, cream of the month. That was what she thought the murmur said. Or *crime* perhaps. Gethin was gently drumming his table with the fingers of one hand, his upper body rocking a little with the rhythm. She watched from the front as she pretended to work. The rest were irritatingly quiet. If they'd just start a bit of talking, it would drown him and then he'd have to abandon, or switch tactics. But they were all scared of him. Some seemed to concentrate on their word-searches. Others looked from Gethin to one another smiling and passing eye signals. Some of the kids looked at her occasionally, judging when she might crack and intervene. The crammed room was getting hot and smelly.

The Careers Library smelt of nothing at all. Perhaps sunwarmed plastic. In the corner behind her there must be the lingering pheromones or whatever they were of Rodent and Curtainhair, but she couldn't detect them. There must be the NQT's dried sweat, too.

Ayers probably smelt of nothing but fresh ironing. If it weren't for his stupid tie he'd look immaterially monochrome, moonsilvery and matted in from a black and white film. One of the angels out of *A Matter of Life and Death*. His smile was that word smiles are sometimes. Beatific. But there were still the little silvery horns. And without his jacket she could see, despite the narrow feint, that he had fat rounded shoulders and a paunch like Little Plum in the Beano. Built a bit like her, in fact. Slightly smaller tits, perhaps. Must have a silly little flap hanging inside there somewhere. So really he was real.

The teachers were shuffling other handouts. The new one was an A3 sheet folded once, air blue. Ayers changed the cell on the OHP. The faces of the teachers took on a subtle blue underlighting from the opened sheets.

Ayers was saying, 'For us to understand the theoretical underpinning –'

Sarah stared at the squared shoulders of the recurring threes strung across the window of her calculator.

'Wait' she said. Her own voice sounded too loud, and strangled and thin.

Ayers waited. Pale blue faces turned towards her. The mesh of numbers in the window waited. Her heart started to thump in time with the drumming heels.

There was a scene in *A Matter of Life and Death* where everything froze when people were playing table tennis. She tried to remember it. Only David Niven could still move.

She looked at the still faces. Things were rushing on and Ayers was rushing something past them and she had to say about how much time. They looked as wooden and other as the ping pong players.

Then the window on her calculator went blank as the battery saver cut in. The film unlocked and everything came back to life.

'Sorry' she said. 'Nothing.' She looked down and unfolded the blue sheet.

Ayers resumed his sentence without any change of tone or pace, the film picking up exactly where it had left off.

But they'd all heard, really. Peter had looked round at her and the NQT had looked across and stopped chewing, and even when he started chewing again he carried on looking at her for a few seconds. She felt his eyes on her as she pretended to study the sheet, and looked up and caught him and he looked at Ayers.

Crime of the month, crime of the month, tumpetty tumpetty.

She looked up through her eyebrows over the rim of her glasses. Gethin kept the murmur teasing her on the limen. He was, literally, setting the rhythm. She couldn't catch him looking at her. Most of the others were hunched over their sheets. Others still spectated.

The blue sheet was as big as a newspaper. A flow diagram. There were boxes, little cartouches full of text, connected by arrows like a map of the underground. The strap across the top said: *The Cycle of Assessment*. Filling the middle of the sheet were whirligigs of boxes arranged in concentric wheels linked by little curving arrows. Ayers talked. The seventeen thousand shades of assessment delineated on the supersubtle clockwise wheel, rotating towards perfection. *Intentions* then a little curving arrow to *Aims* then an arrow to *Objectives* then an arrow to *Planning* then an arrow to *Task Defining* then an arrow to *Task Execution* then an arrow to *Outcomes* then an arrow to *Assessment* – and there, the circle closing on itself, and a little curving arrow hooking once more onto *Intentions*. But spiky arrows reared off from the hub leading to swirls of satellite boxes. So, one arrow eddied up from *Task Defining* to a box that said *Differentiation* which led to one marked *By Task* and another marked *By Outcome* and from each of these other arrows looped elsewhere, sometimes back to places on the main wheel. All verbs, or participles anyway, and abstract nouns.

She looked up and the Martian, who only had two eyes after all, had replaced his Sarahlike glasses and was once more beatifying them all.

A thought clutched at her as she watched him. *This is how I am.*

So what do you do when some Gethin or other sets the rhythm like that, taps dirty Morse on the tabletop and sings the profane song of himself?

The class looked at her, the Martian who brought them unintelligible messages from mysterious other places, and waited.

You try to ease it a little.

She said, 'Well, you lot, I don't mind you talking a bit, as long as it's quietly. I've got a lot to do.'

And the small murmur of ordinary, normal voices started, spoilt Gethin's rhythm a bit. The noise would build and every few minutes she'd have to shut them up, but it spoilt his rhythm a bit, rhythm a bit, cream of the month – *crime of the month, tumpetty tumpetty*. He carried on as if unfazed by the tactic.

129

The chant syncopated complicatedly with her headache and the two were like crosscurrents in the arhythmic murmur of the children's voices. Or not arhythmic. It had an immensely slow and ancient pulse of rising and falling noise and pitch. So slow you had to give it a long time before you even realised it was there. The three tempos – sorry, Mel, tempi – seemed to be at different depths. The collective drone was the most profound. Gethin's, strangely, was an irritating splashing somewhere near the surface. She was somewhere in the middle waters. Faintest sunlights flee. Unbearable the booming in the head and somewhere far away down in the dark the huge slow pulse. You have to hold your breath. The sounds cut across one another restlessly. You have to hold your breath. Just half an hour.

Suddenly she gasped. There was just the beat of her pulse in the pale sunlight of the Careers Library, the blue underlighting of the faces. Ayers' theoretical spheres bubbled on the page in front of her. The music of the Celestial polyphony choiring reasonably, inaudibly. Intricate and delicate as bone china in a glass cabinet. A map of something, elegantly architectonic, filigreed with detail and subtle elaborations, and not possible.

A hand touched hers. Eunice, looking solicitous, mouthed, 'All right?'

Sarah nodded and looked from the page to Ayers and tried to seem as though she was.

Ayers punctuated his talk by clicking off the OHP and peeling his glasses away again. Something was coming to an end. They were going back to the cheesewire grid for the recap. She watched his mouth moving. Something about what he'd like them to take away to their schools and departments. He looked at his watch and another handout came round, this time with bulletpoints, white as Eunice's gin and tonic.

It's all holding your breath really. Till the end of the lesson. Holding your breath till half term. Another few weeks after this one, and the short reports to do in a week. How was it possible? But they'd do it. Holding your breath till Christmas. Surviving in the murk and just bursting your head to the surface now and then to gasp and getting back under. Holding your breath till Friday, swimming down round Wednesday, the U bend of the week. But every time some elasticity in the lungs is lost. Everything leaves its imprint, shaves its piece.

And now he was inviting discussion. Feedback, he said. And Peter was speaking, asking something. She listened for the irony but couldn't detect it. He was asking about something arcane on the blue mandala, and Sarah thought he actually meant it. Come on, Peter.

'Surely' Peter said, 'differentiation by outcome is a more open and inclusive and less prejudgmental approach, but with these changes we more and more have to take the other route, to me the less attractive one, on your diagram.'

Gethin was keeping up his drumming, but you couldn't hear him as the hubbub of the class grew. The three submarine hammerings blent into undifferentiated din until she had to speak.

'Right' she said. 'That's enough. Quieten down.'

She had a few more goes and the class noise died back a little.

And *crime of the month, crime of the month* reemerged, only a touch louder than before, but not loud enough for her to understand the message even now.

She thought she understood what Peter said. He was having a go at Ayers, but seriously, on the visitant's terms. There must be a way to make it plain. Adopt his terms and you're more likely to reach his conclusions.

Gethin was back to doing the glare via the eyebrows, He was holding the edge of his wordsearch up for her to see and he had crenelated it with a couple of dozen tiny rips in the paper. As he watched her he was working at one tear in the middle of the edge, tugging delicately, in rhythm with his chant. With every tug the rip extended a little down the page. She was surprised that his fat fingers could be so precise.

She got up and wandered among the desks. Another rhythm-breaking tactic, acting casual, helping stuck kids to find the words hidden in the grid of letters. But he had forced her away from her pretence of work. She was bowed over one of the children, chatting and friendly, the way it ought to be, her back nonchalantly to him. The background noise was building again, along with the shuffling restlessness of the whole class, but she still heard the chant and the tearing, and then a decisive louder tear, and she knew the sheet was in shreds.

She didn't turn.

'Oi, Miss' one of them said. 'He's throwing paper.'

'Have you heard him, Miss?'

'Stop him.'

She looked at her watch. Somehow it was down to the last seven minutes and no valves had burst. Just hold your breath.

'Miss, stop him. That's rude that is.'

She laughed a bit when one of the boys said that.

Mistake.

Ayers was earnestly answering Peter point by point and Peter was earnestly nodding.

'– I think you have to accept that –' Ayers' arms were earnestly crossed as he disputed. She watched him hugging himself as he talked into the air. 'In a sense I'm only the mediator. The messenger if you like.'

In some obscure, superpolite way, she realised he was what Peter would call on the back foot. But it didn't matter. He'd looked at his watch. He could talk it out. The chances of a Gethin outfacing him were negligibly small, and he could get past them what he had to get past them.

Gethin broke into something between a neigh and a snigger in a parody of her laughter. How long can you hang on? If she could hold it a few more minutes then she could spend some time talking to the whole class, collecting the sheets.

'Miss, stop him.'

A ball of paper hit her on the arm. She had to turn. Slowly, casually as she could.

Gethin had wrapped each of his legs around a tableleg and was rocked forward on his chair, teetering. He held out his elbows and was jerking his head from side to side. He wore the glazed grin of a ventriloquist's doll, and the sneering laugh had changed into a quite creditable imitation of a clucking hen. Pellets of paper littered the floor.

Suddenly he stopped, dropped his chair back, and put on an overplayed look of acting casual.

She did the walk to his desk. In a film there would have been silence. He would have liked that, having got the reaction he'd been working for. So it was good that the others kept up their restless churning of noises. He resumed drumming and chanting, more quietly now she was closer.

132

What do you do? She looked at her watch again. There were still almost seven minutes left. Make him wait outside Billy Thomas's office. He wouldn't wait. He wouldn't go. Go with him. The complaint: flicking bits of paper and making funny noises. She'd get the 'oh come off it' look from Thomas and half term there'd be the veiled threat in a staff meeting about staff not handling minor discipline problems themselves.

There was no formica left on Gethin's table. His fingers drummed on the packed grain of the chipboard. She hadn't noticed it was like that before. There was no graffiti on the chipboard and it looked clean. If he'd ripped the last of the formica off there was no sign of the debris, and nowhere she could see for him to hide it. Perhaps it was like that at the start.

He watched her staring at the table.

She spoke very quietly so as not to satisfy him with a public confrontation. 'Okay then' she said. 'I think we'd better step into the cloakroom.'

He put on the frightened act for a few seconds – 'My, oh my, I'm so scared' – then suddenly sneered, pushed the table away and got up.

Ayers talked, his face skyward. She looked at her watch. It was almost over. People's exhaustion and their urge to leave was stronger than any need to engage in the discussion.

In the dingy cloakroom of the mobile classroom she looked at Gethin and listened to herself speaking. The door onto the rickety wooden steps outside was of wired glass and there were windows in a classroom of the main building opposite that overlooked them, so she didn't think he'd try anything. He'd given up the obscure mimicry and avoided looking at her except in sliding glances.

Through the boom of her headache she heard herself say, 'Do you realise how boring you are?'

One of the sliding glances turned poison, held a moment, then shifted away. He was serving out the minutes. There were the restless noises from 9R through the thin partition. Gethin looked at it.

She heard herself saying the usual things about responsible behaviour and growing up.

Gethin looked at the knuckles of his left fist. They were crisscrossed with tiny straight scabs from cuts that might have been made with a craft knife. His skin was watery and pale grey.

'And what happened to the surface off your table?' she said.

He looked up puzzled. 'What you on about. It was like that to start with. You're just finding anything you can to pick on me with it.'

'First thing tomorrow morning' she said, 'Mr Thomas' – he pulled a face of disgust – 'Mr Thomas will get a full report of your behaviour and it will all go on record.'

'It en fair. I didn' touch the table' he said.

'All right. I'm not talking about the table.'

There was silence. Through the partition the class were listening to the raised voices. Gethin looked at the wall and made himself smile.

Sarah had run out of things to say to fill the minutes, had to find new words.

She dropped her voice. 'And what's all this muttering nonsense?'

'I didn't.'

'All the tumpetty tump crime of the month?'

'Uh?' He still looked amazed.

'You heard me.'

His voice rose. 'I didn' say nothing about crime.' He laughed, but it wasn't really a laugh. It was a display laugh.

'Whatever then, you silly little boy' she said.

And he shouted, '*Time. I said time. Time of the month, time of the month, poor old Baggy, the time of the month.*'

He stared at her in the silence. She felt all the class the other side of the partition soaking up the words.

The bell rang for the end of the lesson. The bell was actually in the cloakroom and ludicrously loud. There was the eruptive noise of chairs and tables being scraped across the floor, and children poured past them and out of the hut, down the rickety steps.

She said, but couldn't hear herself, 'You squalid little bastard,' hoped he could lipread, caught at his shoulder as he moved away, but he snatched it from her and walked out with the rest.

Next was 10L in a room five hundred yards away, and she didn't have the worksheet ready because of the lost free and she needed to write a long note to Billy Thomas.

She went back into the empty classroom to collect her bag and work. All the tables were at skewed angles. When she knelt to gather a few token pieces of litter, she could see on the underside of Gethin's table how he had carefully cemented the formica he'd ripped from the top out of sight using chewing gum.

She looked at the back of her hand spread over the grid and the stacked handouts. The paper was sticking to her palm.

Ayers, his arms still folded so as to display his armlets at their gleamiest, looked around showing how scrupulously he elicited any last questions.

Sarah raised her hand, peeling it away from the sheet. Faces turned to her again.

'Um, time' she said.

Ayers waited, smiling.

'I worked it out for these assessments' she said, holding up the crumpled grid. 'How long it'll take me each half term for all the – the students I teach in years seven to nine. Are we going to be released from teaching to provide time to do it?'

Ayers smiled and simulated a chuckle and then seemed to realise that perhaps she meant it.

In a film there would have been a murmur of agreement from the other teachers, but there was silence.

Ayers talked about nondirected time and time management. Of course nondirected time wasn't legitimately computable as part of their contractual obligations if they chose to complete the sheets outside directed time.

'Choose?' Sarah said.

But he didn't pause. He fully understood that there was never a convenient time for innovations, and he appreciated the – small struggle for the right word – the challenges the requirements presented to colleagues, but these were not insoluble. They should be regarded positively. In part the new arrangement might even come to replace some elements of assessment already in place so that although there would be the usual initial increase of effort, once the process was, um, up to speed it would make no or negligible difference to the input required. Look, this simply confirmed and standardized current good practice. Legally, of course, as he'd already suggested –

Sarah felt half formed answers to all this swim past faster than she could catch at them.

– any work they decided to undertake outside the total allocated time was by definition nondirected time.

Sarah waited to see if anyone else would respond. Nobody did. She watched them. Peter's face was angled to the floor. Eunice stared into mid air.

The number of hours on her calculator had been forty three point three three recurring. On the conservative estimate, thirty one point five. That twice a term. Six extra weeks a year fitted into the interstices of something that didn't have any interstices left. Was there any point in telling the messenger? He'd boiled it down to legalities and that was that.

Sarah looked down, shifted the band of her watch where it chafed her sweating wrist. It was a little sore, but there wasn't the red welt she wanted to see, not even on the tender inward side. She dug at the skin with her thumbnail.

'I give up' she said.

Ayers didn't seem to hear her. He was looking at his watch and saying final things. They'd been incredibly patient. Difficult times. But opportunities rather than obstacles. Thank you.

He packed his materials away into the slim case. Everything done deftly, with the choreography of a conjuring trick. Peter said some hasty thank yous, but people were already leaving.

'Don' worry' Eunice said to her quietly. 'It won' last a twelve-month.'

Sarah was too tired to give the obvious snappy answer. She thought of the pigeonholes yawning in the empty staffroom and looked at Ayers and his jacket and his glasses and his case.

'Some people fart in lifts' she said, too loud.

The NQT looked at her and smiled.

And the lovers had been ejected from their mousy paradise for this.

★ ★

Up the back, the upstairs window of the house where the candle-light had been last night was still open. He looked at the word written on the glass.

The snow had not thawed. It lay in plates upon the tiled roofs of the town. Icicles hung from the thatched eaves of the peasants' hovels and no droplets fell from them. The peasants bound their feet with straw to go about and cats dabbed at the earth disdainfully. The milk grew icy in the buckets and no broth stayed warm when taken from the hearth. When Lech crossed the little yard below, his lantern threw a swinging yellow ring upon the glassy, frozen cobbles, blurred only by the steaming of his breath. The town stood stark in the crisp blue moonlight, and even where the peaceful woodsmoke leaked from the rooftops, the snow had not thawed.

Why, though?

He sat in Gransh's room. His cigarette, in the souvenir ashtray next to his mug, leaked smoke. He composed its angle on the china so that the table looked like a bit from a film which said 'writer, alone.' Except Gransh's table wasn' really a table. It was some sort of forties cake trolley, a bit flimsy and a bit too small to sit at, on gungy alloy castors. The joints squeaked and flexed as it slid away from you when you wrote if you didn' wedge it right against the wall with your legs. He turned the Thunderbirds mug – weak coffee with three sugars and grey with milk – so that Scott Tracy was hidden from the camera. Perrot was opened, lying across the far edge of the trolley and onto the windowsill. The jumbo jotter was wordless white.

Not thawed.

He looked through the window onto the steep back garden. Waz had wedged some wooden factory pallets in the gaps in the fence and tied them together with some sort of orange plastic cord. There were no people and no cats.

But the streets of Frauenburg were empty now, and tense with grim foreboding. Nicholas knew that the people were waiting for the first firing of the crude siege guns, the boot against the door. The closely worked pages of his *De Revolutionibus* were strewn across his oaken table. Would he never have peace to finish his life's work?

He looked at the word on the glass.

Come on. Keep to it. Aitch Seven. How do you place the one life in the rolling of the big wheel? The rocky wooden platform in the North Atlantic. All that stuff the starry messenger had given him to think about. Cabot measuring the sun. New found land. How could Aitch know where that'd lead? America. People getting trod on. The red bits on maps Gransh spewed his hatred on. You couldn' know that. But why otherwise? Some model in the head. Something worked out, yes, calculated, beforehand. Some magic, really. Real magic, not mumbo jumbo tricks. Bloke with cloak.

Model in the head. Anna sleeping face down on the furs, her arse arched upward curving like a world, and peeping from beneath the anus, the lippy cleft swell of.

Keep to it. A model in the head, of the planet, its shape, and working out what to dare do from that. The book of nature. So the slavish stuff about barons and foreign policy and that, do you really need to flog through it? Start with the big things, the whole wheel, and work down to little Aitch Seven in his place. Could be.

He punctuated his thinking with a drag on the fag.

The wheel rolled through his mind.

You could see him, Aitch Seven, a little figure gripping the rim, his crown falling off and his naff haircut flapping. But both him and Nicholas understanding something about how the wheel rolled. Nicholas more than Aitch, though. Qualitatively different knowledge. Aitch looked bewildered and terrified as his tiny face among the millions disappeared into the mud under the rim. Splut. Eyes wide and cheeks sunk, like the picture in Perrot. Like. Like somebody dying.

The paper burned back to his fingers and he dropped the cigarette. Must have been a fuck of a drag. Didn' even know he was doing it.

He pinched the dogend up into the ashtray and handbrushed ash off the blank page. The cake trolley squeaked on its castors.

But keep to it. Aitch Seven could have done with some bloke with cloak. Have Nicholas turn up at the palace, praps. His face on the wheel too. A bit less scrutable than Aitch's, understanding it better, but still there. Died a lot later. You don' escape that.

He looked at Gransh's narrow bed, a little sunk in the middle. The light was beginning to go. The bed seemed to stand in a magnetic field of gathering dark.

He looked back to the swept page.

Keep to it. The shape of the world. How he saw. Start there. Something like

To examine the extent to which Henry VII might be described as modern, we need to examine the way in which the worldview of his day was beginning to change.

He picked up the biro.

Two examines.

To understand *the extent to which.*

Yeah. Crap, but yeah.

He wrote 'To understand' and looked at the words. He hadn't joined the arr and the ess. Two words. Under and stand. Like sub stance. To do with under the surface. What's down there. The book of nature. He stared and the thickness and curiousness of the blue lines dawned on him as they swam on the paper. What's underneath. Anna with her bum stuck in the air like a model in a wank book. Under her tightdrawn anus, the cloven swell.

He rubbed a palm against his penis without undoing his fly.

Nicholas threw back his head as, gently and rhythmically, he fucked her from behind. With infinite tenderness he. Oo. Rubbed his palms across the planets of her arse, opened the book of nature, and there he saw the hairless reddened starburst of her anus.

Jesus, no. Later. Come on. Keep to it. Focus.

To under stand. He looked at the broken blue lines. They had thickness and knots and loops and they swam on the surface. They wriggled senselessly.

This sign, thought Master Nicholas, this message speaks to me. What's at the centre is not mere Earth, dirt, as all the world supposes, but a star, the fiery axle of the heavenwheel.

He put his fingers on the lines to stop them moving.

Yes.

The crisp blue moonlight was indifferent upon the frosty window. And as they made love, he did not hear, far below outside, the opening of the yard gate and the rolling of cartwheels crunching upon the compacted snow.

Yeah. Like a map or something. A model. You simplify. Understand by leaving things out. Looking underneath. Not seeing the window or hearing the cartwheels. For a bit, anyway. The true geometry. What substands. Not dirt. Light.

He stared at the two – or three – words he'd written and still saw the texture of the paper, the thickness of the lines. What had he meant to say? Gransh told him the thing about the blind men and the elephant. The world is the elephant and everybody's the blind men, and to work it out you have to measure and remember. Make the map in your head. What's out there is either too much or not enough, or both. You have to interpret the evidence. Outthink it. Weird science.

He looked out at the tumble of gardens. Waz had been cutting
his grass this summer. Most of the other gardens were overgrown.
This was the first bit of the elephant Gransh had seen every morning for years. The leaning fences and the odd bush that was
turning into a tree. The old woman lived in the house with the
open upstairs window. Sometimes she came out and emptied
tealeaves into the drain. Steve didn't know her name.

The UPVC backdoor of her house had a panel kicked in. There
were cans and broken binbags near it. He stared at the broken
panel and then higher, at the open window, and the scrawled word.
Not scrawled. It was quite neat really. It was spraypaint, or maybe
that fake snow they put on shop windows Christmastime, and it
said SHIT, with the ess backwards, because they'd done it, the
people with the candle, on the inside of the glass, carefully reversing
the order of the letters, just getting that one thing wrong. But it
showed that the writer in that room wasn' only writing for himself.
Thinking of his audience. Sending his message to the world. Shit.

He looked down to the message he was writing for himself and
Baggy. The kid spraying the graffiti was so decisive. To under
stand. The blue lines waited for him. What was the rest of the
sentence?

IAU

It was raining. From her institutional armchair in the crowded staffroom the shoulder of hill was nearly invisible in the rainhaze. You had to know it was there to be able to see it.

Gron fell into the seat next to her, laughing. He reached into his pocket for his pipe, remembered, and stopped reaching. But he still smiled.

Peter looked up from a disintegrating Penguin edition of *King Lear*.

'What are you laughing at?' he said. 'It's only Thursday, and it's only October.'

It was morning break and a good day for not being on corridor duty. She thought of the wet oozing in the corner of the mobile classroom, oozing in the women's toilet, the rooms crowded with wet steaming children.

Gron laughed again.

May, who had been going over some of her painstaking notes on children in 8SN with Sarah, pulled a face.

'Early retirement come through?' she said.

'Aye. I'm demob happy' Gron said. 'Sarah's in charge of History next term.' He looked at Sarah, smiling, and saw she wasn't taken in. 'No, don' worry, lovely girl' he said anyway, as if she had been. 'No remission for me. 7C have been telling me jokes, that's all.' He settled back in his chair, hand in mid air in front of his face, holding the stem of his nonpipe. He laughed again, but nobody asked him what the jokes were.

Sarah went on checking the notes. May liked to look after her nonspecialists with this series of detailed essays and statistics on each special needs kid. Sarah'd taught 8SN that morning and was beginning to get to know the fourteen boys and one girl.

His learning has been hindered by inability to concentrate for more than 10 minutes, poor short term & long term memory skills, non-

143

existent listening skills, and other emotionally immature characteristics.
It was hard to concentrate and she had to stop listening to May to read.
Is being referred to the Ed. Psych.
10L next. She'd finished typing the worksheet just as *Newsnight* was starting last night and would have to collect copies from the reprographics technician in ten minutes, if they were ready, just ahead of the lesson.
Generally, concentration skills improve slightly if isolated from peers.
Gron laughed again. 'They sang me a song' he said.
'Bugger off' Peter said.
'There's something godlike about true laughter' Gron said.
'There's something bloody irritating about it.' Peter looked back to his text and mumbled, 'What the hell's a trundle-tail?'
'Kind of dog' Sarah said.
Peter pencilled 'kind of dog' in the margin without looking up.
Marie has mastered some simple number operations, but is unable to make appropriate methods of calculation.
Calculation. Forty three hours, she'd said to Mel during *Newsnight*. Forty three bloody hours extra. Why don' they work these things out? Mel half listened, about Gethin and Ayers. Talked about the quarry when she went quiet.
She stared at the character sketch in May's careful handwriting.
All of these children are me.
A quiet, withdrawn girl, who is fairly well motivated.
There, what did I tell you? Well, except for the last bit, maybe.
Gron sat wearing his Zero Mostel like godly laurels, undamaged yet, even by the rain when he crossed the yards. Every day we get up and recement ourselves, repoint and make good and let the winds and buffets knock the corners off us and then start again tomorrow.
Gron's constrained laughter bubbled like far thunder in his tar-polluted bronchi. May laughed too and Sarah felt herself going a bit.
'What are we laughing at?' May said.
Sarah shook her head, shaking. Peter looked fraught and bent closer over his book.
Sarah had fresh tights on. Different shoes – the boots with the zips that hid her unMandyish ankles. At the end of *Newsnight* she'd had a hot bath to soothe the haemorrhoids and the subtle aching. She looked at the finger of her left hand where the scab was forming.

What if you don't bother with the repairs? What if you just leave the corners unreplaced, let the bricks work loose? People walking around with bits missing. Limbs and eyeballs lying in corridors. Like children or the old, suddenly waking up in one shoe, dribbling and dizzy.

'Did you hear about the sanitary inspector who hated his job?' Gron said.

'His wits are gone' Peter said.

Billy Thomas came into the room. There was the usual slight tensing of the atmosphere. Everybody glanced at Billy's hand. A fat bunch of supervision slips. She looked up from him to the clock above the door. Nine minutes and collect worksheets.

Thomas worked his way round handing out the supervision slips personally. Casting the Runes, Peter called it.

Encounters difficulty in most subject areas. Unable to construct sentences. Requires constant encouragement.

All these poor 8SN lambs. Marie delicate and tiny, Benlike, like the 8C boy (shit, find book), and out there now, in steamy classrooms with rain streamering the glass, avoiding the Gethins.

'So, he hated his job so much, he just used to come in every day and go through the motions.' Gron reddened and convulsed with the suppressed bubbly thunder.

Sarah smiled. May laughed the etiquette laugh of the person who doesn't get it or hasn't listened.

'Sanitary inspector see' Gron said. 'I don' think the kid who told me understood it. Said his uncle told it him.'

Peter looked up from his book expressionlessly without straightening, then looked back down again.

Billy Thomas's shitcolour sleeve was in front of her and he shoved a slip in her hand.

'Sorry again, Sarah' he said. 'Last lesson, too.'

She looked up at him. He was already moving on.

'No. Wait. Sorry, Billy. I can't.'

He looked back.

'I'm going to the dentist's.'

'No.' His face puckered satisfyingly with distress. He looked at the sheaf of slips as if they should tell him what to do next. He looked back to her. 'There's work set for them this time.'

'Listen, I'm going to the dentist. I've cleared it with Dave.'

Dave. He won't like that.

Billy took the slip back, looking thwarted.

'Did you get my note about Gethin Devereux?' she said. A double whammee.

But he was already rushing on. 'Yeah' he said, passing. 'I've passed it on. That's not my pigeon. Oh aye.' He stopped and turned. 'Glenys wants to see you, she asked me to ask you. She's there now. No kids with her.' And he was gone.

Clock. Eight minutes. Well, I can cut it short if I want to.

She got up and left the others, who were mildly impressed by her repulsing of Billy Thomas. Gron was still rumbling and red, barely holding back the godlike.

★

Not Twirlyhair, please.

Down the tidemarked corridor, past the Men's and then the pisswiffy paintcurly Women's, the on duty teacher leaning on a jamb clutching a mug, the dinning wetrooms.

Because she was sure that's what Mandy had done. It's not fair, Mrs Fylfot. We all opted thinking we'd have Mrs Waters and instead it's Mrs Bowen and Mrs Bowen doesn't know anything about it. Elizabeth of Lancaster she said and it's not fair on us so the others asked me if I'd come and.

Bloody right too. That's the trouble. So today's thorns: lost book to find for Benlike boy by lesson six; avoiding Devereux; this.

Past the year tutors' office. Gwil Evans processing the usual breaktime queue of complainants, miscreants and walking wounded. Then to Glenys's door, shut for a change and no children waiting to see her.

Sarah knocked and was called in.

'Hiya' Glenys said. 'Have a seat.' She was slipping papers into a folder.

The striplight blazed on the blue carpet. Her room seemed somehow brighter, sealed off. Instead of the revolving geometrical shape, this time her computer monitor's screensaver was the one with the pattern of dispersing stars, as if you were flying or falling through space.

Sarah sat. As they exchanged broken bits of smalltalk, she saw how Glenys had everything cemented into place – hair formered into a frozen wave, cantilevered shoulders. Like an air hostess. She almost looked permanent. Almost a concrete noun.

'Gethin Devereux' she said, tapping the file and picking up her mug of tea. 'Thanks for the memo.'

'Billy passed that one on quick.'

Glenys looked straight at her and widened her eyes, nodding a little. 'Yes. He's very efficient at *that*.' She swivelled on her chair and slid the folder into a filing cabinet. 'Another chapter for the horror story.'

Through the wall behind Glenys's stickercovered year planner came Gwil Evans's voice as he worked his way through his queue.

She turned back to Sarah. 'Since he came off the At Risk Register I thought he'd improve, but there you go. The trouble is the so-and-so never does anything bad enough for us to do something about it.' This was code for exclusion. 'I'm having a "word" with him dinnertime.'

Him too?

'Thanks' Sarah said. 'I'm sorry, I've only got a minute. I've got to collect some photocopying for next lesson.'

Glenys was sipping her tea.

'If it's about having to take over from Eileen' Sarah said. Glenys did her eye widening and nodded as she sipped. Ryan's phrase. Get your retaliation in first. 'I'm not very happy with it myself. I've talked to Gron numerous times. And –' she struggled to say the name twice in one day '– Dave.' That's a lie. Actually failed to when I had the chance. Too busy bleeding. Retrieve. 'I've been meaning to talk to him too.'

Glenys looked sceptical. 'Well –'

'On paper I'm qualified to do it, but I've never even taught history before, except when I was a student, and that was only form one. Seven.' Take that, Twirlyhead.

'Well it is to do with Eileen in a way.'

'I'll be glad to get shot of it. It can be fairly stressful, and it's not fair on the kids, either.'

'Well I appreciate all that, but going like she did at the end of August, everything was locked into place. There wasn't really a better alternative at short notice. Anyway, that's not permanent of course.'

The back foot.

'Nothing is' Sarah said.

'But that's not really it' Glenys said. 'Not so much history as the future I wanted to see you about.'

Not really it? Glenys was quiet a moment and the drill of Gwil Evans's voice took over. More distantly there were rainy breaktime classroom noises.

'What it is' she said, 'is with Eileen dead and a lot more staff going this year we'll be in for a fair bit of reorganising. Course, Eileen was due to go the end of the year anyway. I think that played a part in it. Anyway, I've been having a look at possible reshuffles.' She was speaking chattily, as if this was gossip. But *reshuffles*. Political word. She listed some possible retirers. They included Gron, May and Eunice. 'I think Dave's seeing Eunice this week sometime to talk it through. Plus the usual turnover' she said. 'What I'm saying is, I'm pretty sure there'll be a year tutor's job going at the end of it. You'll be second in the English department if Eunice does go, but the way Dave's looking at it there won't be any money in it, and Peter's probably going to be there till the crack of doom. He'll be lucky to get anything better than this.'

Sarah thought of Peter with white hair in the same staffroom in thirty years' time, rushing through *Lear*, asking what festinate means rather than looking in the notes.

'So thinking of your career, think about going for a year tutor's job when it comes up.'

My career.

There was a far off explosion of children's godlike laughter.

'You're good with the kids and quite well organised. There won't be much else coming up unless you move on altogether.'

Me? Is this the same me as the me I know?

She looked at Glenys's silk scarf, asserted with a modest brooch, and realised that by her own lights this woman was being kind to her.

'Thanks' Sarah said to her. Then again, relieved and smiling, 'Thanks.'

Glenys talked on about staffing changes. If they appoint for History but get someone who can do a bit of English. Free up a few lessons for you and the year tutor job will be possible.

Gwil's drill continued. It would mean she'd have a desk in the year tutors' office with him and a few others, a filing cabinet and some shelves. Kudos and queues through breaktime. The manu-factured sternness of mandatory ballockings delivered to order. That was *not* a nice thing to say to Mrs Davies. Is that me? Calling the next one in. A row of Gethins to outface. Me and them knocking the corners off one another. Cruel routines and routine cruelty. Disintegrating by design, almost. Like being a surgeon or something disinterestedly paring flesh. They repair, I suppose, too. Often just paring. Dentists pulling bits away systematically. Incremental removal of the face. Something positive in that. The slow striptease. Eileen the ultimate positivist.

A gust threw rain against the metalframed window. Sarah felt the draft lightly on her face. Glenys's room wasn't airtight after all.

'Mind you' Glenys was saying, 'don't mention this to Eunice or anybody. Maybe nothing will come of it.'

Sarah said she'd certainly think about it and it was certainly a possibility, although it had never occurred to her things might go that way and really she was more interested in. But she didn't have an end ready for that sentence and let it fade.

Glenys, practised in picking up cues for turntaking, came in efficiently. 'Well look, what I'm saying is, I know you could do it, and what I think is to be honest there ought to be more women in the management team in this place. The more there are coming through the more chance there is of some of us going on further. Just have a think about it.'

So that was it. Not entirely kind after all. A counter in a game. Counter caster.

Sarah glanced at her watch so that Glenys could see her glancing at her watch and made minimal I am leaving signals. 'Well thanks for thinking of me this early on. I'll bear it in mind.'

Glenys stood up so that Sarah would feel comfortable standing up. The bell was close and the reprographics room far. Sarah left quickly.

So not the first probings into incompetence. All these crises appear like pinpoints and swell as they get closer and you think this is it this time and they burst over you and nothing really happens. A bit of agendadriven encouragement. Sarah, Troubleshooting Year Tutor. In a montage in a soap opera she rushes down corridors, puts a friendly arm around a crying child, shows NQT how to do the register, turns from files marked Confidential and smiles nobly, earnestly into the camera as it tightens for the closeup. But really perhaps protecting the Maries and all the other Benlikes from the Gethins, shifting, ultimately, to a silk scarf and getting her own carpet. And it bursts over you and nothing really happens. That is, until it does. *Career* is something you do down a wet road without any brakes.

The bell had rung. She fell through the perspectives of small wet faces in the corridor. Among them were Mandy's freezing eyes. Sarah did her best to smile.

★ ★

These days, toothless old Margarita kept the door of the tower barred. For good measure she had got the blacksmith to nail stout iron grills across the windows, because not far away the great guns of the Teutonic Knights were firing. The icy little town was under siege, and old Margarita had her feet firmly on the earth, even if others did not.

She laughed the laugh of a late medieval Sid James and cast her eyes to the ceiling at this thought. No. She laughed her withered crone's laugh and looked meaningfully to the ceiling as she thought this.

As she sat by her fire and slurped her broth in the late afternoon, the shadow of a cart trundling into the yard fell across her window. The trundling stopped ominously close and presently there came a knocking at her door. Even so, she got up and waddled to answer it without fear. After all, the enemy would hardly be so polite.

But when she had swivelled the heavy bar aside and swung the lancet door open, she was a little chilled to see the dark, motionless hooded figure standing before her. In the moment's silence she observed the dark wagon, long and high-sided and shuttered, standing in the yard, and the steam rising from the nostrils of its two black horses.

The dark figure leant towards her and in the cave of its hood she saw the dull gleam of its eyes.

"I have come to visit Master Copernicus," rasped a dry voice.

The high and stippled cloud was incarnadine with the going sun. Incarnadine. Oo yes. The sallow-faced magician put down his brush and sighed. The light would soon be gone and candles would not do to paint by. He left the darkening canvas, threw open the door of his observation platform and stepped out.

The wintry air hurt his throat. Beneath him lay the fortified wall of the Cathedral enclosure and the snow-whitened roofs of little Frauenberg. The snow had not thawed. Woodsmoke drifted from the huddled houses. Already the redness of the clouds was cooling, disappearing into the deep blue and green shadows of their darker recesses. There were but a few gaps through which he might in a little while observe the stars.

Now that he had sent Mistress Anna and her children away to the country to safety, there was nothing to distract him from his work.

Looking to the horizon and listening to the thunder of the far guns, he did not notice the black cart rolling into the yard below, nor hear old Margarita answer the door, nor hear the footsteps on the winding stairs.

He stepped in from his observatory and called, "Come in," when he heard the knock.

The short grey hair and wizened face of old Margarita appeared.

"A stranger to see you, Master Nicky," she said. "A wealthy gent." Her deep old voice turned to a hoarse whisper. "I think he may be ill. He'll be wanting your doctoring skills."

"Let him enter," said Nicholas, taking a taper from the fire and lighting a candle.

Old Margarita withdrew.

The stranger, when he stepped in, felt a little confused. He had spent a long age in the black cart listening to the solid wheels turning. He was cold. Where he clutched his cloak under his chin, his fingers were white and thin as bone. And now that he stood here, he was no longer sure why he had come to see this man, though he knew something compelled him to travel the earth and speak.

Before him he saw a sallow-faced man well into his middle years. The face was thin, the forehead broad, the eyes and nose large. The man stood by a table where pages of a manuscript were spread and a candle flickered. Behind the table stood the instruments of a man of learning – shelves of books, an astrolabe and a quadrant, and other equipment he did not recognise. A half finished portrait stood upon an easel. The man in the portrait wore a fine, fur-trimmed gown and carried in his hand an image of the sun upon a stick. The stranger looked from the picture to the living man and realised that they were the same. From some hidden place in his cold brain he began to remember that he once had been dressed as well, or better, not in the ashy cloak he wore now, and had sat for an artist to paint him. He was starting to remember who he was.

Nicholas observed the dead white bony fingers clutching at the stranger's collar.

"Please," said the magician, "take a seat by my fire."

The stranger shuffled forward and sat. Dirty ice dissolved and dripped from the hem of his cloak. In the coming dusk Nicholas could only dimly see brows, nose and cheekbones deep in his visitor's hood. The face seemed to be angled to regard the fire as if it saw its future there. Perhaps that was why he had come, for a horoscope. The credulous often came with present ailments they wished him to cure or future ills they wished to avoid. War was good for charlatans and Nicholas protected people from them by treating them and seeing their futures free of charge.

"You've come perhaps to have your horoscope divined?" he prompted, at last.

The stranger's head moved a little as if he were startled.

"No," he said. "I don't think that could be it. I have no need of horoscopes." He spoke in Latin, and with an accent Nicholas had never heard before.

The stranger looked back to the flames. He felt their warmth through the rough wet cloak and upon the numb mask of his face, but their restless coiling and shifting filled him with unease. Though the endless miles of icy dark had bitten him to the marrow, he feared the flames. But most of all he began to feel the smallness of all that he had been and done, and he began to remember something of why he had made his journey. He looked to the astrolabe and the manuscript pages, the image of the magician gripping the sun.

"How can I help you then?" Nicholas asked, in Latin also. The man, he surmised, had a chill which needed treatment.

"You have all the learning of the world gathered in this room," said the stranger. He spoke slowly, as if the words were charged with meaning.

Nicholas sat at the other side of the fire. He did not speak.

The stranger looked back to the magician. It was odd, to wake like this, after the cold and dark and tumult of a life, in a calm room where everything was known. There was some conversation he must have before it would all be over.

"I think," he said, "that when I was alive, I was a king."

He lifted his hands and pushed back his hood.

Nicholas thought that he must have misheard, but the visitor's face quickly took his mind away from that.

It was beardless, long and thin. The deeply sunken eyes and cheeks accentuated the prominence of the cheekbones, which, with the broad brow, were as dead white as the stranger's knuckles. His lipless mouth was withered and slightly open, so that Nicholas could see the narrow, darkened stumps of teeth. The hair was long and straight and had been dark, though much of it was now grey. The magician was perturbed by the feeling that he was looking into a distorting mirror, into his own future.

The stranger looked to the unfinished painting, which was growing indistinct in the dusk. The candle-flame twisted in the draft.

"I see you paint yourself as if you were a king, Copernicus," he said.

Nicholas smiled uncertainly.

"You even carry a sceptre in your hand."

"It is both greater and less than that. What power I have I've accepted reluctantly."

"When I lived," – the stranger spoke his words haltingly, as if he were discovering them – "I sought power. I was not born a king. No. I waited, and chose when to act. I believe I rewarded some people and killed others. That has always been the technique. And when I had grasped the crown, I studied to keep my hold on it by the latest methods."

Nicholas watched the white fist tighten at the stranger's chest. In the gloom he thought he saw one of the knuckles come loose and drop soundlessly into the folds of the muddy cloak.

"I learnt," the visitor continued, "yes, I learnt to hold everyone to account. I concocted lists and inventories, and became a great arithmetician. A loyal army delivered me the world and a keen eye and a grasp of number enabled to me keep it." He looked at the magician, amazed that he had done and been these things but found it so hard to hold on to the ideas now. Why was it not firmer, more important to him? He wanted it to be so.

Nicholas looked at the glittering, half comprehending eyes. He thought of the Prince Bishop cowering with his retinue at Allenstein and Grand Master Albrecht with his guns outside the walls of Frauenberg. He thought of the tithes he had collected and the bodies he had counted.

"I have kept some such accounts for my own masters," Nicholas said, "and I know how wearying they can be."

The glittering eyes turned towards the fire once more. "I thought, I thought they were the essence of things."

"There's some truth in that. The book of nature," said Nicholas anachronistically, "is written in mathematical characters."

"I hoarded and arranged and made laws, to make my House safe for my heirs."

Nicholas nodded. No man could do more. It did not need saying.

"This was my destiny, you understand. Seers told me in my own tongue that I was the son of prophecy. That knowledge gave me tenacity. And when I died my tomb was more magnificent than any seen in my lands." Yes, the stranger thought. It was the rest of the journey that he must ask the magician to explain. That and his own uncertainty. He looked at the calm, wise face, which was beginning to vanish in the darkening air. "Tell me, Copernicus. I grasped the muddy nature of the heart of things and remade it for myself. At least, I think I did. You are the wisest man in the world. They say you have seen the shape of the universe. You have all the knowledge of the world. I have travelled long years in my carriage across the cold plains. I no longer know myself. Tell me the way I must take now so that my journey can be finished. Give me back my certain path."

Nicholas sat back and regarded the stranger for a moment. It was almost dark enough for the stars to be observed. He needed to work. "Magnificent tombs," he said, "like castles with thick walls, have more to do with uncertainty than with certainty." He glanced a little nervously at his portrait. The right hand gripping the image of the universe was tensed. "We are alike in some ways. I cannot give you certainty, but let me tell you what I think may be the truth." He looked back to his visitor. The light was growing very dim. "When I was a young man I studied for many years. In Italy where I lived all the knowledge of the ancients poured in from Egypt and Constantinople. Some of it sits on those shelves now. When I put the learning of Ptolemy and Hipparchus and Pythagoras and Aristarchus together with our modern mathematics, and then looked to the sky, I made a wonderful discovery."

The stranger leant forward.

So many came to hear this explanation and so many went away puzzled or unconvinced. But none of them were quite like this one. He did not want mere marvels. Nicholas, as simply as he could, elucidated his new system. The neglected Aristarchus of Samos, in his sketchy notions, had been right all along if someone had only checked. "There are details still to work out," said Nicholas, frowning, "but I am close to doing that. I need to chart the place of Jupiter tonight, in fact." He looked to the place where his visitor sat. "We are alike. We have both changed the world. But I have had to kill no one, my friend, and I have nailed the sun to the sky and made the Earth spin about it, simply by counting and looking." He could not tell in the half light whether the stranger was disappointed or not. The bony hand was up at the stranger's chin.

"What does this mean for me?" the visitor said. He already thought he knew the answer, that he had always half suspected it. The magician's face was reduced to a yellowish brow and cheekbones and nose and chin in the dim flame-light. All the rest was shadow. The yellow face rose as Copernicus stood.

"All the premise of your life was wrong!" said Nicholas. He could say to this shade what he dared not put in his writings, what he could only present hidden in abstruse calculations. "By your actions you made yourself nothing more than the rolling ball in a game of bagatelle. And the dirt you devoted your life to is not at the centre. The earth beneath our feet is no more fixed than the soot that whirls in a chimney. Everything is dislocated!"

The stranger dropped from his chair onto his knees, his hands raised. "And my journey? Which way do I go?" The magician grew fainter by the second.

Nicholas smiled. "Everything is changed," he said. "Nothing is where it was. We are not at the centre and all the system of the spheres must be wrong. Hell cannot be where we thought it was, nor the empyrean nor heaven itself."

"Then where are they?"

The magician looked down at him. It seemed to the stranger that he was a tremendous distance away.

"I don't know," said Nicholas. "I suspect –" he hesitated "– I suspect they may be nowhere."

The stranger emitted a ghastly sigh and reached out as if to clutch at Nicholas's clothes. In the distance, the thunder of the cannon rolled.

"Hear that," said Nicholas. "The ancients thought that thunder was a god's laughter, but men like you made that thunder. Men like you, demolishing the walls of the world you made. I believe there is no journey left to you, my friend."

The visitor lunged towards his host but the magician was too far away. His face, like his voice, was tiny and diminishing, until there was nothing but blackness.

As the stranger fell towards him, Nicholas caught at his arms. The white wrists, all the bones of the hands, the greying hair, the gaping white face, splashed on him, disintegrating into fine white dust.

Nicholas, clasping the stranger's empty cloak, staggered out onto his observatory platform.

The moon had risen and Jupiter shone like a lamp. Far below, the silvered courtyard of the cathedral, where the stranger's carriage should have stood, was empty.

Copernicus clutched at the material and could see no traces of the ash. When he looked closely at the cloak, he could see that it was his own.

★ ★

She dumped 11E's books onto the back seat of the car. The column broke and slithered, fanning across the upholstery. Only a couple missing. Extra work for them. Names in the diary and note in markbook. And black bag on the floor. These are the chains that I have forged in life. She slammed the door and got in the driver's seat. But that's it for today. Escape.

In the upstairs windows of A Block a few tiny faces turned from desks and saw her, looked at watches, and then others turned too. Look, she's mwtshing off early.

She sat and looked at them for five seconds – she saw the time arc noiselessly on her wristwatch out of the corner of her eye – then fired the engine. Should be the thrill of a small triumph. So long, suckers. But she felt merely treacherous.

The windscreen was like cinemascope. Only a boring French film showing, no subtitles. But then there was no dialogue, the director eschewing plot or selfregarding concern for composition in the frame. Instead, a lifelike impression of the wipers smearing drizzle with a rhythmic squeak, the desultory succession of encounters with roadsigns, the crumbling kerbs at junctions, tail-lights. The sky suitably grey and heavy with a premonition of November.

Her dentist was in another town, a little to the north up the valley where Mel went to work. When her car slid onto the dual carriageway she could see through the drizzle, high on her left, the mountain, looking healthy and green in its trees, but then the treed craterrim of the quarry drilled into it, the drab limestone amphitheatre, and the top row of an estate of semidetached houses precarious on one edge, the ones they were going to buy and pull down. Shreds of cloud and some crows blowing about like rags. But Jean-Luc or Francois, or whoever the nonexistent director was, swivelled the camera back to the kerbs, the taillights of the dual carriageway. Just a bit of her face caught in the corner of the rear view mirror, an alternative bit of cinemascope matted in to the main screen. Future and past like two ends of tunnel. The flat front of a lorry like a cliff with its headlights on rode in the drizzle a yard behind her. She only needed to touch the brakes and the past would catch up with her and collide, buckle over her. She leant to her left so her face blocked most of the lorry out in the mirror.

'Moi' she said, Frenchly. 'Mwah.' Like a kiss.

When she moved back, the lorry had shifted, straddling the lanes looking to overtake. She eased the accelerator down and enjoyed the surge, watched the cliff recede. Then eased off again, watched it grow. But there was the drizzle and the headlights, and when the lorry caught up, the cab was too high for her enjoy the look on the driver's face. The headlights and grill grinned at her like the stupid face of a doll.

Suddenly there was the roundabout and she took her turn off a bit fast, felt the centrifugal tipping of the car. The lorry, taking a different route, lurched on its brakes and its lights flashed. Sweet.

At the edge of the dentist's town there were deserted roadworks draped with a parody of bunting. The makeshift traffic lights slipped from amber to red in time to stop her behind a cement lorry. She switched the tape deck on. A tape Mel had left in. Gloopy slow piano music with lots of longheld bass chords. Like something submarine. The drum of the cement lorry was striped in black and dirty yellow and it was revolving slowly clockwise. There were steel flanges to make a vortex milling around the black aperture. Cement or concrete? Chips of mountain in there, maybe, churning in sync with the revolving cassette. An ironic soundtrack, perhaps, underscoring (ha!) the unbearable oddness of other. Glassy and elegant against the submerged grey light, the sustain peddle letting the chords hang and shimmer in the underwater valley like stunned shoals of fish.

She pressed the eject button and the music cut, the tape poking its tongue out at her.

'Mwah' she said to it. 'Well timed.'

The humbugstriped lorry chewed on its mouthful of stone rhythmically as it rocked forward.

*

The dentist tilted the chair back almost to horizontal so that she felt like a specimen of something dead laid out on a board. Any bit of her could be picked at. But they kept the tray of hooked and pointed instruments discreetly out of view nowadays, at least. And on the ceiling next to the mount for the anglepoise light the dentist swivelled into position above her face, was a poster. A therapeutic landscape from the endpapers of an old Rupert annual. Some of the animal characters from the stories, little Edwardian schoolboys with animals' heads, clambered on rocks in the foreground, but they were tiny in the frame of trees and hills. The immense country below them was undulating and mottled with the greens of late summer, shifting towards blue in the distance. It was broken here and there with patches of woodland, and a castle and a village, and a chinoiserie tower among spiky pines. On the unhurt mountains in the top right there was a blue blur that might be a jet of rain, but it was a long way away. And beyond that, in a dip in the ridges, so far and small you might be wrong about it, was a flat place that could be the sea.

The dentist's face came close. You could see his pores, and the blood vessels on the inside of his nostrils. He had sung the litany of her teeth to his assistant and switched to English to talk to Sarah.

'I'm afraid this one, upper right, needs a filling. Just a little one, nothing much. And.' His huge head shifted. He pinged the steel hook against old amalgam. 'And this one next to it really ought to be replaced at the same time.'

He repeated the check round her mouth, ran the probe along seams, looked for cracks and leakages. His face was the colour of dough. They always look like a photo through a fisheye lens.

'Any other problems?'

'The front two' she said.

'The top?'

'Yes.'

He looked, tapped, picked at the interstices, twiddled the mirror into play.

'They're fine' he said. The gums are. Well, but they'll be all right for a. They're all right.'

'I onk ung ouk leethe.'

He took the mirror away.

'I want them out, please' she said again.

His face retreated a little so that he could look at her whole head. His expression didn't change.

'What's the problem?'

'I just want them out.'

The face retreated further. He looked away at the clipboarded record card. I am a busy man. I keep detached and calm.

'Some pain, is there? Do they rub your lip?' He turned back and ran a latex fingertip along the back of her upper lip, got close again and looked. 'Perhaps some sensitivity.'

'Lun og ungs cacked a git.'

He took his fingers away.

'One of them's cracked a bit' she said. 'And there's a chip off the other.'

'No pain though?'

'Yes' she said. 'Aye there is. They're awful sensitive.'

The dentist glanced across her to his assistant and back to his patient.

'In the cold and when I drink.' She thought of the toothpaste advert with improbably young and beautiful models who drank from iced cocktails and then their mouths were hit by computer animated lightning. They winced woodenly and put their fingers to their cheeks.

She looked up at him through the fisheye and simulated a wince.

He watched her a moment, wagging his little mirror like a pendulum. 'You can get –'

'I've tried the special toothpaste. It's useless.'

He paused. 'It takes a while to work.' He was very calm. 'It's incremental. You've got to give it a few weeks.'

She looked straight at him. Come on. Acknowledge the unbearable oddness of other.

But he had opened her mouth and was busy there again.

'Eye hake gung.'

He moved his hands away.

'I hate them.'

But his fisheye eyes were still looking at her front teeth as if they were the opened pages of a book that took some thought. His face wore only the small, customary professional frown.

'We could x ray them, in a while' he said. The latex finger gently tickled the roof of her mouth just behind the teeth as he thought through growths and complications.

Her eyes and brain were at the edge of his world. Hinterland on the mountains away from the roads of the busy. A place you don't go, where waters plunge endlessly into space. To him she was just a damaged mouth on stilts. Everything else shrivelled away. Shoulders, breasts, trunk. Like Ben's drawings. An enormous head on tiny legs. In one of them, one huge hand with twenty-odd fingers. The other one not even drawn. Because that's where all the perception is, where all the nerves cluster and are busy. In our heads we bubble and change shape all the time like cartoons. Those fertility carvings focussed elsewhere. All piled swags of tit and belly, stupendous clefts and gigantic cocks. A race of dentists scratching on their cave walls with little lowspeed drills would depict you as an enormous trumpetbell of cracked enamel turned upward, the eyes gone to dots, the brain shrunk to the innards of a walnut dangling, then the useless stilts stretching almost horizontal on the electronic couch.

'They're aligned pretty well. They're really good solid teeth. Aren't they?' He looked again at the assistant.

She smiled with her mouth only and made an obscure affirmative sound.

'I really don't think –'

'You could take them out the same time you do the fillings' Sarah said.

'If it's the colour and the alignment, there are things we can do without –'

'That'd be a bit extra for you in the same session. It'd suit both of us.' A new one on him. Trying to talk a patient out of having work done.

He moved away and picked the clipboard up again. Though he held it in front of his face, she could see that he wasn't looking at it. The dough looked a bit sweaty. I am a professional. I am nonjudgmental. He tilted his wrist a little to see his watch. The half full waitingroom. In a moment another set of records will be brought in. The meter's ticking.

He swung the anglepoise away decisively and levered the chair upright. Perhaps he was actually going to. He put down the clipboard, put his hands on his thighs and sat forward, signalling the end of the consultation. He looked from the assistant to Sarah.

'Well what we'll do is, Mrs Bowen, we'll keep an eye on that.' He stood up. 'We'll keep it under review.'

No. Of course not. She watched him a fraction too long before she got up.

'If you go to reception and make an appointment for the two fillings, we'll check again then and I can x-ray your front ones then and we'll see how it's looking, okay.'

The okay was said as a full stop rather than a question mark. Power punctuation, like Glenys and her quotation marks. Dismissing me.

'I've got a walnut, you know' Sarah said. 'Brain.'

The assistant's empty smile didn't change, though the glaze on her eyes seemed to dull. But the dentist had turned away and was reaching a sample tube of toothpaste from a cupboard.

'This is good stuff for sensitivity' he said, presenting her with it. He explained how rather than brushing with it you should massage it onto the tooth and gum. 'You'll find it'll help, with time.'

'Help with time' Sarah said, and she felt herself smirking.

She took the little tube and shuffled awkwardly towards the door. She looked from the tube to him and said, 'Okay. I'll try.'

He smiled, the tension left him, and he started to unpeel a glove. More power punctuation.

'Then you can take them out' she said.

Momentarily the unpeeling slowed. Take that, you bastards. She watched them resisting the instinct to exchange a look.

'Nice poster' she said as she shut the door.

She paused in the corridor and listened. He would be throwing the gloves into a bin and drying his hands. She would be feigning busyness at a bench and watching the drizzle. There was a satisfying silence.

*

Outside, Sarah went into the newsagents next to SupaSeconds. She stood for a long time enjoying the colours of the rows of magazines. They all seemed to be covered in pictures of computer monitors or young women. Lots of pouts and smiles and dazzling eyes, and the babble of lure lines. Up Your Orgasm Count. The Secret You

– Numerology Reveals All. 25 Brilliant Ideas for Vegetables. They were shiny as toffee apples at a fair. She bought a glossy that always had some fiction, and at the till a bag of boiled sweets for herself and jelly babies for Ben.

On the road out of town in the cinemascope slot of the windscreen she saw far off the smudge of the red traffic light, where the bunting would be, and the long tail of standing cars. The valley wall on her left was steep and roadless, but on the right, across the valley bed, was the ribbon of stranded, pitless pit villages. Beyond them the mountain was patched with pine plantations and gorse, and in a couple of places roads climbed into the hinterland.

She took the next right and drove till she hit one of the mountain roads, from then on going slowly so she could see the view as she followed the switchback. The road was unknown to her. It sort of went in the right direction. Anyway, what if it didn't? She checked the fuel gauge. Plenty. Mel kept it topped up come autumn for some finicky reason. She could just drive till she hit somewhere she recognised.

There was no hilltop estate here. When she got to the cattle grid on the brow of the mountain, she had an uninterrupted smirchy view down on the sodden clot of traffic at the lights she'd avoided. Further east the roundabout and the dual carriageway were fuzzy with spray.

The drab intense arrow of Jean-Luc's plotless film had changed course, and she had made it change. Not just kings, then. She gripped the wheel harder.

Instead of crossing a ridge to drop into another valley and another road, the wet screen had dissolved to broad upland dark with massed pines. Surprising how much space there was. The car dipped into a hollow in the mountaintop following the three dimensional wind of track through the unnatural forest. It poured flickering over the screen like the walls of a tunnel. She crawled past a shut pub, one of those solid Victorian stone buildings that looked like it might have been built for a railway station, though it couldn't have been. There were two picnic benches outside it, weatherwarped and black with wet. It was hard to imagine that there could ever be a time when people might sit at them. Further on, on the other side of the road behind a drystone wall was a church.

She pulled the car in by the gate and switched the engine off. Suddenly the slishing of the tyres and the squeaky wiper were replaced by the tick of rain on the roof.

The church was small and huddled, with a squat tower. It looked shut too. The pointed door in the back of the tower facing her looked boarded over. It and the blank backs of the gravestones gave her the feeling they'd turned away and pulled a shawl around themselves. They were looking back across the upland hollow at nothing. The low clouds blurred the tops of the highest trees in places. The set had assembled its desolate self ready for a scene to be played out. In a well made piece, not something by Jean-Luc, things would mean things and things would happen. But she knew that nothing would happen.

She reached the magazine from the passenger seat. It was dark under the fraying cloud and she switched the dim interior light on. She flicked through the shiny pages.

Breast Implants – Boon or Bane? Stop Feminine Itching. Lucy Purbright says – Count Your Blessings.

Why? was Lucy worried some may have gone missing? Perhaps she did a daily blessing audit. Do a bar chart, Lucy.

Lucy smiled fetchingly from a small colour photo, her legs crossed and one unplanetlike knee braced against her laced fingers. She was wearing a suit a bit like Glenys's.

'Mwah' Sarah said to her.

The short story was called *Of Burning Gold* and it had a Chagallish illustration of two figures curling round one another symmetrically like the Pisces symbol in a floating soft focus blue sexual swoon.

Absently Sarah groped for the bag of sweets.

A New Story from Philippa Ducasse. No photo of her, so maybe floorward jowls and stellar patellae. Nice to think so. All about Penelope who works for a publisher and whose husband is a barrister.

Her eyes ran down the columns of words as she fumbled at the sweets and pulled one out of the bag. Done modishly in the present tense, as if that could make it realer.

Penelope Weaver frowns, but it is no good. The thread of her concentration has snapped for the umpteenth time. She sighs and turns away from the manuscript. Ever since she met the man whose words she has to edit, she cannot stop his voice from. Penny shakes her head, nervously. Penny smiles and touches her hair. "Dominic," she says, but Dominic is busily immersed in the papers of his latest case, and she turns towards her own briefcase with another sigh. At the publishers, Max smiles. Max's eyes linger just a little too long. He raises a querulous eyebrow and they laugh. "Take care, Penny," freewheeling Paula advises in the kitchen over morning coffee, "but if he's so." But Max turns up at the office, at functions, at launches with wine and celebrities. She glitters. He glances. She hovers. He stands close. "When we finish your book, Max, perhaps." Something gleams in Max's eye and he turns away. Paula points to the baby indignantly. "But nothing's happened," Penny insists. "But in your heart?" asks Paula. I thought she was my friend. What shall I do? she thinks. The crisis. The inner tussle. When I finish your manuscript. When I finish. But Dominic's casual cruelty. His rushed, oblivious entrances and exits. Old Mrs Fennesy the cleaner picking up his dark gown. "Shall I put this in that there machine, Mrs Weaver?" "No, it has to be dry cleaned, Mrs F., I'll hang it up." But wait. A distinctly feminine and familiar scent upon its shoulder. Penny thinks hard. *Paula.* Her fist clenches on the cloth. So. The tussle resolved. She shuts the completed manuscript and picks up the phone. "Max?" That voice, so rich and dark even on the phone. "We'll make some time to discuss it at the New York conference." In the half light her jewellery gleams. From the luxurious window they watch snow fall on Times Square. Oddly, it makes her bolder to be lying defenceless like this. Slowly, he runs his. Continued on page 98.

She flipped the page. There was a wet technicolor landscape of broccoli and diced carrots. 25 Brilliant Ideas.

She chucked the magazine down so she could concentrate on her boiled sweet. Penelope Weaver for nonexistent god's sake. Fuck you, Penelope. And on page 98, he will.

The wet landscape outside was almost monochrome, not quite unintelligible through the fractured spurts of rain on the screen. Just the artful, near washedaway dark greenblue of the pines, cold, nothing like the warm blue of the coiling sexual fish in the picture. In that direction somewhere beyond the trees the set ended, and then close, a mile or two off, would be the pile of houses on the mountain drilled hollow for its rock. Then wires and roads, and pipes running south, their outfall in the sea, which would be steelgrey and rainhammered.

A gust spattered the screen with rain and shook the car and then the wind dropped. The rain sound stopped. She looked at the blurred treetops and the cloud wasn't moving. She blinked and it still wasn't moving. Again? Congratulations, god, or Jean-Luc. Twice in one week. Nor breath nor motion. But she was breathing, minimally. She could feel the faint passage of air through her nostrils, the lob and dub of her heart, the whisper of fluids in capillaries.

For the first time since she'd left school that afternoon she looked at her watch. The second hand was standing still. Yes. I have made this happen. *Arrows of Desire*, a new story by Sarah Bowen. Grab the arrow by its fins and point it any way you like. Or stop it dead.

She thought of the dentist frozen at his chair, his drillbit stopped mid gouge in a patient's molar. The assistant's smile was more wooden than she intended, the summer country of the poster fixed perfectly on the staring patient's retina. Mel in the quarry was struck motionless hitching up his trousers in his portakabin office. In the shut pages of the magazine Philippa Ducasse's story was stalled simultaneously in all its moments. In Hampstead Dominic pored over his papers. Feathers of snow hung in mid fall over Times Square. The Laertean robe of their manuscript at once finished and not finished, Penny lay bold and defenceless on the blue carpet in her adulterous coil with handsome greying Max. Still unravished ravished bride. The spray on the dual carriageway lit from inside with head- and taillights stood in the air like a sculpture of frosted glass. Clint and Dustin were tired on the bus home that would never get there, coconut heads leaning together.

And the second hand snapped forward again. The wind rocked the car and rain hit the sidewindow. The film unlocked.

She was gripping the sweet very tight. You can't escape. She held it up and pulled the cellophane lugs. The little drum of the sweet revolved as the plastic untwisted and the words printed on it rolled past her eyes like the credits on a film. PURE CONFECTIONERY PURE CONFECTIONERY. And then the breaking in. She sniffed, looked at the moulding. At first it was too large for comfort in her mouth. All that taste releasing through her head. She tongued it to the right and wedged it against her upper teeth as she let in the clutch and turned the key in the ignition. So bad for the teeth. So bad. Oh wonderful.

GWENER

I stood by the handrail next to the steps down, shivering a bit and watching it all splashing and I thought, is this it? Well it is. It is all there is. Trouble with this country is you can't have a road movie, don' matter if you got Crosby, Stills, Nash and Young tapes and you read the right paperbacks. Specially not if you do drive a Fiesta one point fucking one pissbucket. Drive for a bit and you come to fucking England, which is bad enough. And the only alternative's this. Hundred and twenty mile on the road and wallop. Seventeen thousand million acres of fuck all. The wild west. Ireland next stop.

I was holding the car key by the leather tag, dangling it on the handrail. That early in the morning everything's a particular shade of grey. It's grey that do say I'm grey because you can't open your gritty eyes properly because it's so fucking early. Specially when you been driving in the dark like that. It's stuck to everything like when rain's dirty sometimes and you get sand from the Sahara or some fucking where stuck to the windows.

So I watched all the foam and stuff fifteen foot below me like washing up gone wrong, all rolling back under itself and there was that sucking noise when it do drag back through the sand and stones. Sand. It en sand. The colour of wet cement. A turd after a night on the Guinness.

Sandra like doing it on the landing. She do put a pillow by the bathroom door and put her head to one side like she do and there's just enough room for us diagonally. Play havoc with the knees, so sometimes we come to the edge of the stairs and I do go down a step or so and the angle's just right. Or there's the piano stool. We never had room for the piano from my mother's, but I got the stool. It sound good when you play it from that distance, Sandra do say. So it's by the dressing table. We push it against the bed and she go face down with her knees pointing

169

down either side of a corner and it do press up against her lovely
and I slip it in kiff from the back. She got a lovely back. She never
take long and once she's going she like it wanged up her pretty
strenuously, but sometimes we do just undulate in rhythm and
smile at one another in the mirror on the fitted wardrobe.

I was the only person and my rusty old fartwagon was the only
car on this stretch of the front. From the stump of pier one end to
the cliff the other it was empty. All that salt spray and the car
'ouldn' be there long. They needn' bother towing it away. Be a
heap of grains in no time. Just blow about, a red streak on the
beach.

Thing in work half way through yesterday afternoon put the lid
on it.

Simmonds the senior engineer calling me and Roy and Maureen
in and trying to make it seem like a casual chat. He ought to try
on the assembly line with a fucking tachometer keeping count on
him for a bit. That'd show him casual. He live in Usk or some
fucking where. Come to work in an Espace. On his own.
Possibilities of retraining, he said. Probably to him it was being kind,
giving us an early signal in case it happen. You got to hand it to
those kids. I 'ouldn've thought they could've done it, specially with
that tired tosser Mr Wazzock with his moustache in charge of em.

Terry's more of a one for the bed. She like to keep her bra or a
top on and I do feel her through the material. She got different skin
and she do take ages and when she get close sometimes her fingers
and her face do go all numb. We do stroke and cwtsh for ages and
sometimes I can't even manage after all that. But sometimes she do
say, Oh Ken, my face've gone numb. And sometimes she do just
moan and sometimes she do burst out laughing and once she give
this huge hoot like a fucking foghorn. And the look on her. It set
me alight.

No more of that.

New gadget could be ready in less that a year Simmonds said.
Affect about six of us. The best ideas are the simple ones he said.
Best. I had a long talk with one of the kids. Lanky fucker, taller
than me, with a pointy nose and a crewcut. Quite reserved. Nice
boy when you got to know him. Think he twigged Simmonds
quick enough. Keep out of this bloody game, I said. It was just a
school project to him. And inside a twelvemonth six of us'll be up
the road.

That was it, on top of everything else.

The funny thing is, since Sandra come back – she was only gone a week – but since she come back, after I blew everything to fuck about Terry, we been at it like knives. Every time the girls are out the way pretty well, which is a lot now they're older. All the bloody time. I must be a late developer or something. It's fucking wonderful, but it's a bit funny.

The grey wasn' getting any better. It's looking west, so it's like looking back to where things were a couple of hours ago. Like a grey slot between the clouds and the sea, and the sea just a bit steely and getting darker and darker towards where they meet.

A man come past. The only other person in sight. He had a rolled umbrella and an old grey mac with a belt and a hat. Old bloke. He obviously wasn' going to work. Just walking, not even with a dog, that time of day. He said something in Welsh. Good morning, I expect. He wasn' the sort to say How's it hanging? or Hand over your wallet. Aye aye, butt, I said. And he toddled on right down the far end, the dead end of the front, under the dirty looking cliff. Look more like an old coal tip than anything, though it couldn' be up here.

How much do you know for definite, Brian? I said to Simmonds. I been there twelve years. He's all right like that. No misters. This is all up front, Ken, he said. I can't tell you any more than I know. But they're going to make this gizmo and that's it. I think he'd be all right away from that place. It's work, what it do to you. Destroy you. But what are you without it?

When the girls were out of the way watching telly upstairs I told Sand. She went loopy like it was my fault. It was displaced, see. All the built up stuff after Terry, all spilling out the wrong time. Trouble is after it all I just got to take whatever she do throw. No reason why I shouldn't.

The old bloke went right up to the far end under the rocks and he just stopped for a bit, kicked the handrail, and turned round and started back. My eyes were pretty sore and the light was murky grey, but that's what he did.

I just kept calm till she quietened. It's funny. Big bust ups on telly do finish and then they cut somewhere else. But really you still have to sit there after. So after she ballocked me she got me a cup of tea and we went and fucked. Quiet, because the kids were in. Bloody strange.

Then two in the morning I woke up and she had the light on and she was sitting on the edge of the bed. Not depression. Not crying. She was beside herself. Quivering and talking shit. She just pulled a drawer right out of the chest and it went everywhere and she picked stuff up and she was throwing it at me. Pairs of socks and insurance policies.

I hung on to her and in the end she quietened and had a cry and then she hung on to me and she hugged me and the same time she said, Get out you fucking bastard, I hate you.

I looked at us over her shoulder in the wardrobe mirror. What's left? You know how you see your reflection and most days you look okayish and then you see your photo and you really look your age. Even with the pinky bedside light glowing I looked fucking old. Both of em gone really. Her and Terry. And the girls heard everything by this time, even though I worked it past em when she left for a bit. And in a bit thanks to Mr Wazzock and his junior fucking scientists, no job and no money either. Look in the mirror that day and there'll be no face there at all.

I dangled the key. The old bloke was coming back, a bit stiff and slow. I nodded to him. Hello again, he said. In English, otherwise I 'ouldn've known. Nice this morning. I couldn' tell whether he was joking or not. I said, Enjoy your walk? and he told me he always woke up early and come down if the weather was anything like. It has become something of a ritual. Every walk for me is the walk home, he said. I like to think of it as a circular stroll in a straight line. We stood there on the empty prom smiling at one another.

Sand kept crying and ballocking me and telling me to fuck off. In the end I said, Sand, I can't take this any more, like in a film, and I went and I got in the car.

You? the old bloke said. Are you staying here? He was awful polite but he must've clocked the state of me. Just arrived on spec, I said. To tell you the truth, it's such a lovely morning I was fancying having a dip. He kept smiling. Yes, he said. Every morning I think of shinning up the cliff, and then I think, not this morning. But one morning I will. He knew what it was about. Well, very good luck to you, he said. And I just wagged my hand to say good-bye and there goes the fucking key, out and down fifteen foot, into the shingle and the wet cement by the bottom step. I leaned over and I could just see the gold lettering on the tag and the steel ring and the water hit it. Jowl, the old bloke said. Something like that.

I shouldn've cared. It shouldn've mattered. But it did. I felt sick as a dog suddenly because I thought I couldn' get home, and I knew something.

But the old bloke was already down the steps. I saw it, he said.
Meantime the washing up had come and gone a couple of times
and shifted the pebbles and cement and made the sucking noise.
Watch out, butt, I said, and I was half way down the stone steps
behind him. But he was there second step up, leaning out over the
suds and jabbing his brolly like Zorro down in the water. And
pretty quick he lifted it up quite gently and there the key was,
speared through the steel ring on the ferrule of his umbrella.

He give a quiet little laugh, delighted, even though his feet
must've been wet. I imagine you will need this? he said. He was
right. Good job you come along, I said. Oh I don't know, he said.
If I hadn't been here you wouldn't have dropped it. He could've
been wrong about that.

And where is there other than back?

⋆ ⋆

but where was I yes eight see nine tee eleven ee then, no wait that's
Mon this is Fri, two days start the same and you never get it. Try
again. So eight see nine tee, yes then break and after break, wait,
on duty so corridor then after break after break *not* eleven ee, their
books for Sunday to mark, not them. Try again. Eight see nine tee
then break in the corridor and then, double eight ess en for May,
her notes, the maries and the unable to concentrates, the benlikes,
so yes, then dinner (sorr no fuck off) and then, then, hang on. Try
again. Eight see nine tee break in corr double eight spesh needs din
(sor) nothing in dinner no meetings no detention so mark then,
then seven see and a free a FREE if Billy Shit don' come for
revenge and, wait, dinner seven see free corridor duty for afternoon
break and double hist lower six to top off, confusing symmetry to
the week, both ends the same, in my end is my, that's the way the
week ends not with a bang but a, then shopping, pork peppers rice
yogs marj wine chocs, pay the minder or did I? and tea and telly
and Sat to mam's, phone tonight, ask about Kenny and Sandra, ask
dad praps get more sense, and Sun there's the nine tee worksheet
mark that and eleven ee books and have a look to sort out Mon,
type wksht on the quarry ha bloody ha, pork making minnowlyric
with fan oven, then eight see nine tee eleven ee et cetera the wheel
rolling towards half term short reports coming and departmental

meeting was it? after hours Peter doing the debrief on Ayers and disgraces my turn to do the minutes or is that a week Mon? this Mon I think but one thing at a time. So today again, eight see nine tee eight ess en for the double and din and remember corridor break, eight ess en, what was it? oh dinner time find benlike boy's book, ben, my darling, but eight see's first so have to go in early look for book first then ben thenben are we on   a

River. Stone. More river than stone. I am a fountain of gardens, a well of living waters.

Really, when you swim, you're almost weightless. Flesh levitates. You fly.

The world was spread like a storybook with all its fields and gardens and wildernesses, with passages of sun and green and blurred blue jets of rain on far hills. Two small children were chasing a bright red paper kite which had snapped its tether. They ran along ridges and it flew high above the billows of the trees. The red kite sails above the earth. The two chums run for all their worth. 'Come back!' they cry as on they run, And yet the chase is splendid fun. It flutters brightly in the breeze Then plunges down among the trees.

Because gravity see.

Her finger was pushing in her room, her fountain, and the radio was already talking about roads and wars. Round and round the garden. Hid in the grove's a garden fair, And, oh, my red kite nestles there. Come on. Stroke it. The Red Sea. But the voice already with wars and things, because this late in the week you come to later.

And his hand was on hers. Fat and firm and rocklike and a little cold, pushing hers aside and then brushing at the raised button of it. And rolling her and his broad knee, pyjamaclad, between hers. And oh, yes, yes. Somebody interesting, somewhere exotic, down among the wild trees where a river is. The sound of liquid trickling and air moving. Process making its progress. Yes.

His weight rolled onto her like a mountain moving, the heavy bag of his belly, and the beard slid against her mouth and his beige breath came on her. He was murmuring something. A tune. Some tune, but you couldn't tell what. Aubade. Oh, bad. Wiggling absurdly. His tumid willy was trapped somewhere in the braiding and button at the waist of his pyjamas and he stopped the flow of movements and the tuneless song to disentangle it and she was wet enough for there to be no need of further adjustments and they shut on one another with the ease of old practice and she was irritated.

'What are you doing?' she said. 'It's only Friday.'

So he stopped and she opened her eyes.

The air was dim milky grey. No chink. No Newtonian finger. She checked the time and shut her eyes again.

He'd slid off her and the bedsprings unclenched as he got up.

She laughed down at the two small animalboys in their odd uniforms. Can't catch me, you silly pair. I flick my tail and swim through air.

A hand knocked at her face as if it was a door. She started and looked at the clock again. It was fifteen minutes later than it had been a second ago.

Ben stood and Mel was kneeling next to the bed. Light splayed from the landing door. They looked funny in their pyjamas, smiling.

'Happy birfday, mummy' Ben said. He held up two wrapped presents and a card and started to clamber onto her.

Hence the murmured song.

Mel put a mug of coffee next to the clock.

'Well there's lovely' she said, sounding like her mother.

She cwtshed her son and Mel was opening the curtains and there was a confusion of tearing paper and Ben's excited voice and huggings, the little chimplike muscular movements. I'm still a bag of blancmange he can squidge about. Thirty years he'll be hair and muscle and some little chimp will be clinging to him. And me a voice bubbling down the phone, tiny. So is this a node? How count what flows? The occasionless occasion. Sticking a flag in a wave. Half way ought to be a node, didn't it? Something to do with wavelengths and strings vibrating.

The grey daylight refused to acknowledge that it was. She listened to herself talking to Mel and Ben, reacting to the unwrapped things.

Shortly, Mel went to the bathroom. Ben got engrossed in the thinginess of wrapping paper and boxes. Soon he would have to be put on the toilet. There. The usual, node, involving gravity. Same chapter again. All incidentals, no incidents. Even if one day you try to lose your face but can't because the dentist must save his, it passes and the sun rises the next day. So you pour your own gloop into a temporary mould and pretend to be a concrete noun for a few hours. Disintegrate, then do it again tomorrow.

She hugged Ben and slid her coffee mug to one side so that she could read the clock. She needed to move to get in early to look for the lost book. The chocolates gave her a target for tonight. She wasn't so sure about the flatpacked ornamental windowbox, but it did have some profound advice printed on it. Assemble yourself, it said.

★ ★

If you don' wash your ballocks for a bit, black stuff gets in to the grain of the skin. It don' quite have the same quality as the black stuff you get between your toes. It doesn' have that, like, squashy, plastic quality. But it does have a similar air of being meaty and nutritious. You can almost understand the motives of parasites that live in hair and feed on blood, sweat and shit. If you collected the black stuff like they recycle paper and that you could probably use it in animal feed. Probably full of protein. Look good on the label. Free range chicken, fed on a diet of organic corn supplemented with the black stuff off your ballocks.

He considered this as he soaped his balls.

A waste really, all that food being washed away. If you add it all up, think how many chickens. You could probably save pumping them with all the hormones. All natural. Not an additive in sight.

He'd put some of his mother's bath stuff in the water. It was in a pink plastic bottle and it didn' smell butch. In fact it smelt like his mother, and it was very strong because the foam was plentiful. But it got the black stuff off your cobs.

He lay down in the water.

It could work up into a nice standup routine. Next to the re-cycling skip, the blackstuffoffyourballocks collection point. It'd have to be a tall container so the dogs didn' go for it. Try it out in the Adit later on today.

He considered.

Mand and Trish and them. Maybe not, really. But it'll pep up the day no end, a quiet pint early on like that. A nice prelude to my talk.

He lifted the head of his penis above the foam. The Birth of Penis. Botticelli. Strange what you find out when you start looking up who was around at the same time. Nicholas might even have met him. How be, Cop. Aye aye, Bott, butt. They could've swapped renaissance appercus over a pint of Albright down the Florence Exy. He peeled back the hood and bent it to face him, so that the split bit smiled at him. It was like the hemispheres of a smooth brain.

In a minute or twenty he'd shave. Choice of three. The Gillette Sensor she got him for Christmas, the rechargeable electric one he never took with him when he went and she left lying there as if he'd just nipped down Maggie's, Gransh's silvered one with the tooled chrome handle and a little screw thing at the bottom. A Brief History of Blokes in This House, in the bathroom cupboard. Gransh's still had the blade in, watermarked with rust, tiny shavings of white whisker trapped in hardened lather along the edge.

In Gransh's room the jumbo jotter on the cake trolley was still opened at a page on which two words were written and then crossed out. But that'd be all right. He was better just talking it through on the spot. He could do it. Aye, a wet shave, sitting here, because all this foam.

Did they have the word bagatelle back then, in fifteen whatever? What was it anyway, exactly? Look it up the day I check sallow. The day I start writing it down. All day yesterday on that. Grilling potato waffles and telly and finishing Hoyle, thinking, stinking and wanking. But then, what are Thursdays for? But Fridays. Yes. You scrub your nuts and jingle dosh. Unthink, destink and – well, okay, come on. Two out of three. The birth of.

The smoothed brain did some standup of its own. He watched the steam taking on the grey morning light and condensing messagelessly on the frosted window, and thought of nothing for a long time.

★ ★

Assemble, did I say?

Because it was her duty day, after failing to find Benlike boy's book she barked at kids in the corridor and escorted them into the hall. Chatted to some year nine girls. Stationed herself by the serving hatch and surveyed the panorama of young skulls with the steely expressionlessness of the warder with the mirror shades in *Cool Hand Luke*. Except of course here there was no fucking plot. She saw Tina's highlights – late essay due there – but Gethin's hairless nape wasn't visible. Glenys's "word" probably scared him off today. Clint and Dustin, whose bus must have got home after all, stood by the main doors guarding and distributing the stacked hymnbooks. Peter, on duty too, stood on the opposite flank of the hall. His face was khaki and puckered under the warming lights, and expressionless. Three year eight children stood on the podium, nervously fingering copies of their readings.

So everything assembles and something should happen, some great orchestral node. But instead Gwil Evans comes in and calls for quiet and the kids stand and Glenys and Billy Shit and eight or ten other members of staff, no Ryan among them, come in and sit, and everybody sits except the on duty teachers and then Glenys blah blah and the gay boy in year nine plays the opening bars of *Morning Has Broken* on the piano and then there's a pause and everybody stands – why is it always that way round? – and everybody is silent and the kids mime halfheartedly when they think Glenys is looking at them and all the staff mime except for Alun Brown head of Modern Languages. Aubade. Everybody stares at nothing and tries to think of nothing and they all try not to listen to Mr Brown as he widens his nostrils and sings the descant on his own.

★ ★

The Common Room was dead, it being Friday and almost dinner-time. Apart from the odd fragment of shattered mug and a couple of upper sixth people doing work, it looked quite tidy. And no sign of Pod and the others.

Steve went on down the corridor past its double doors, clutching the black hardback, keeping an eye open for Shattock. His work-shop and the staffroom were in another building, but the bugger might be lurking.

Steve pushed the door of the Sixth Form Library open warily, like they do in films. But no Captain Kirk. Just Melanie and Rob Morgan poring over a large sheet of paper on the teacher's desk.

They looked up and Melanie smiled and said, 'Hi.'

Rob nodded and said, 'Stick' and gave him a measuring up glance and turned back to the desk. He always had the look of a policeman who's just hung his hat on the back of the kitchen door

178

but who hasn't quite come off duty. Still being nonjudgmental, but actually totally pissed off with the entire universe.

Steve walked in, acting casual.

'Seen Pod and them?' he said.

They hadn't.

He went to the bookcase. He could feel their eyes on him. He stood at one end of the cupboard and checked. There was no sign that anybody'd noticed where he'd prised the back panel away. The butter knife from the Common Room had dropped down inside, so there was no chance of getting that back.

'It's locked' Rob said.

'Yeah yeah.'

A carpet tile was a bit ruckled where he'd slid the cupboard away from the wall and then back. Nobody had straightened it. He went back towards the teacher's desk.

'Um' he said, 'Melanie, you going to this um.'

Melanie looked straight at him and smiled and shook her head ever so slightly.

'Well, no. Sorry to have.' He looked at the sheet. They were drawing a poster for a meeting of the Christian Union. 'Bye then.'

He'd have to put the book back another time. Just before the talk maybe.

In the corridor, Pod and Trish were standing by the Common Room door waiting for him.

★ ★

Coming out of 8SN's lesson at the end of the morning, she walked across the carpark and along the railings by the road with Ryan, back towards A Block. In the first lesson, with 8C, Benlike boy had been generously forgiving about the lost book. Sarah promised him she'd try harder in future. 8SN had been lamblike as usual under the day's routine acts of butchery.

She smiled at Ryan and didn't know what to say. Didn't smirk. Thought of the tissuestiffening Moment on Wednesday. A mild electricity down my near arm today, though it's almost not there at all. But it's Friday and I'm tired.

His knuckles were pushed down in the patch pockets of his white coat. He and she did mistimed glances at one another.

His lip unbuckled. 'No rain' he said.

'No' she said. 'Wasn' it terrible yesterday.'

He agreed as to the terribleness of yesterday.

An air sandwich. You assemble and disassemble and there's nothing in between.

Then she thought of something to say. 'Steven Leyshon was in my lesson Wednesday, by the way.' The wrong thing to say, naturally. It sounded like point scoring.

But his lip didn't rebuckle much. 'Yeah. He actually made it to registration Wednesday morning' he said. 'I had a word with him about attendance. No sign of the bugger since of course.'

'Not today?'

'No.'

'He's doing a talk for me this afternoon.'

His walking slowed only fractionally and he looked at her face, the look of one who's won a small victory and doesn't want to look like it.

An unnaturally clean red car slid past slowly on the other side of the railings. Sarah got a good look at Mandy at the steering wheel. She was wearing a turquoise chenille sweater and small gold earrings and lipliner and eye makeup, and her eyebrows were even more eyebrowy than usual.

Sarah turned and watched the exhaust pipe for a second. The gears crunched.

She followed Shattock into the main building and up the stairs towards the staffroom and drew level with him on the landing.

'I' she said. She was going to say 'enjoyed the drink', but it felt wrong so she stopped.

★ ★

When the tables were crowded with drinks and everybody had sat down and all the smokers had lit up, there was a sudden silence as if the world had stopped, and then everybody laughed.

Mandy had just passed her test and had driven like it, though having seven people in her dad's Orion couldn't have helped. They'd all met the car a street away from the school. Pod had sat in the front because he was the biggest. Trish had hesitated, looking into the crammed back seat, until some skinny bloke next to Steve patted his own thigh and said, Come on, don' be shy, and she'd folded herself in on his lap. Mm, the skinny bloke said, somebody's fragrant, and Trish elbowed him and Steve sniffed his own wrist and realised it was him – the pink stuff – and tried to shrink into the seat but there wasn' enough room and they went round a corner and Trish fell against him. The book, tucked into the back of his trousers, dug into him. A few people who lived close to the pub hadn't gone to school and had walked to the Adit. There were ten or so all together. Steve only knew a few of them.

They were in a corner which was partly screened from the rest of the pub by a half wall topped with a partition of yellow glass frosted with squirly patterns. That was left over from when the Adit had been Bubbly's Wine Bar, but now it was supposed to look like a drift mine, with the walls painted black and white and photographs of pitheads everywhere and a case on the wall full of lampchecks.

The two picture windows onto the carpark in this corner spoilt the effect a bit. Outside, by the entrance, there was a fluorescent sandwich board with a crossed pick and shovel on it and the name of the pub and 'Music Wednesday's' and the times when food was served and the challenge: 'Why haven't you come down an Adit?'

There was a sign behind the bar, too, which said 'Persons in school uniform will not regretfully be served', which was why some people had changed sweaters and removed ties in the car. Mandy, like some of the others, was already changed. Tight white trousers and a blue top made of some slinky furry stuff. Steve looked at her across the tables as she talked to one of the girls about her boyfriend Russell and going clubbing on Saturday.

Pod drained his pint. 'Come on, butt' he said to Steve. 'I'll buy you one.' He tapped his watch. 'I'm your co driver for today.'

Steve gulped on his lager and handed his glass over.

'Is this the Sip Rate Theory?' Mandy said, interrupting her own conversation.

'Yeah' Steve said, a bit surprised. 'Oo, we'd need all day for that really.'

Pod glanced at his watch as he squeezed past chairs towards the bar. 'Over two and half hours, mun. We can have a trial run.'

The rest of the pub was quiet. Round the edge of the partition, down a perspective of corners hung with Davy lamps and helmets, Steve could see some boys in baseball caps playing pool. A little nearer, two middleaged men with earrings and bellies were having the first of the day. Parked next to their table they had a double buggy into which two small children were strapped.

Trish and a couple of the others next to Steve were talking about somebody he didn't know who'd died in hospital.

'Eight minutes' Pod said handing the pint over and looking at his watch. You're a bit behind schedule starting your second.'

'Who's this dead?' Steve said to Trish.

She told him, and he realised it was somebody off a soap opera.

'Oo' he said. 'That programme old people watch.'

Trish ha haed sarcastically. She was drinking a half of Strongbow.

'Apparently the death rate in soaps is worse than in any real place on earth' he said. 'People always die in soaps.'

'I think you'll find, Steven' she said, 'they sometimes die in soaps. They always die in real life.'

The wheel. Aitch Seven and Nicholas. Yes, undeniable. The shavings of white whisker.

He bit into the new pint. It was the colour of Dettol and it even smelt like it a bit, but it tasted of nothing.

'I see there's a new porno soap opera starting' he said. You got to be fast. He waited for the feedline, like: Is there? or, Oh really? or, Get away, or something, but she just looked at him. 'Yeah' he said. 'Starting next week. It's called PudEnders.'

She looked blank. Pod spluttered in his pint.

Steve dipped back into his drink to drown a smile, then took a big gulp.

'Is that wise, Steven?' she said, watching his Adam's apple sliding as he swallowed.

'Well you know these telly people' he said. 'They usually do their research.'

'No, I meant.' She stopped and did an irritated face. 'You know what I meant.'

'Leave him alone' Mandy said.

'Yeah, leave him alone' the skinny bloke said.

'Oh you meant this' Steve said, pointing to his glass. 'It's being done scientifically. Laboratory conditions.'

'Well at least you don' smoke' Trish said.

Steve, who was blowing Embassy Regal smoke over himself to try to blunt the pink smell, raised his eyebrows at her.

'No' she said. 'You know. You don' smoke.' She looked at his eyes. 'Do you?'

Steve briefly considered lying and decided not to. 'What is this? A job interview? Actually, when I grow up I'd like to be the first theoretical physicist since 1965 not to be on something.' He took another slug of disinfectant.

'You don' need to be' Mandy said.

'Which implies other people do.'

They smiled at one another.

He flicked the tail of his cigarette to drop a punctuation mark in the ashtray and missed.

⋆ ⋆

Darren, standing in the doorway, looked at her, puzzled. He didn't move to let her in.

'I aven got you now' he said.

She stared up at him. Double eleven ee lessons five and six wasn't it? She looked away to think and then at him again.

'I had you yesterday. First after dinner' he said. 'You took the books in and give Tina and them essays for not doing it. Remember. Monday Tuesday and Thursday you are. Friday today.'

The points of his hair gleamed and his breath smelt of Cheesy Wotsits, and he was right.

'You *were* yesterday' she said, remembering.

The books were still fanned across the back seat of the car. That's Sunday, or possibly tonight, but Sunday definitely. So end of today, it's, yes lower six double hist. I was doing yesterday today.

She turned and walked back up the corridor.

And now? There's never any now. That's in the middle, between what was and what will be and so's a point without any extension, or come to think of it, point. The traffic behind and in front constantly squeezing and teasing you, bunching and stretching like the fins of a groaning concertina. The same catastrophic banal noise of uprush and withdrawal, like the sea on shingle. Something breathing. Shit. Spare me the metaphors. So, this morning was eight see nine tee break with Peter in the corridor, eight ess en Shattock, turquoise Mandy in red car – hm – pisswiffy sandwiches marking registration register totalled for the week and. And.

★ ★

Steve stood at the stall next to one of the men with an earring and a belly, and pissed.

The bar was getting hazy with smoke and busier with people ordering food. After it, the bogs were suddenly quiet and filled with ambient grey light. He could hear traffic. It was funny to think of the world spinning on with its daytime things, people working. His mother in the shop.

The bogs didn' try to be a driftmine. You could see grouting and botched bits of plumbing. Surprising somehow. It all glowed with certainty about itself in the softened light. That could be the title for something. the certainty of light. The Certainty of Light, by Steven David Leyshon.

'Plenty of cunt over by you' the man said.

'Uh?'

'In your corner. Plenty of cunt with you.'

'Oh. Aye' Steve said. He didn't know what to say.

The man shook the drippers off with a scarily vigorous technique, flexing his knees as he did so. Steve zipped up and turned to go.

'Ey' the man said. 'I got some seed for your budgie if you want it.'

'Uh?'

The man said the same thing again.

'Er, we got a cat' Steve said.

The man looked puzzled as he zipped his torn jeans and then laughed like somebody joining in a joke too late. Off his fucking trolley. Steve opened the door and the bar noises got louder.

'Ey' the man said, a bit indistinct in the noise. 'You want to watch that scrawny little fucker mind. He'll have yours off you if you don' watch.'

'What the fuck are you on about?' Steve said as he went, too quiet for the man to hear.

In the bar, the pool players had suspended their game temporarily to watch a telly on a high shelf. They held or hung on to their cues as if they were mallets and shepherds' crooks. On the telly he glimpsed two beautiful young Australians on videotape looking straight at one another and then away and going through a crisis. As he floated past them in the haze, the pool boys cheered some line of dialogue and the reaction shot of a pouting face, as if a try had been scored.

The two picture windows lit up the corner he went back to. Through the yellow glass Mandy's slinky top was a blur of iridescent green. He passed the double buggy, in which one of the small children was asleep and the other was sucking a titty bottle full of squash, looking round with big eyes.

Pod was fiddling with his watch. Everybody was laughing.

'How are we doing?' Steve said. He squinted at the watch. An enormous amount of time had passed. 'Fucking hell.'

Everybody laughed again. It did seem incredibly funny. Steve laughed and they laughed some more.

'According to Leyshon's SR theory' Pod said, 'we should be on at least number five and you've only had three.'

Steve tried to remember the diminishing formula. It didn' seem quite right.

'I think I must have slipped through a wormhole in the space time continuum or something' he said, taking Pod's glass. 'But you're the navigator.'

'You ought to put some weight on then' Pod said.

Actually, that wasn' bad, for Pod. Steve laughed again and they all laughed again, except for Trish.

He took the two glasses and bumped into the buggy on his way to the bar, but the sleeping one didn't wake.

★ ★

And seven see. 7C.

The received wisdom is that a reading lesson's a nice way to end the week. But you have to concentrate so hard on watching them and the time and the words and the stumbles and misreadings of stops and take care not to embarrass the ones who're nervous – half the time you can't spare the effort to follow the story. The slabbiness of the language, the things you could teach, slip through your fingers.

She was late, having gone to the wrong room, and the kids got up a head of steam waiting. When Sarah walked in there were hisses of *effbee! effbee!* and kids scattering back to desks and one left standing at the front, one of the quiet girls whose name she didn't know yet, in redhanded consternation holding the remains of a copy of *The Silver Sword* which had just lost its cover in some joyous skirmish.

The tableau took a second to unfreeze and Sarah tried to muster the energy for giving a ballocking. The restrained quiet but deadly kind was all she could manage, though they're as good as any. But ended up talking herself into a detention on Monday.

Poor little redhand looked close to tears.

You too.

Next week's double page in the diary was clogging with the falling soot of notes. She wrote in the margin 'FB' and then crossed it out. She didn't really want to find out what it stood for.

Redhand said, I didn' do it, Miss, I never been in trouble before. So the whole reading lesson went with Sarah's eyes slipping from the page to Redhand, taking her emotional temperature. Some sort of node in Redhand's life, perhaps, though not a birthday one. There ought to be something real about half way. Press a string in the middle and it goes up an octave. But actually, no. All the moments fall past you like faces in the corridor so that they're not moments at all, might just as well never have been. They break noiseless as bubbles. No music.

And then after seven see, yes, Billy Shit's revenge for yesterday. Her free eaten supervising year ten maths, though this time they had work set. Kids bored with all the mechanics of it. Christ, who'd be a maths teacher on Friday afternoon. No wonder the sod's away.

Afternoon break, late for downstairs corridor duty coming from the maths lesson so she didn't get any coffee, she stood with Peter and thought of nothing. Peter trawled the classrooms along the corridor, kicking kids out. ('Is it raining?' 'Why, sir, you going for a walk?' 'Is it raining?' 'Not really.' 'Out. Now.') A couple of times, reluctantly, he let small dancing children into the building to go to the toilet.

It went quiet and he settled against a dingy wall under one of the low energy lights with a paperback of *The Mill on the Floss*.

Two small girls approached Sarah. One of them murmured to her and she sent them upstairs to get a Lil-let from Glenys.

'Good god' Peter said to the book. 'What an ending. The upper sixth are going to love it.'

'Are they?' Sarah said.

'No.'

A small head appeared round the double doors that opened onto the carpark.

'Out' Peter shouted.

The small head vanished.

'It knackers me, this, on a Friday' Peter said. 'No they're not. They couldn't give a toss. And it's crap, isn't it?'

'Incisive critiquing there, Peter.' She struggled to remember. 'The brother and sister stuff.' She stood close to him to see the book.

'After all the vicissitudes' Peter said in a melodrama sort of way, 'reunited at the end.'

She thought of Tom Tulliver. A name even more unconvincing than Sarah Bowen, though Eliot, on the whole, was otherwise a better novelist than god. Earning a living crippling him. Poor Tom shut up in the Counting House.

Peter was looking down at the book, seriousfaced, his skin like clay under the white light. She saw, down the corridor beyond him, some boys sneak in through the double doors and into the boys' toilets.

'Jesus' Peter said. 'And the flood.'

'Oh yes' Sarah said. 'Everything got washed away.'

It occurred to her that they were in a corridor. She knew already, of course, but she could see it, suddenly, its long windowless emptiness and the studs of the pale lights. As if a bit of Now had jostled itself some space, had broken through so you could know it. The tidemark of dark smirchings along the walls up to about year eight shoulder level. A place between places. This could be a Moment. She looked along Peter's body. Taller than Kenny, but the same stringy build. He was leaning against the wall with his feet crossed, so that she could see his socks. One was white and the other yellow. A day of high desperation.

He flipped some pages and read: 'Never to be parted; living again in one supreme moment, the days when they clasped their little hands in love, and roamed the daisied fields together. Good god all bloody mighty.'

Sarah heard a toilet flush in the distance.

'Oh dear' she said. 'Had a bad week?'

'Bloody awful. You?'

She considered. 'Average.'

'Why do I do this?'

The boys sneaked back out of the toilet and escaped through the double doors. Peter didn't notice. She wanted to touch his face but she didn't.

'We've all got to earn a living' she said. We all work in the counting house.

She was still standing very close, though she was no longer looking at the words about the drowned people. She noticed and felt its awkwardness and moved back from him.

'Tell them it's a well made piece' she said.

He shut the book and looked at her. 'It isn't.'

Down the corridor something gleamed under the pale lights. Water was seeping across the floor from under the door of the boys' toilets. Once in a while by way of celebration of the week's end, they would block the pans with paper towels and flush the cisterns.

The moment, supreme or otherwise, was gone. No tissuestiffening, not really any electricity down one arm, even. Which was perhaps what Mary Anne had in mind for Maggie and Tom. The little death rather than the big one. That'd get Peter thinking. Better not mention it or it'll be in twenty A level essays. Too tired anyway, for banter or electricity. What next? Bell in a minute, then – who? Last lap. Lower six double hist then pork peppers rice.

She yawned and Peter yawned, catching it.

'Peter' she said, through the yawn. And she nodded down the corridor and down to her feet.

He looked down and lifted a brown shoe out of the spreading film of gloop. He seemed too tired to be surprised. He handed her the book and turned, pulling up his sleeves.

'Fuck' he said. 'Again.'

★ ★

It turned out the skinny bloke was doing physics. Steve couldn' remember him, but then, he'd only been to two lessons when he'd had the bust up with Matthews about chaos. Or maybe one. Skinny Bloke talked about some topics Steve hadn't heard of. He couldn' really hear in all the babble anyway. Pod kept saying How about a game of fuzzy duck? and sometime or other the baby with the titty bottle had started grizzling. The man with the birdseed wheeled the buggy back and fore with one hand and supped his pint with the other. Trish, sitting between Steve and Skinny Bloke, was talking across them with somebody else.

'See' Steve said, 'the thing about fractal image compression is, it's, like.' He stopped and thought. He couldn't think what it was like. Something about geometry and nature. 'When that bloke.' He wanted to say Benoit, the father of fractals. Did it rhyme with Renoir, or Detroit?

'What bloke?' Skinny Bloke said, straining to hear. His hand, with knuckled cigarette, brushed Trish's skirt and left a streak of ash.

'Oh, Steve' she said, pushing Skinny Bloke's hand away. 'Get him off me.'

Skinny Bloke concentrated hard on Steve while he leant against Trish.

'My grandfather' Steve said.

'What?'

Steve looked down the black and white perspective, past the middleaged babysitters and the lampchecks to the pool players and then back.

He used to pronounce Engels Enjels because he'd only ever seen it in books.

'Nothing' Steve said.

'What about him?' Trish said. She was angling herself away from Skinny Bloke, who was still leaning into her but was looking away and had jumped into a conversation with Mandy.

Steve shrugged.

Skinny Bloke was squeezing Trish against him. Steve leant away a bit, but everything was so smoky now there was probably no chance of her getting a whiff of the pink stuff.

'Talk to me, Steve' she said quietly. She looked sideways to indicate Skinny Bloke.

'Oh' Steve said, pointing. 'Is he irrit –'

She mimed a sh, touching his hand, and said in a fake conversational way, 'Oh, really?'

He looked at her, feeling stupid and feeling stupider for knowing he felt stupid. The table was jolted and a fresh pint appeared next to his three quarters empty glass.

'Ten minutes behind, Leyshon' Pod was saying. In real terms you've still only had three. This one's off Mandy, by the way.' Pod's digital watch appeared against Steve's face, too close for him to focus on it. 'Get cracking, professor.'

Steve raised the glass and spilled a bit. 'Cheers, Mand.'

She raised her coke and smiled brilliantly. Her blue arm seemed to leave an electric trail in the air.

He looked back to Trish, who was looking from Pod to Mandy. Her forehead, it seemed to him, carried evidence of a tiny frown. A funny neat fold between the eyebrows. Then he noticed he was sipping his new pint.

'Mm' he said to her, putting it down, 'yeah. Really. Conversation. Tricky stuff. Um. Nice year for the time of weather. Um. Have you ever noticed how if you don' wash your ballocks for a bit, all black stuff gets into the grain of the. Well, no, obviously. Um, do you believe in god?'

She looked at him, her chin on her hand. 'I'm a Catholic.'

'So, is that a yes or a no?'

The kid with the bottle was only crying now when it remembered to, in a cursory, stylized way. Pod had undone his belt a notch and was threatening to sing a song. Skinny Bloke had spotted an empty seat closer to Mandy and moved in. Trish watched him. She muttered something and then looked back to Steve.

'So, you off out anywhere tonight?' she said.

Is that a yes or a no. Shit. He reached for his drink again and realised there were two glasses. He poured the three quarters empty one into the three quarters full one. He had to concentrate. 'Probly not after this, actually.' And drank. Shit. She does that stuff. Mass and that. Mass times the speed of light squared. Life after death. Bugger. 'Sorry' he said.

'Look, I don't care whether you're going out or not' she said.

'No, I meant.'

She looked not quite at his face and he looked not quite at her face.

Suddenly people were getting up. Mandy was jangling the keys of the Orion and one of the boys and most of the girls were shaping to leave. Steve looked at them blocking the light.

'Are we off then?' he said.

Skinny Bloke stood up too, looking a bit uncertain. Mandy looked at him and stopped jangling the keys. Skinny Bloke pretended to reach for his lighter from his back pocket and sat down again. Steve made to get up.

'No, have a wiff, butt' Pod said, holding his arm out. We got a hool pint left. Anyway, they en going back up the school.'

'Oh' Steve said. He thought about this but he couldn't get anywhere with it. He looked round at Pod, but he just looked redfaced and pissed.

Mandy mouthed something to Trish and pointed to the door

with her eyes. Trish shook her head. And then the standers were all leaving. The birdseed man leant out of his chair to watch them go and said something to the other one and they laughed.

And immediately the corner was quiet and full of light and the tension had gone. Steve watched the light gathered in his bubbling Dettol. There were empty glasses gleaming and blibs of liquid on the tabletops.

'So have you prepared your talk?' Trish said. It sounded real, not like smalltalk.

'It's all up here' Steve said tapping his temple.

She looked at him.

'No' he said.

Skinny Bloke was sliding back along the seats to get closer to Trish again. She watched him and pulled a face at Steve.

'I suppose you don' need to though, do you?' she said.

'Nuh' Steve said emphatically. 'Well, maybe.' He looked at the empty seats. 'Where've they gone?'

'God, you're observant.' She paused. 'They've gone to Cardiff, most of em. You didn' know, did you? Mandy gave Fylfot a list of names. Yours wasn' on it. She told her we're all going to Cardiff to audition for the youth theatre.'

'Be fair' Pod said. 'Two of em are.' He was squirting a sachet of tomato sauce into a bag of crisps.

Skinny Bloke was leaning against Trish and looking at her as if he was part of the conversation. She shouldered him gently away without looking at him.

'What about History?' Steve said.

She looked past him down the black and white pub. It was quieter. You could hear the pool balls clicking.

'They've gone shopping' she said.

The windows looked burnt out white, like a photograph taken in a desert. The carpark and the dayglo sandwich board and the mountains were pale.

'So, you didn' go' Steve said.

It was all going a bit slow for Skinny Bloke. He gave up jostling and started playing the air guitar. It wasn't a rampant lead solo though. More of a rhythmy, slumped forward headshaking sort of bit.

She was wiping the sweat off her half a half of cider with one finger.

Well fucking obviously she didn' go, Leyshon, you dickhead.

'Obviously' he said.

She looked at him and didn't say anything. Something sarcastic about being observant again would have done, but not a word.

'Shit. Only three of us left' Pod said through the crisps. 'No fibre some people. I en even pissed yet.'

'Why not?' Steve said, looking at her glass.

'Because' Pod said, not getting it, 'according to your theory, which is a very good theory, we've still only had the equivalent of a glass of orange juice and a scotch egg.'

Her fingers pressed on the tabletop. She leant forward to see Pod better. 'Look, Mike, will you just bloody.' She stopped and looked away.

Steve watched faint haloes of condensation dissolving away from her fingertips on the varnished wood.

'What's he done to you?' Steve said.

'What's he done to *me?*'

But Pod was putting his arm round Steve's shoulder.

'So, Stick, butt' he said. 'How are you? You pissed?'

Steve thought. 'No. No, I'd say a bit gone, like. Like we planned.'

'Yeah' Pod said. 'I think I'm, like –' he waggled his hand in the air '– say, tight. Tightish.'

'Not pissed though.'

'Oh no. Not pissed. Maybe not even tight.' His hand waggled again. 'I'd say, nice.'

'Nice?'

'Nice. Like prematch nice on international day.'

'I'll drink to that' Steve said, and they drank.

'I think it've been a successful experiment' Pod said. 'How about you? You nice?'

'Oh, easily nice' Steve said. 'Probably very nice. I'd say there's nice, then very nice, then –'

'Tipsy?'

'Tipsy. Good one. Then tightish, then tight.'

'Then you start on your pisseds' Pod said.

'Then you start on your pisseds' Steve said. 'What about him over by there?'

They looked at Skinny Bloke, who had finished his concert and was staring into space with an unlit cigarette in his mouth.

'Now he's pissed' Pod said.

'Aye' Steve said. 'Hammered?'

'Oh no. Steady on. Early yet. He will be though. On the Pissed Level at the moment. Working towards getting Hammered.'

Suddenly Skinny Bloke got up and walked in the direction of the toilets. Trish was rubbing the tabletop as if she was trying to erase her fingerprints. The birdseed man got to his feet, hitching up his jeans, and followed Skinny Bloke towards the bogs.

'Bet he tries to sell him some birdseed' Steve said. He gathered his thoughts. 'So there's pissed' – he tapped his finger on the edge of his glass as if he was counting time – 'very pissed –'

'Arseoles' Pod said.

'Yeah, arseoles' Steve said. Tap. 'Pissed, very pissed, arseoles, then steaming, hammered, bladdered, wrecked.' He watched his finger tap with every word. 'Dead.'

He stared at the droplets and the empty glasses thronged with light.

Pod laughed.

Trish was standing up. 'I'm going while he's out of the way' she said. She didn't look at either of them but glanced at her watch as she edged round the tables.

Steve watched the door close behind her.

'I think she's angry about something' he said.

'Fucking furious' Pod said.

'Think I've narked her?'

'Stick my boy, you are without doubt the stupidest fucking nitwit I've ever met.' He wrapped his arm a bit tighter round Steve.

'Mm, yeah, but clever with it.'

'True. Hand me her cider.'

Steve did.

Pod released him and took the glass. 'You do realise' he said, 'she fucking fancies you?'

Steve watched him sipping the cider. 'Yeah, course.' The digital watch gave a time far too late for him to get back for his talk. 'Well no, actually. Shit.'

There was a pause.

Pod stopped sipping and stared at him. 'Well?' he said.

'Well what?'

'Well get after her, you fucking tool.'

Steve took a token swig of lager and got up, clutching the back of his chair. 'Okay. I think I'll, um.'

'Yeah yeah yeah. Fuck off and leave your butties. Fucking

typical. No fibre some people. Mind you, a couple of sips of cider and I can shit through the eye of a needle.'

He left Pod muttering theatrically, passed Skinny Bloke and the birdseed man who were chatting as they walked back from the bogs, and stumbled out into daylight.

Although it was cloudy and a bit cool the air was bright. He ran across the quiet carpark and past the noisy sandwich board, and caught her up at the beginning of the terrace of houses. Everything felt strange, as if the afternoon had sneaked into the wrong place. The bright paint on the brickwork around livingroom windows grinned at him hilariously.

Trish looked at him and carried on walking and he walked alongside her. He wanted to say one of Gransh's things. So, do you believe in life before death? but stopped himself. Too smartarse.

'Um, oo, en these windows funny colours?' he said.

She stopped walking. 'You en going to Baggy's lesson like that are you?'

'Like what?' Even the straight dark hair was a bit burnt out in the desert photo. She had long sleeves, but he imagined the clean elbows. She seemed to be fading to white, atomising, as if the signal was breaking up. He squinted and she came back, but there was still something wrong with the contrast button. 'Do you check your elbows in the mirror?' he said.

'My what?'

'Your, um. You've got.' Beautiful elbows. Shit. Don' say it. 'God. These windows.'

'Steven, you are *not* going to Baggy's lesson like that.' She put her hand on his arm and the signal faded then strengthened again and there was that funny neat fold between her eyebrows.

'Oo, yes, Miss' he said. 'Well I can't anyway can I, really?'

The fold folded a bit more.

'I mean it's too bloody late, en it.'

'No' she said. 'No it isn't. You don' know, do you?'

She smelt like clean sheets and his arm felt thin under her hand. Then her hand moved away and she was showing him the time.

'Look' she said.

The dial was swaying. He held her wrist to steady it.

'It's nearly an hour ago' he said after looking for a long time. 'I mean nearly an hour slow.'

'It's right, Steve. See. Every time you went to the toilet they set their watches forward. To get you pissed.'

It sounded funny her saying pissed.

'Did they?' he said.

Like always, she didn't give an answer when there was no need for one.

'Quite funny really' he said. He leant a shoulder against the hilarious brickwork. The signal was breaking up again. He could scarcely see her. 'I been thinking about the talk all week.' The book was sticking to the sweat on his back. 'It's about something.'

'Sorry' she said.

The wheel turning and people's lives. Stuff. Matter.

The signal came back and she was watching him. He unstuck the book and pulled it out from the back of his trousers. It was clammy, but somehow it hadn't buckled. He thought of Mandy buying him the last drink, just before she left. In the famous portrait on the cover the old astronomer gripped in his hand the image of his universe.

'You coming to History, then?' Steve said.

'Don' go, Steve. You mustn't. What for? You'll get in trouble. What does it matter anyway?'

'It's all. I mean it all matters. Anyway, there's this library book. I got to go back. Do you know you got a little fold?' He pointed between his own eyebrows and then backed away. He gripped the book tight. In the picture, the earth made a ring round the blazing sun. Go on, Leyshon. Go on. 'I'll' he said, 'I'll, um, ring you.'

Christ! Man of action. Can't be many Henneghans in the book. The fold disappeared. And he turned and ran.

★ ★

Last lap because circles and all that. Last lap that is, till the next one.

She unlocked the Geography Room door.

Markbook, diary, Perrotbrick, deployed on the teacher's desk. She was a minute late from corridor duty in the other building, having left Peter and the caretaker paddling, but none of the sixth form had arrived yet.

Five sixth form names in the diary. They gleamed uncertainly in her memory. Be grateful I'm in the right room and close to conscious this late in the week. Steve of course, and two who were absent Wednesday and two there wasn't time for. Should fill the hour plus easily. Yes.

She sat and slipped her shoes off. It was quiet, the Geography Room cool and dark. The black blinds had been left down but with the louvres angled open. Only the tiniest beginnings of the headache – miracle – even yet, so keep the lights off. The slide projector was on its stand loaded with its circular magazine of pictures ready for something on Monday. How the head of Geography keeps sane. Keeping his kingdom in order, keeping its borders closed, switching the light off when he leaves.

Through the louvres she could see, hitching up her socks and untangling string, Girl with Kite, preparing to run as if she'd been there all week on the strip of grass by the hall. Some ghostly parallelism in the timetable. Not red, though. Cardboard with a hint of, of course, Beige.

And he wanted to fuck me this morning. Strange. Or put on a show as if he did. We each of us feel like it most when the other's unconscious. The secret of comedy. Timing.

She rubbed her eyes and massaged the flesh of her cheeks.

The floorward flesh. Some days you want to tear your face off, but after a while it starts to leave on its own anyway. When you get to thirty five – have to think of a new rhyme.

Melanie came in. Sarah smiled at her and slipped her feet back into her shoes, smoothed her face, looked at her diary. The sixth former threaded among the empty desks fastidiously, as if they were occupied, and took her seat at the back. There was silence.

'Our friend with the kite's back, I see' Sarah said.

Melanie's hair winnowed a little light out of the gloom as she turned to look through the window and then back again.

'Oh yes' she said, perfectly audibly. 'Technology.'

'What?'

'It's Technology, Miss. What she's doing. I found out. Somebody told me.'

Somebody ratlike, I suppose. 'Is that with Mr Shattock?'

'Yes.'

How did I guess?

'They have to plan a project, Miss, and make it and test it. She's doing a modify and retest.'

Sarah watched Girl with Kite hold up her creation and test the breeze. There wasn't any.

A modify and retest. 'How disappointing.' She pretended to

study her diary some more and then looked up again. 'They're late today. La*ter*.'

Melanie tugged at her curtain. 'Do you know about the auditions, Miss?' She explained about Cardiff and a youth theatre, and in sixth form assembly one morning Mr Brace had said about initiatives coming from the students being a good thing, carrying more weight on applications for things. On your CV, she said.

'I haven't heard about this' Sarah said.

'I think Mandy only went to see Mrs Fylfot about it yesterday, Miss, or the day before, praps.'

So. Her. And on duty today and haven't looked in my pigeon-hole. 'I see.' I suppose I ought to be grateful. So that's why crunching gears in the smooth gear. Should feel pleased the lesson's wrecked. But you little bitch. 'Well, that's very good, isn't it. Good luck to them.' She heard herself sounding unconvincing.

Melanie watched her.

The technologist made her first pass with the modified design. the kite twirled on too short a string.

'Well look, Melanie' Sarah said, 'I don't think we're a quorum are we? You may as well go back to the Common Room, if you've got something to do.'

A big smile. 'I was doing a poster, Miss.'

Things assemble and then nothing happens, but this late on things can hardly be bothered even assembling. Presents that might as well be absent. Music that isn't music. A flood that washes nothing away. Not with a.

After Melanie had gone Sarah took her bag and books to the back of the room and leant across the plate glass of the map tracing desk. She clicked its light on. The ceiling whitened and the dark globe cast an elongated shadow above the door. She switched it off and leant on the sill and watched Girl with Kite.

The satisfaction of a mystery is that it's unsatisfying. Girl with Kite Mystery Solved. See the headline. Set that for year eight next week perhaps. Write the story to go with this headline. But really when you solve it it's over. All the possibilities that swam are gone. Everything shut down.

Girl with Kite ran, gripping the string.

Really, the story's end you pursue so hard is always empty. The marriage or death of the hero. Nowadays, the Maxes and Penelopes fucking in the present tense. Interchangeable annihilations. But here, G with K re-enacting Sisyphus, the serpent gripping his own tail in his mouth, a negative feedback loop, Mr Ayers, and that makes the week's zero.

Short reports. Cyclical and interim. But really in the end, you can let it happen or you can make it happen and that's all you've got. Eileen ending herself took truest control of her own story. A woman of action. Now there's art. Simply a matter of having enough of the right kind of foil wallets, or that other phrase they use. Blister packs. Blister packs.

Suddenly, Steven Leyshon appeared on the other side of the glass. He'd been running. His shoulders rose and fell as he fetched deep breaths. He looked into the window, a little to one side of her. She started, but realised he could see nothing in the darkened classroom beyond the black louvres of the blinds.

He stared and straightened his hair, or failed to, with his fingers. The window was a mirror. She watched his long lashes. In daylight, the green of his eyes was startling. He said something to his reflection, then looked around without noticing Girl with Kite, who hadn't noticed him. Although the sill came up to his upper chest, she could see from his shoulder movements and the hunched, eyesdown posture that he had set about urinating. She even saw, faintly, a little steam. He stood like this an implausibly long time, then one shoulder jerked as he shook. Mel did that. She imagined men all over the world doing it, time after time each day. He looked at his reflection again, smiled, then marched towards the entrance. Escape.

When he got into the room she'd packed her black bag and was about to move towards the door. Shit. Timing.

'Afternoon, Mrs Bowen' Steve said.

The room was dark. He looked round to get used to it. Rods and cones in the retina have to adjust after all that blaze on the pavement by the grinning windows. Retune to this signal.

There was the dusty planet hanging from the ceiling, and some bit of equipment on a stand, some books. No portrait though. Instead, a curlycornered poster about meteorology. And Baggy with her bag, leaning her arse against the long map table by the blackslatted window.

'I come' he said. 'I come to do the talk.' He licked his teeth. His mouth felt a bit dry and thick.

'Well, Steven, I'm afraid you're my only customer today. So.' She paused. He wasn't good at hints.

'I sort of expected it. I heard about the trip and that.'

Another pause. 'Did you, did you do a lot of work on it?' she said.

'Yeah. Yeah, I did, actually.' He came forward rubbing his mouth with the back of his hand. 'Research and everything. I just took a stack of books back to the library.' He waited.

'Why don't you, why don't you do it on Monday afternoon.' She was ready to get her diary out. 'We'll all be here then.'

She held her bag under her arms, which were folded across her midriff like they do. You could barely tell she was tubby when she stood like that.

A chair grated on the tiles as he walked into it and he realised he was walking forward and stopped and looked down, a bit surprised. You couldn' run all that way and almost puke up for nothing. It had to happen.

'Oo. I don' fancy that' he said. 'I'm, like, psyched up for it now.'

She looked at the disruption to the patterning of the head of Geography's chairs. 'I could, I could just look at your notes instead, if you like.'

'Notes?' He waved his hand to dismiss the idea. 'Never use em. Never catch a standup using notes.'

He was close and he smelt of cigarettes and beer and sickly perfume.

'Are you okay, Steven?'

'Yeah, course. In fact I feel bloody great.' He laughed suddenly. 'Sorry. Look. Look. I'll do it. Let me do it and it'll be over, Like I promised, sentences and everything.'

And his face shone. Literally. The shadowy furze below his sideburns was shaved shiny. She felt herself smiling and had this picture of the two of them grinning stupidly at one another in the half dark while outside people drove cars and blew up mountains and ran around with kites.

'Okay' she said. 'Go on then.'

'Great. Thanks, Mrs Bowen.'

Mandy had a sense of irony after all. He'd never come to a Friday lesson and now he was here she kept the rest away.

'See, the thing about it is.'

Thin as he was, he looked as if he'd burst with the things he had to say, but he didn't seem to know what they were.

'See, we do History, no disresepect, but we do it all wrong. We don' see it real. Real. It's, like, it's somebody else's Now. Look.'

He caught her by the shoulders and dragged her away from the map table. Beer breath. They nudged desks and chairs aside as they moved in a rhythmless dance.

'The thing is, we got to get their worldview. It's like, we don' believe in god and they did kind of stuff. It's vital. Vital.'

He brushed the slide projector with his shoulder but didn't quite push it off its stand.

'Look, you sit by there and I'll show you.'

He pushed her down onto a chair in the middle of the room. She sat with her bag clutched on her lap. He backed away, looking at her and she felt how huge her calves must look, and slightly scared and less tired.

'Um. Worldview. Oo, I should've.'

'Steven' she said. 'Be honest with me. Have you had a drink?'

'No. No. Well yes, obviously, but not really. But listen.'

He backed away further, urgently, bumping into desks and skewing the entire kingdom.

He stood still and felt lost a moment and then the signal came back and he was charged with certainty. Like when you turn the dial and it hits the station exactly and you get clean air.

'Clean air' he said, and opened his eyes, because suddenly he realised they were shut. 'You stay there. You're the earth.'

He looked at her seriously and started to walk clockwise around her.

'Let me be the sun' he said.

He picked his way among the chairs and desks, twelve feet off, making a ragged circle with her at the centre.

'No. Don' turn. Watch me cross your heaven.'

He was behind her and she heard him clattering, felt his eyes on her back. And he came up on her left. Dreaming when dawn's left hand.

'I rise in your east' he said. 'Cross. And set in your west. Nod your head. Go on. Right. You tilt to and away from me as the seasons turn. When you nod to me I wake your earth, suck clouds out of your sea and drench the mountains with them, draw forests up like mats of hair, and sometimes I parch a desert on you.'

A chair went over and he kept going.

'You count your days by me. It's like a beat. And out there' – he stretched a hand away from her and towards the wall as he moved but didn't take his eyes off her – 'there's the enormous globe studded with the fixed stars, and that's rotating too, a bit faster than your clocks. Just think. If you count time by them you get a whole extra day every year. Star time floating round out there nobody uses. And beyond that' – the hand wheeled past the blinds and the year niner – 'god and the angels live. And here' – he raised the other arm and suddenly stopped his orbit and came towards her.

The hand got closer. He accelerated. She tensed, and his palm slapped against her clutched bag.

'Here's hell. In the mud and stone. Inside us.' He sank on his haunches.

He'd stopped and was looking at the floor. She looked down at his head. Their fingertips were touching on the bag.

'And that was what the brainy ones thought' he said. 'Just imagine the ballocks the stupid ones must have come up with.' He belched. 'Oh shit.' The magician and the ghost. What was next?

A whole extra day. She felt hell inside her like a cave.

'What does bagatelle mean?' he said suddenly.

She was staring at his dark hair. 'Bagatelle?' She thought of Mel's CDs. 'A piece of music, isn' it?'

'Bugger. I got that wrong and all.' He got to his feet, only a little unsteadily. Henry. Had to get him in somehow. What the hell did Henry think he was doing? 'That' he said, 'that was the frame Henry lived in. I don' think he thought he was inventing imperialism or anything. He was a wannabe who got to be. Wanted to be kinglet. The nation state thing was, like, just happening anyway. He sort of flowed with it. He didn' do much that was different.'

'Right. What's this extra day thing?'

'He lived in Ptolemy's universe. I mean, I know I said it was dynamic the other day, and they must've had some idea because of Cabot and that. But I don' think they knew what it meant. See, with everything nailed down like that, maybe they couldn' picture things shifting. Shifting. Yeah. What they didn' know was it was all shifting anyway. That would've put the willies up em. In fact it did when people started to twig.'

He stopped and looked at her and against the background of the fixed stars, he swayed a little.

'See what I mean, Mrs Bowen?'

The green was only a little dulled indoors without the striplights on. The thick lips were slightly parted.

She stood up. No. 'I think that's a very good point.' Why don't.

'A lot of it's just accidental and slow. Like the fall of Constantinople, like I said.' Constantinople. He thought of the word, how it weighed in the mouth with gold and sureness. Unchanging city. How wrong can you get? 'Con stan tin ople.' The signal was suddenly clearer again and it was all lucid certainty. 'All the old learning came into Italy because of that. All the Greek stuff from Egypt and that. And castles were on the way out because of gunpowder. And there was printing. That was another one. A lot of it was just to do with technology like that.'

Oh god, god. There it goes. Undifferentiated gloop resolving into architecture. Summon up the tissuestiffening blood. Always the right one first. Why don't you.

He held her shoulders again. She kept still, looked at his mouth. Suddenly he smiled.

'Your turn to be the sun' he said. 'Stand up this time if you like. But keep still.' He skipped away from her. 'I'll be the earth. See, this is bigger sh-stuff than any king thing.'

When he'd moved back far enough he started to trace the same orbit, but this time anticlockwise. That's right, because viewed from above the sun's north pole the planets move that way. 'See, to us, we know it's like this. I'm the earth, a lump of dirt flying through the dark – or falling really, depending how you think about gravity – and there you are, the sun burning. But back then, then, that would've looked crazy. But when he looked and he considered the sky, the paths of the planets didn' add up. Literally. And he looked, and he had the maths to work it out.' Wait. I ought to spin. Tricky. Leave that a bit.

He stopped his treadmill and pointed at her.

'See' he said. 'He put energy in the middle. Light. Did I say it was Copernicus? Copernicus. He put energy at the centre.'

He was pointing at her breast and she felt electrified.

He dropped his arm. 'Only I ought to spin as I go.' He resumed his orbit, this time revolving anticlockwise as he circled her. It was hard to do this and talk and stay on your feet. 'See. It still all look the same. You rise in my east and set in my west. Oo. This is. Tricky.' The vertiginous universe hurtled past him. 'Whoa. But now the planets. Moon and Mars. Mercury and Jupiter. Venus. Saturn. They all. Add. Up. Nearly do. Have to do an ellipse. For that.' He stopped speaking to concentrate on his double spin. He'd bumped a path through the desks and chairs but now he staggered out of it to make the ellipse. 'Whee! Goodbye.' Tilted and spinning he surged to the far end of the room and slowed near the rollerboard, tried to wave, then raised both arms, almost stopped, and shouted, 'Aphelion!' Although he was trying to be still, distantly she whirled by him, simplified by the backlighting of the shaded window. The signal had gone faint. 'But you got me on a string. I can't escape.' Yes. Light. He accelerated towards her, tilted and spinning. He shouted, 'Perihelion!' and the edge of something struck his thigh and he was knocked out of orbit and flew past her, brushing her shoulder, falling.

He slid across the tiles and into the legs of the map table. She dropped her bag and helped him up, unnecessarily.

'Oops' he said. 'Good job planets don' escape. Think of the mess.'

Her palms were on his ribs just under his arms and his hands were on her shoulders. She squeezed and felt how bony he was and let go, a little slowly.

He leant against the table's edge. 'You just got to look at the evidence and then make a model in your head to figure it. Observation.' And suddenly he thought of Pod looking at his watch and laughing, and Gransh's window and the cake trolley and the snowword written on the glass. The acidity of the lager in his stomach came back into his mouth, but he swallowed it.

Baggy looked a bit anxious.

She was dead, of course, the old woman with the tealeaves. The kicked in panel and the burst bin bags and the hearse bumping in the potholed road.

The slats reflected on Baggy's glasses. He tried to get the thread again, but he felt heavy and slow.

'And everything changed. He changed everything. Hardly anybody could understand it back then but it did change everything. Just by looking and thinking and saying. From then they could work out dynamics and gravity. The lot. They couldn' even keep the sun still after that. It was only a matter of time. They go on about Darwin, but I reckon Copernicus gave god a hell of a bloody clout hundreds of years before him.'

He slid up to sit on the plate glass and sank down on one elbow, tucking his feet up as if the table was a Roman couch. She looked at the angularity of the arm and the upthrust shoulder, the slung curve that went from the other shoulder to the hip. He smelt faintly of vomit, and his face had clenched as if he might throw up, but that was gone, along with the urgency in his voice.

'Perhaps a mystery's a good thing sometimes' she said.

He let his elbow slip and laid his head on his arm. It's only in comedies and horror films that the box bursts open and the shroud sticks its arms up and goes, 'Woo-oo!'

'No' he said. 'Do you believe.' His voice was quiet. 'Do you believe in life after death?'

He stared straight at her. Hard to tell if he was really drunk or not. He might be at the deeply meaningful stage, but then he always talked like this. Even in this light the striations in his irises were naked and intense, as Mel's eyes had been once. She wanted to switch the lamp on in the table and underlight him.

'You always go for the big ones don't you' she said. And after a pause, 'No.'

'Neither do I. I used to talk to my grandfather about it. He's dead now so I don't talk to him much about it any more. Sorry. He was a what you call it. He had a word. Autodidact. But I think everybody is really, if they learn anything at all. He taught me to swear in Welsh. Cachu. Uffern dan. Days of the week. Dydd Llun, Dydd Mawrth. Stuff like that. I don' think he could speak it much, he was just showing off. Knew his politics though, and history.'

'How old was he?'

'Oo, you know. Seventy something.' He tapped his chest.

'You're seventeen, plus.'

'Yeah. Got held back a year. Extra time.'

'I know.' Seventeen. Thirty five. Seventy. Ought to mean something, but it doesn't. A pattern instead. A shape made in time, like a piece of music.

'I tell you the funny thing though.' He rolled onto his back and lay at full stretch with his head on his hands and his long shins overhanging the table's end. 'About Copernicus. I was reading this book yesterday, and in the end he changed the world, but he didn' even prove anything. If you fix the maths this book says, him and Ptolemy are physically equivalent. Sun or earth in the centre, you can model it either way. After Einstein, see, because there's no such thing as absolute space. Ironic or what?'

Or what. Her hand brushed his side. 'Yes, that's amazing.' Not with a whimper but a.

He licked his lips. His eyes had dulled.

She looked out at the year niner sitting on the grass, looking at her creation and waiting for the bell. 'To be honest with you, Steve, I don' really understand at all. Any of it.'

He heard her voice like a slowing tape. Something was rubbing his hip. He tried to scratch it.

'Aw, simple stuff' he said. 'Neither do I.' He laughed tiredly and then stopped. 'I tell you, the great thing about not believing in life after death is it makes being alive feel so fucking marvellous.'

His fingers were playing soft arpeggios on her knuckles. She heard herself laughing a bit, hoping it might be so. Apart from his hand he was keeping very still. Outside the girl was staring at the kite and waiting. His fingers slowed and he just held her hand.

Everything that happens is somebody's now. Everything's important. What if you don't have a now? Things may have happened and they may be going to happen, but they don't actually happen. You don't live through them. You have, and you will, but you don't. If you wait long enough and keep standing in the right places, Ryan will make his little pitch, or not, and there'll be a mess, like with Kenny, or not. But it'll be nothing much. Penelope and Max fucking in a perpetual now is only something in a story.

The girl outside was still. Steve was still. Sarah reached across him with her free hand and tugged the string on the blinds so that the louvres rotated and closed. It was surprising how dark it was.

There. I made that happen. Perhaps I have got some Now. You had the trick of it, shooting it into me with the electrified finger. An Event. It leaked through you from all that unused time swimming among the constellations.

She could see his shape dimly on the table. Like the stupid machine in the open evening, or possibly not. Dead king. Living man. She pressed her hand on the black sweater, lightly and then harder.

'Steven' she said. Make it art, artful as Eileen's death. You can arrange these things.

His chest rose and fell against her palm. And rose and fell. She felt his chin and lips and smooth cheek and the unmistakable rhythm of the breath from his nostrils on her fingertips.

She reached under the table and switched on the lamp under the glass.

Oh, somebody different, somewhere exotic. I could have fucked you now. Even if it had been no good it wouldn't have mattered, not much anyway.

The light fell upward unreally around him and she looked from his sleeping face to his spreadeagled map thrown on the Geography Room ceiling and she switched the light off and opened the blinds.

★ ★

When Steve woke up he had a stiff neck and drool was coming out of his mouth, which felt dry. A bell was ringing. He sat up suddenly and he felt the table legs shift in their joints a bit and he knew where he was.

Baggy was sitting at the teacher's desk at the far end of the room. She had her glasses in one hand and was rubbing her eyes with the other. The desks and chairs stood in their perfect grid, and the blinds were open. The bell stopped.

'Phonecall' he said.

She took her hand away and her eyes looked red and tired. 'Welcome back' she said in a teachery way. 'And how are you?' She put her glasses on like a mask.

He looked around and at himself. There was a streak of tomato sauce on the shoulder of his sweater and he felt wobbly. 'Okay. Yeah, good. There can't be many in the.' He wondered what he was saying and then he remembered. 'Um, how was the talk?'

'Bloody wonderful. You should have been there.' She sniffed. 'I've got to lock up, Steven.'

He looked at her. There was a noise outside the window, like corny crowd noises in a radio play. He looked out and people were pouring past, going home through the bottleneck between the Geography Room and the windowless hall. They made patterns as they moved.

'Oo. Come and look at the people' Steve said.

Baggy came close by him. She looked tired and pissed off so he smiled at her, and they watched the people. People from eight see and nine tee, the twat with a blazer in the upper sixth, and Elis Richards, and Gron, with his hat on so you couldn' check, a Christian union, two coconuts, eleven ee and ten ell, the pelvic pair and maries and benlikes and barrys and gethins, though not Gethin himself and only Melanie from lower six hist. As they walked their heads rose and fell in syncopating waves.

'Watch this now' Steve said.

He rolled on the table and leant across the sill and misted the pane with his breath. None of the people noticed or looked round. He wrote with his finger on the glass a backwards capital ee. In mathematics that meant something but he didn't know what, or it could stand for earth. And to the right of that a vee, which is symmetrical and needs no reversing, and which could be the number of a chapter or upraised wings or a wedge of hair or somebody's initial. And next to that an oh, which is also symmetrical and could be an egg or a planet or a bubble or a nothing, or the mouth a fish makes. And he came to the last letter which was also the first letter, and his finger hesitated above the moisture because he wasn' much of a writer and he was still pretty drunk and he didn' know whether to write it forwards or backwards, and as he hesitated the backwards ee was already starting to vanish.

Other novels by Christopher Meredith

Shifts

This is a compelling novel.... The prose is spare and poetic, at once plain and rich, musical in its rhythms of speech and clear descriptions ... a beautiful, understated first novel – *New York Times Book Review*

Meredith's prose captures the Welsh accent, as well as the hard-nosed working-class flippancy.... A first novel of consummate skill
– The Sunday Times

A fine young writer. His closely observed description of life in a declining steel town is remarkable for its unsentimental chronicling of working-class life, written superbly, with a poet's eye, mind and voice
– The Guardian

A novel so good it is difficult to believe it is his first – *Western Mail*

Griffri

The language is earthily poetic, the overall effect is beautiful
– The Observer

Writers are too often tempted to write about writing, and it rarely comes off. Meredith has found a way which does
– The Independent on Sunday

A book of uncommon interest and appeal – *The Guardian*